WHAT SHOWS
THE HEART

Karen A. Wyle

Published 2021 in the United States of America
Oblique Angles Press

Cover design by Kelly A. Martin of KAM Design

Author photo by Holy Smoke Photography

Dedication

To those who go their own way,
and those who find it.

Chapter 1

MAMIE inspected the bottle of blonde hair dye, almost empty, and set it on her overcrowded dressing table, where it barely fit between the silver-backed brush and the flask of perfume. There should be time for the next bottle to arrive before she needed to touch up her hair again. She'd just managed to stay on schedule and get the job done before the party guests had started showing up. Most of them, anyhow — just one more, and she could lock the front door. Ten men altogether, enough to fill the special dining room, and one of them the marshal — for three more days.

Here Cowbird Creek had finally got big enough to have their own marshal, and he'd gone and got himself engaged to a woman too fainthearted for the West, and smart enough to do something about it. Men always underestimated the power of a timid and clever woman. First she started on about how the only decent dressmaker had run off with a medicine show, and she just *had* to get her wedding clothes back East. And then, how important it was to have everything fitted in person, but she couldn't possibly make the trip without her strong brave protector by her side, and it was all right because they were engaged already. And then, oh, she'd gotten the most wonderful letter from her daddy, who knew about a grand opportunity for a man like her husband-to-be, an office job where he wouldn't be risking his life and leaving her lying awake at night, and he wouldn't want her to risk her health with all that worrying, especially once she was in a delicate condition . . . . And now it would be a wedding in New York, and the city council would have to find another marshal or do without, and hardly enough time for them to give him a good sendoff.

Good thing for all those men that she knew how to throw a party, and had better booze than most any of the saloons. And good for her that they were willing to pay her prices for the booze and the space, so long as she let them make all the noise and mess they wanted — up to a point — until morning if they didn't drink themselves unconscious first. (One of the younger council members had told her they'd talked about having the party at the church. She'd laughed out loud at the thought of it, and the council member, after a moment's self-consciousness, had laughed along.) She'd made them pay enough that she could close down for the night, and not have to keep the usual customers from busting in on the mayor and council members and banker in their fancy suits.

Right on time, there went the first broken bottle, the crash and the laughter loud enough for her to hear it up in her office.

She'd need to make an appearance soon, just to remind them not to start breaking the furniture. She checked her hair in the gilt frame mirror, making sure she'd covered the red roots (darker than they used to be) and put the color on even. No gray hairs yet, at least. No telling how much longer she had before they turned up, what with her less than a year from turning forty. Her mother had died with no gray showing, and Mamie hadn't seen her sister — gone now too — since she was newly grown and Mamie far from it. They'd had an aunt who went silver quite young, before she got to Mamie's age, and it had looked fine enough, but

Mamie couldn't let her own hair go that direction. Can't have customers look at her and start thinking about their mamas.

The sound of shouting, now — but not the sort of shouting she should be hearing. Mamie hustled out of her room to the stairs and leaned from the top of the banister to see what sort of trouble she'd have to deal with next. Girls were spilling out of the small parlor — they must have been having their own little party to celebrate the night off — and out of bedrooms. She started down the stairs as fast as she could without running. "All of you go back to your rooms! I'll handle this."

This being a cowboy, dirty and scruffy and belligerent, and big and drunk enough to be giving her latest bouncer some trouble. The cowboy was slurring his words, naturally, but she could more or less make out what he was hollering as the two men shoved and wrestled just inside the doorway. "I been on a drive, and I've got my pay, and what do you mean you're closed, you've got all these women and I hear men inside, and I'm comin' in, and you'd better get out of my way before I lay you out and walk over you!"

Well, whatever happened, and however she got rid of this fellow, she'd be hauling her bouncer over the coals. What was she paying him for, if some cowboy could push him around?

And just what was she going to do now? Pry the marshal away from his party, she supposed, and wouldn't that just make the guests happy. They'd be demanding their money back next. Mamie gritted her teeth and headed for the party room. The fellow was still marshal, though he might be too drunk by now to walk straight, let alone do his job.

* * * * *

Jake reached the outskirts of the town — Cowbird Creek, that farmer had told him, not that it mattered much — and wiped the sweat off his forehead. It'd been a hot one, and not cooling down fast enough to suit him. He would cut the trail dust at the saloon with the tallest beer they had. And find Wrangler a whole trough-full of water.

Maybe the town would have a bed-house. He hadn't had a woman in a month or more. Maybe that's why he was so quick to fly off the handle these days, spoiling for a fight. A good brawl had its own satisfaction. And just like a willing woman, it reminded him how far he'd come from his younger days. Not so easy to push around now, and women not so hard to come by — when there were some around, and no husbands or fathers to get in the way.

Hmmm. The town wasn't big, but it was bigger than he'd guessed. It might have two saloons or more.

But while he was looking and listening for signs of one, he caught a glimpse of red. A red lamp? He rode toward it. And once he could see the building plain, he kicked Wrangler into a trot. That was no ordinary hookshop. That, unless he'd fallen asleep on horseback and dreamed it, was a parlor house! It was almost a shame to walk into a place like that covered in caked-on dirt and baked-on sweat. He probably smelled worse than Wrangler.

A place that fancy would have its own bar, like as not, and maybe even a piano player.

But as he got close, what he heard was a far cry from piano music. Someone was cussing a blue streak, and another fellow was shouting back. By the time Jake jumped off Wrangler's back and threw the reins around a post, he could see which was what. A cowboy almost as grimy as Jake was trying to push his way in, and for some reason a fellow in a fancy jacket was trying to stop him. And not doing too great a job of it.

Did this parlor house make its customers clean up first? That could annoy a man — it'd annoy Jake, with how he was feeling at present — but he didn't much care for how the cowboy was handling it. And while the doorman, or whatever he was, might not appreciate a stranger horning in, it looked like he could use the help.

In the meantime, just the other side of the doorman, a crowd of gents had turned up inside, all dressed to the nines, and none of them offering to get their hands dirty. And they sounded like they'd been drinking pretty deep. Was every son of a bitch in this goddamn town drunk except for him? And him riding with a throat as dry as desert for the last five miles?

Jake grabbed the cowboy by the shoulder, yanked him out of the door, mostly ducked the man's wild punch, and threw him halfway across the street. The cowboy landed hard, the wind knocked out of him, but after half a minute or so he managed to get up and limp back toward the door. Jake waited for him to get close and gave him one good shove.

The cowboy collapsed in a heap, and seemed inclined to stay there. Jake turned around to see the doorman slinking away. A crowd of ladies had appeared behind and around the gentlemen, and one of them squirmed on through, grabbed Jake's hand, and pulled him inside. There he stood, surrounded by the smells of beer and whiskey from the men and perfume and face powder from the women, and it looked like he was minutes from being the middle of a tug of war between the men wanting to congratulate him and the women wanting him for other things.

And then a voice cut through the noise, feminine and commanding. "Girls, get back! And gentlemen, if you would, give the poor man room to breathe."

Had the cowboy got in a punch Jake hadn't noticed? Why was he feeling like Wrangler had thrown him, disoriented and confused? How could that voice sound so familiar?

The crowd had backed away, just like the woman had told them to. He could see her now, standing on a big polished staircase, a few steps up so she could see better. She had a grand shape to her, and blonde hair up in some sort of do, and a handsome face that had him as mazed as her voice. He stared, and then he gasped.

Jesus God, it was Mamie. Mamie from home.

* * * * *

This was just plain impossible. But here he was — Jacob Flint. Jacob, that she'd been the first to call Jake. Because he was such a Bible-reader and carried a name out of scripture, and Jake was just one letter shy of meaning an outhouse, and someone needed to tease the serious out of him.

The hair was the same, dark enough that lamplight got lost in it. And of course the light gray eyes hadn't changed. But he'd been skinny, and still beardless, and the one time he'd taken the chance of stepping up to help her, he'd been laid flat so fast she'd barely had time to blink, not that the hooligans left it at that. Then she'd left town without thanking him — thanking him for trying, at least, when no one else did or would.

And now there he stood, tall and muscular with broad shoulders and a thick neck, looking a little like a bull that had got into locoweed, staring up at her like he couldn't believe what he was seeing any more than she could.

And in the meantime, all the most important men in Cowbird Creek had just seen her lose control of her place and needing some stranger off the street to get her out of trouble. She had to do something, and fast, to change that story.

They'd quieted down, at least. She gave herself just enough time for one deep breath and called out, "Gentlemen, I do believe you may have found our next marshal."

It got quieter for a few seconds, and then four or five of them started talking at once, to Jake or to each other. That gave her the chance to herd the girls to the small parlor, except the few who'd been napping and were still blinking and yawning. After all the excitement, her guests might well be wanting some of the house's brand of company.

The delay also spared Mamie from figuring out anything to say to Jacob — or Jake, if she'd heard right in all the confusion, and he'd taken the nickname for his own. But she'd have to talk to him sooner or later, and she hadn't a clue where to start, or what he was thinking. It looked like he'd recognized her, but how did he remember her? As the girl everyone had treated like a hussy, before she'd as much as lain with a man? As the girl he'd been unable to protect? As the girl who gave him nothing in return for taking a beating trying to help?

And now she owed him thanks again, little as she liked to admit it. She made her way through the men gathered around him and caught his eye. "I hope you'll accept a bottle of whatever you're most inclined to drink —" She almost said "these days," though he hadn't, as far as she knew, touched any kind of alcohol back in the day. "Compliments of the house."

She hadn't actually said thank you. From the glint in his eye, there and gone in an instant, she thought he'd noticed as much. But he bowed a little and said, with a bit too much emphasis, "Thank you kindly, ma'am. I could use a glass of some decent whiskey."

Mamie instructed the bartender to get out the second-best whiskey and keep the newcomer supplied with it. She could be wrong, but she guessed Jake's taste wasn't refined enough to tell how it differed, slightly, from the best and more expensive one. Then she headed for the party room and beckoned to the men. "Now that the unscheduled entertainment is over —" She waited for the obligatory chuckles. "— you can resume saying farewell to our dear marshal. Perhaps he can tell his possible replacement all about our little town."

She almost added "and why he should want to settle here," but she didn't know what to think of the idea, even though she might have ended up setting it in motion. Did she want a piece of her past intruding on her present? What other memories would insist on trailing along with him?

When the party broke up, hours later and after a few of the men had gone off with girls and come back again, she could finally sit with a glass of sherry and take stock of the evening. It was, she lectured herself, too soon to have much idea of what Jake's startling reappearance would mean, if it meant anything. As for the embarrassment surrounding it, her distraction seemed to have worked well enough. And as to her negligent or overpowered doorman, she'd get his story and excuses tomorrow. It might be time to find another strong young farm boy who'd love nothing better than to earn actual cash money showing off his protective skills to a bunch of painted ladies — if he could keep his mind on the job.

As she put her glass aside, hung up her satin robe, and slid beneath the covers, a moment came back to her, one she'd noticed and forgotten. When Jake had seen her, after his first confusion and shock, he'd looked her up and down, the way any man would. And even with all those younger women crowding around him, his face had said he liked what he saw.

Chapter 2

THE MAYOR had insisted that Jake come home with him for the night, and waved away his protests at coming into what must be as fine a house as the town boasted without a chance to wash. He used the well behind the parlor house — declining the offer of the kitchen, which he wouldn't feel right dirtying — to sponge away the worst of the grime. The mayor assured him that Mrs. Mayor would have gone to sleep, so at least he could make himself presentable before encountering her the next morning.

The mayor casually mentioned, as well, that his household boasted a luxury Jake had heard about but never thought to find in Nebraska, let alone a town this size: a bathtub with hot and cold water, which one could fill as much as halfway. He found out where it was so he could take advantage of it in the morning, not wanting to bother with it sooner. Then he declined the offer of yet another drink, accepted a huge towel for the morning, and shucked off his clothes in a bedroom big enough to get lost in, decorated in a frilly taste that made him want to laugh, or maybe sneeze. He pitied the maid — this place would have a maid, if not two of them — who'd have to wash the soft cotton sheets after he'd spent a night tossing around in them.

He'd long since trained himself to wake with the sun, and there it was out the bedroom window. He made his way to the bathroom, wrapped in the towel with his spare clothes in hand. When had he last had a hot bath? He didn't indulge in them as a rule, not wanting to get soft, nor to put some hard-working woman to the work of hauling all the buckets back and forth. With that not a concern, he scrubbed long enough to rid himself of all the dirt he still carried, even in his hair — and then let out the water and filled the tub again, just to soak in. The water had a brownish tinge, probably from rust, but that was the mayor's worry, not his.

By the time he finally got dressed and left the tub behind, the household was stirring. He followed his nose to a table off the kitchen, with a feast — scrambled eggs, bacon, ham, toast, butter *and* jam — on a sideboard next to it. As he pulled a chair out, the mayor's wife, unmistakable in her over-curled hair and expensive day dress, hurried in with a plate and a mug. "Good morning, Mr. — oh, isn't that just like him! My husband didn't tell me your full name."

"Flint, ma'am. Jacob Flint. Thank you for letting me impose on you in this way."

"You're most welcome, Mr. Flint. I've heard *all* about how helpful you were last night. Please help yourself to some breakfast, and I'll get the coffee. Cream and sugar?"

"Just black, please." There was a limit to how much he was going to spoil himself in one morning.

He was pushing himself away from the table after his second helping when the maid, or a maid, came in and presented his hostess with a small envelope on a silver tray. She turned it over, looked at it, and reached across the table toward Jake. "This just came for you, Mr. Flint."

Jake leaned over to take it. "Thank you, miss." Would

it be from one of the other men he'd met last night? But the handwriting was small, flowing, feminine. There was only one woman he knew in this town.

Dear Jake, if I may so address you — I hope you'll give me the pleasure of taking tea with me this afternoon. And then, if you're interested, I can give you a tour of my establishment.

The maid was still hovering. "How did this come?" he asked her.

"Sir, a boy brought it. He's waiting in the hall."

Sir? Good God. But he'd best ignore it, rather than telling her she'd got it all wrong, or washing her mouth out with soap.

He had a stub of pencil in his shirt pocket, and used it to draw an arrow under the message toward the other side of the paper, where he wrote, *I'd be happy to — Jake.* He stuffed the paper in the envelope, wrote *look inside* on it — he didn't want her thinking he'd sent it back without an answer — and handed it back to the maid. "Please give this to the boy and ask him to make sure and give it back to the lady who sent it."

The maid didn't quite manage to hide her eyebrow twitch at his saying "the lady." He didn't look at the mayor's wife to see what she thought of it.

His spare clothes weren't much better than what he'd worn riding, but at least they, and he, were clean.

He'd expected one of the girls, or Mamie herself, to open the door, but instead it was the doorman from last night, dressed neatly but still somehow looking like he'd been held upside down and shook by the heels. Jake guessed this new Mamie, grown up and transformed, could make a man look like that.

The man shuffled his feet, his expression shifting back

and forth between resentment and shamefaced gratitude. He stepped back out of Jake's way and half-grunted, "Madam Mamie is in the room where the party was. You remember where?"

He did. But before he reached it, Mamie came out, looking like she'd somehow got plenty of sleep, her hair up again, her dress fitting just as close as the one from last night, but quieter somehow — not so many ribbons and geegaws shining all over it.

She held out her hand, and when he hesitated, not knowing just what he was supposed to do with it, took his and gave it a little squeeze before letting him go. "Thank you for coming, Jake. Welcome to Cowbird Creek."

* * * * *

She'd never had occasion to feed the man before — or the boy, then — but she'd seen him eat, at town picnics and the like. Back then, skinny and not yet tall, he'd packed it away like he had plans for the food. To look at him, he'd made good use of it.

He'd favored anything sweet, but not squishy — no jelly-filled cakes. So Mamie had had the cook bake up crullers and muffins and cupcakes, but also what a more elegant tea required — crumpets and thin slices of bread, with plenty of butter available, and slices of meat and cheese. When she led him to the table in the party room, he looked it up and down and sideways like he was looking at a woman.

Which reminded her of the arrangements she'd made, a reminder that didn't do much for her own appetite, but she pushed the thought aside and waved him to a chair. She ate enough to make him at ease with eating more, but left herself pauses in which she could speak without mumbling around mouthfuls. "How do you come to be here? And what have you been doing with yourself since whenever you left Deliverance?"

He gulped down half a muffin and wiped his mouth — with the napkin, though she'd seen the movement toward his sleeve before he caught himself. "I've kept on the move. Most recently, I was boss of a cattle drive. It wasn't the first, though I'd never been boss before. I've done some blacksmithing, and been the bouncer at a couple of big-city bars. Did some boxing for folks to bet on. And I've been down a coal mine and a copper mine. Didn't much care for that — I like seeing the sun from time to time."

Always some job that showed he was strong. Did he believe it yet? He must, at least some part of him must, seeing as he might've been crippled or worse in some of those places otherwise. How long would he have to keep proving it? It might not have been such a good idea suggesting him for marshal, at that.

"And I've been a sailor — on the rivers during the war and after, and at sea. I can climb a rigging and tie a line with the best of 'em. I got me three tattoos — want to see 'em?"

Mamie raised an eyebrow, but felt a smile coming and didn't fight it hard enough to win. She didn't look to see how he answered it, just poured him more tea and took another sip of her own.

When Jake had finally eaten enough that even he must be satisfied, he pushed back from the table and said, "That was mighty welcome. You've got yourself a fine cook."

She stood up. "I'd be content with nothing less. And it keeps my employees more contented as well." She wouldn't go so far as to say it kept them happy.

As she got up, Jake asked, "Speaking of employees, I

see you haven't fired your bouncer yet. Are you giving him another chance?" He didn't sound as if he approved.

"For now. I don't have anyone at hand to replace him. And I know you may have brighter prospects."

Jake opened the door for her without commenting, saying only, "Is it time for that tour you mentioned?"

"It is." She heard the dryness in her tone and forced warmth into it. "We'll start down this hall, with the main parlor. You'll have passed by it last night, but it wasn't in use." She led him in through the open door from the corridor. "There's the bar, and the piano — though we don't have the piano player start until our busier time. There are more ladies then, but whenever we're open, some of them are available here for incoming guests."

She let him take a good look around, and waited until he asked, "And your other ladies?"

The smile she wanted to produce didn't come, so she fell back on a businesslike tone. "They're in their rooms. A few will be working, but I've arranged for the others to be . . . awaiting your pleasure. Lucette will show you."

He studied her face. Whatever he learned from it, he said only, "That's all very kind of you. Where is Lucette now?"

"This way." She led him to the small parlor, where Lucette was passing the time doing her embroidery. Lucette rose gracefully as they came in. Mamie had told her that if Jake didn't seem sufficiently interested in any of the other girls, he was hers for the rest of the afternoon. From the way Lucette was looking him over, she'd have no objection.

* * * * *

Lucette had a round face, pointed chin, dark curls, and

a dainty but curvy figure. She dropped a curtsy as they approached and extended a plump little hand. "Thank you so much for helping us all last night. Whatever would we have done without you?"

That was a good deal more than Mamie had said, but somehow he hadn't thought to expect it from Mamie. It wouldn't be her way. And in fact, Lucette's thanks made him a little jittery. He'd just as soon not think of all these ladies, and Mamie, having come that close to trouble, if he'd happened to go on into that first saloon. He changed the subject. "You're French? I've heard the accent before, but it sounds a lot sweeter from you than from a sailor. And I'd wager you don't cuss as much as he did."

Lucette smiled, showing dimples, and said, "Merci, m'sieur. And if you would lose that wager, I will not tell you so. . . . Shall we go upstairs? That is where all our bedrooms are."

They passed several closed doors, as Mamie had told him to expect. He had heard the sounds of people joining often enough, in rented rooms and seaside brothels. It felt odd to hear the same in a house like this, with polished wooden banisters and chandeliers and wallpaper scrolled with velvet.

The first open door showed a room decorated in white and pink, with a large bed on which perched a tall young woman — hardly more than a girl — with long blonde hair, lighter than Mamie's, and a figure less full than either Mamie's or Lucette's. She smiled up brightly as they paused in the doorway, but he thought he could see the fatigue behind it. He returned her smile and headed on, Lucette smoothly moving to catch up with him.

Next door, a woman with smooth brown skin and

shining black hair lay back on her mattress. A leather canopy over her bed gave it the look of a teepee. She turned her head toward him and gave him a look more like a challenge. His heart sped up, and he turned toward Lucette. "Maybe. But let's keep going for a bit."

Another closed door. By now, the sounds behind it got his pulse pounding, and he stopped. "Actually, let's go back. That native girl will be just fine."

Lucette startled him by pouting prettily. "And here I was hoping none of them would please you, and that would be my good fortune." She dimpled again. "Perhaps another time."

* * * * *

Mamie was looking through bills, adding figures and making more mistakes than usual, when Lucette poked her head in. "Monsieur is with Summer Dawn. I told him to come here to say goodbye before he left. I hope that is what you wanted."

She hadn't let herself think about what she did want, once he'd taken his pleasure with one of the girls. She didn't much hanker to see him just after, all smug and satisfied the way men got. But it wouldn't be much better to have him just slink out the door. "That'll be fine, Lucette. Thank you for your help. Oh, and close the door as you go."

The knock on the door came about twenty minutes later. Not bad for a man who'd been on the trail for who knew how long and was likely starved for it. She pushed the papers aside, checked for straying hair, and called, "Come in."

He did look more relaxed, and a little shamefaced along with it. The urge to tease him, as she had so often, rose up, and she welcomed it. "Well, Jake, all better now? That big meal doesn't seem to have slowed you down."

Jake started to shuffle his feet and then caught himself. She smiled wider. "No need to be embarrassed. We always appreciate a satisfied customer."

The last word seemed to take him aback. True enough, he hadn't paid for Summer Dawn's time, but then he had it coming for services rendered. He recovered quick enough, sitting down without an invitation and saying, "Well, I am that, sure enough."

"Where are you headed now?"

He hesitated. "The mayor invited me to stay longer, but I booked a room at the hotel instead. I'd rather be able to come and go without bothering anyone." Or, she figured, anyone keeping too close track.

"Were you planning to just pass on through? Do you have a job waiting?" Or a person, but she doubted it, and wouldn't mention it even if it seemed more likely.

Another thing she's forgotten: how he could sometimes act like he'd read her mind. He gave her one of his knowing looks before answering, "Nothing and no one special's expecting me. Not that I'd thought of being a marshal. What has your marshal had to do, anyhow?"

Mamie snorted. "Not a lot. What you saw last night would be toward the exciting end. But you could always hope for *two* drunk cowboys, or an Indian uprising actually getting here, or a gang of outlaws. Do you have any outlaws as sworn enemies, who might follow you here?"

He took longer than she'd expected to answer. "I've tangled with some folks who had it coming, and no doubt didn't see it that way. I'm not expecting them to come trotting into town. But then, I didn't expect to come into town and find you."

He let that lie there, as if expecting some sort of explanation. She'd be damned if she'd go explaining herself to him, as if she should have stayed in Deliverance, Indiana and become the cheapest sort of jade, or married whatever man was willing to put up with what everyone called her. A man who'd expect her to be grateful for his overlooking how soiled and tainted she must be.

Which got her wondering something.

"Come to think of it, Jake, I didn't expect you to fall in my doorway, throwing a drunk cowboy around. If I'd been guessing, I'd have guessed you'd stay in Deliverance and grow up a preacher like your grandpa. When did you leave?"

His sudden glower made her scoot back into her chair before she could stop herself. She'd hit on a sore point, seemingly, one that probably had to do more with "why" or "after what" than "when."

That certainly put a damper on any more talk of his days back home. Even as it made her mighty curious about what had chased him away.

* * * * *

Mamie probably hadn't meant to rile him. Or if maybe she had, it served him right for steering the talk the way he had. He could guess why she'd left town, and some of what had probably happened after. He'd been as likely to see her here as anywhere — the least likely part about it was how well she'd done, what she'd built for herself. There wasn't a building back home that could hold a candle to this place. Nor a woman with her combination of strength and style.

And he'd better smooth things over, and quick, if he wanted to see her again. Which he did, whether he actually stayed in town the way the men last night had urged him to, or whether he rode out again after a couple of days of hot meals and hot water.

* * * * *

The scowl fell away almost as fast as it had appeared. Jake even hung his head, for all the world like a boy caught lying to his mama. Not that she much cared for the idea of him thinking about her that way.

He opened his mouth, most likely to apologize, but she beat him to it. "I've no business quizzing you about why you do this or that. May I apologize with another corn muffin?"

He seemed stuck between stubborn and relieved before he gave in to the latter. "Thank you kindly, but I'm full to bursting. In fact, I'd best take a walk to work off some of that grub, or my horse'll refuse to carry me when it's time to ride out."

That didn't sound like he was much considering the marshal idea. Whether that was good or bad, she could puzzle out later. She stood up as he did and held out her hand. "Do come and say goodbye before you leave town."

"I surely will. And thank you for the finest and most bountiful tea I've had in many a year."

She waited until he'd gone a few steps out of the room before moving to the doorway and watching him stride down the hall.

Chapter 3

JAKE had seen something of the town on his way from the mayor's to Mamie's, but he'd been telling the truth about needing a walk, so he may as well take a better look around. Not that it was likely he'd decide to turn marshal, even if the offer held up in the light of day and notwithstanding the hangovers the town worthies must be enduring.

Madam Mamie's occupied one corner of the town square, so he made his way around, resisting the temptation to detour to the center of the square and stretch out in the sun on one of the wrought iron benches. A few of the townsfolk were doing just that, leaning back with heels on the ground or draped longways as if the bench was a cot. He wouldn't fit if he tried that, anyway.

He passed a general store and a separate dry good store, an ice cream parlor — another temptation, even after all the baked goods he'd crammed into his belly — and then the churchyard, which he decided to take as a warning against eating himself to death.

When he'd walked around the square and was almost back to Mamie's again, he struck out down a still-unfamiliar side street. A blacksmith was hammering away at something inside his shop — Jake could see sparks flying as he passed by. If Jake was getting sweaty just walking in this heat, the blacksmith must be plenty worse off.

As he shook his head in sympathy and prepared to keep walking, he heard footsteps behind him and turned to see a pretty little family party. A man in a frock coat, carrying what might be a doctor's bag, escorted a woman in a white uniform somewhat the worse for wear. The woman pushed some sort of wheeled carriage with a bright-eyed baby girl sitting upright in it, dark hair only sparsely covering her head but equipped with a cheery red ribbon. Jake stood aside to let them pass, but they stopped instead, the man tipping his hat before he said, "Am I by any chance addressing the newcomer who stepped in to assist our Madam Mamie?"

Now that was an interesting way to put it. These two good citizens, or at least one of them, claiming Mamie as their own and evidently approving of the man who'd aided her? He tipped his own hat and answered, "You are indeed. Jacob Flint at your service. And as we're guessing, would you be the town doctor and his —" What did that uniform mean? And how did it fit with her pushing a baby?

The man rescued him with a smile. "Doctor Joshua Gibbs, at your service, and my helpmate in both life and work."

The woman put out her hand, in a gesture more forthright than common. "Clara Gibbs, also accompanied by Alice Gibbs. And I thank you — I can, I believe, safely say we thank you — for protecting Madam Mamie and the town peace last night. Joshua saw to patching up the troublemaker you ejected."

"I'm sorry the matter disturbed your evening, and possibly your sleep."

Dr. Gibbs smiled wryly. "It comes with the job. My patients don't always have the forethought to injure themselves before supper." His face shifted toward sober.

"There's plenty who have more to contend with than interrupted sleep. And not all as fortunate as I am, to return from my labors to safety and shelter."

The man was the right age to be a veteran, if he'd joined up as an eager young lad. Something in his expression suggested he'd had to leave that young lad far behind. Mrs. Gibbs put a hand on his arm, her expression echoing the pain in her husband's. Sympathy, or something else?

The baby chose that fortunate moment to start babbling. Both parents broke into smiles, and Mrs. Gibbs released the little girl from the carriage, picked her up, and put her in the doctor's arms. Dr. Gibbs kissed the baby's forehead, then blew noisily on the top of her head, leading to gales of giggles and flailing arms. Meanwhile, Mrs. Gibbs leaned forward and inspected Jake's cheek. "You've a bruise there, and a scrape. From last night?"

Jake shrugged. "I suppose so. I didn't notice, then or since."

"Well, it doesn't look as though it needs tending, but if it takes a troubling turn while you're here, or if you have any less obvious souvenirs that do, please come see us. Anyone can tell you where our office is."

That was about enough of being fussed over, even if the woman's manner was some ways from fussy. "I'm glad to've met you. Enjoy your walk." He tipped his hat again, wondering where to take himself that'd look like he'd meant to go that way all along.

Mrs. Gibbs' eyebrow didn't quite go up. If she could see through a man as well as that, the good doctor must have a lively time of it. "The same to you, Mr. Flint. Perhaps we'll meet again."

And that summed up his dilemma in a nutshell.

* * * * *

Last night had been especially busy, maybe from people hoping the drunk cowboy would come back with friends and cause an exciting scene. It took extra effort to wake the girls up, and she'd given in and let the most stubbornly sleepy ones stay abed another hour. She could always haul them out if necessary.

She indulged herself as well, having a third cup of coffee and putting her feet up while she drank it. By the time she'd finished, the early customers were trickling in. None of them picked Summer Dawn, which gave Mamie the chance to indulge herself another way. She pulled the girl aside and said, "Tell me about last night's helpful stranger. What went on?"

The girl's expression rarely changed. Mamie had given up telling her to smile at the customers. Some of them apparently liked that almost-glare she gave them instead. Now, though, her mouth curved ever so slightly upward. "Strong man. Good to have strong man in bed."

That was another thing. For all Mamie knew, Summer Dawn's English was as good as her own, and she used those short sentences with words missing as part of her act.

"Did he say anything much?"

The mouth got closer to a smile. Or a smirk. "Called me Indian princess. Said thank you."

It could have happened. Or the girl could have guessed that if Mamie was asking, she had some unusual interest in Jake and what he got up to. Too late to figure out which. "All right, go back and look — exotic." If the girl didn't know what that meant, too bad.

It was Joshua's day to give the girls their monthly

checkups. She managed to get the laggards out of bed and reasonably awake before he turned up, bright-eyed as usual — usual since his marriage, at least. Bless Clara.

Mamie led him up to a vacant bedroom — not the one that had been Amanda Jane's, because Mamie still couldn't go in there without her stomach turning, and was using it for storage. As Joshua set down his bag on the dressing table, which made an odd enough picture, he asked, "Everything all cleaned up and tidy after last night? I gather the cowboy didn't get far enough inside to break anything, but what about your esteemed guests?"

Mamie grimaced. "Two of them threw up, and both of them missed the basin. And the banker broke a chair, which was no surprise, fat as he's become. I charged enough to make up for it. And speaking of things that got broken, I assume you had that cowboy to tend. What shape was he in when Jake got through with him?"

Joshua tilted his head. "Jake, is it? The gentleman introduced himself to Clara and me as Jacob."

Damnation. Well, she wasn't going to get into their shared past and origins, not now anyway. "So how much work did you have to do, so late at night?"

Joshua twinkled at her another little while before he let her off the hook. "Dislocated shoulder. By the time his friends got him to me, he'd sobered up enough to tell how much it hurt. Clara took note of some of his cussing in case she ever needed to expand her vocabulary."

Mamie laughed out loud at that. Who'd have thought it, all that time Clara made her way around town without showing anyone a word or a smile? Some married couples really did do each other good.

She turned a little away and swallowed a lump in her throat, hoping Joshua didn't see, as Joshua added,

"Sprained wrist, too. That should keep him out of trouble a little longer. But he was probably able to ride out of town. I hope we're shut of him."

She was tempted to go back a step and ask what Joshua had thought of Jake, though why it should matter was another question. She said instead, "I told the men last night that maybe they'd found their new marshal."

Joshua chuckled. "That was quick thinking. What did they say?"

"Damned if I know. They were all talking at once. Let me know if you hear anything."

"Yes, ma'am. . . . Are your ladies ready for me?"

They had better be. "I'll start sending them in."

* * * * *

The marshal and his bride were leaving town on the evening train. With nothing else to do, and not all that clear on why he was still in town anyhow, Jake figured he'd follow the crowd going to see the couple off. At least it wasn't so hot that strolling to the station felt like a preview of hell. The station itself was nothing much to look at, but better kept up than many he'd seen, with plenty of spittoons and bins to throw trash in.

The bride hadn't been at the party, naturally, but a woman he'd guess to be her was getting on the train when Jake arrived, calling goodbye to the other women clustered nearby and waving handkerchiefs at her. She seemed a fussy sort, overdressed and busy, with a high-pitched voice that would have driven Jake mad in no time. Funny how a fellow manly enough to be a marshal could pick a woman like that. Maybe it made him feel more manly than he did to start with.

Jake hadn't figured on doing more than watching, but all of a sudden one of the men from the party — a member of the city council, if memory served — grabbed him by the elbow. Jake, already feeling jumpy, barely managed not to punch the fellow. Oblivious, the man said, "Let's get up there where we can say a proper goodbye! Maybe he'll have some advice for when you take his place."

The council member tugged him into the thick of the crowd and elbowed through it. The marshal-as-was stood on the platform on the last car, waving at the crowd like a politician. Jake saw no further sign of his fiancée. She'd probably gone to sit in the best car the train had to offer, fretting about when her husband would join her.

The marshal spotted Jake and hailed him. "Mr. Flint! Good of you to show up! Wanted to make sure I really left town, did you?" He laughed heartily at his own wit and then put on a more serious air. "I wish you the best, sir. I hope you'll take care of my little town. These are fine people here — you'll see."

Jake had some questions he'd like to ask the man, but not with so many people here to listen in. He settled on, "What's been the hardest part of your job?"

The marshal stroked his beard, which was awfully well groomed for anyone that worked for a living. Maybe the future missus insisted on it. After hemming and hawing until Jake expected the train to haul the fellow away before he got a word out, he replied, "I'd say it's having to manhandle or arrest folks I know." Present tense, Jake noticed. The man might have his misgivings about leaving for that desk job back East. "Like I said, they're good folks, even if they drink too much and get out of hand now and again, or have bad luck and don't handle it as well as they might. It gets tricky, trying not to be too rough on 'em and still getting the job done."

That was a good attitude for a lawman, Jake supposed, for all it sounded dull. "What about that cowboy? Was he someone you knew?"

"Naah, he was just passing through. We get a lot of them cowboys stopping here, before or after a cattle drive. And we get some traveling salesmen, and lawyers or judges riding circuit — not that I can tell a lawyer from a judge, without they tell me!" He guffawed again. "We're growing, too, being as there are always folks wanting to go west and the grasshoppers haven't been as bad hereabouts. So you see new faces, but after a while they turn into friends."

From the sound of things, the train would be leaving any minute. People the marshal actually knew were calling to him, saying goodbye, wishing him well, making wedding-night jokes. Jake had to raise his voice to ask one more question. "What was the best part?"

"What was that?" Jake had to try again, pretty much yelling this time. But the marshal managed to answer just as the train started moving. "Helping my neighbors. Making Cowbird Creek a better place to live. Good luck to you!"

Jake edged around the crowd and left, heading back to his hotel and thinking hard. Before he could care much about making a town better, he'd have to care about it in the first place. And the job still didn't sound like enough to keep a man busy — at least, a man that had made a point of staying busy for more years than he cared to look back on.

Did marshal have to be a full-time job? And what could he find out about this town, to see if it was more likely to keep him than any of the places he'd left behind?

He could only think of one person to ask.

Chapter 4

MAMIE had been wondering when she'd be seeing Jake again. If she'd placed a bet, she'd have lost — it was only one day after the marshal left town that Trudi knocked on the office door. "That good-looking stranger who threw the cowboy out, he's back and asking if you have time to see him."

Jake had got good-looking, she had to admit. He'd shown signs of it even as a shy, weedy youngster, under his pa's and grandpa's thumb, tagging along after his big brother when his brother would let him. She'd given the brother, Ethan, a nickname too — Esau, because the Biblical Jacob had a brother by that name, and because he was supposed to be awfully hairy, and Ethan was a little on the hairy side. But he probably never knew about it, unless Jake had mentioned it.

Anyway, if Jake wasn't a stranger to her, there was no need to mention it to Trudi or anyone else.

"Send him up, and I'll find out how much time he wants. How would you feel about taking care of things around here for an hour or two, if it comes to that? It'd be instead of seeing customers."

It could be that Trudi might have the makings of a second in command. She'd thought Amanda Jane would —

if she'd lived, if she'd been as strong as Mamie had always thought her. Trudi might be tougher.

Trudi hustled down the stairs and came back leading Jake by the hand. Of course she would. Jake was looking at their hands and away again as if he wasn't sure what to do about it. Mamie met them at the office door. "Thank you, Trudi. I'll let you know whether I need you to help out as we discussed. Why don't you go and see if there's a customer for you in the meantime."

Trudi let go of Jake and flounced away. Mamie sat back down at her desk. "Still here, I see?"

Jake didn't quite snort. "Still here. For now. That's part of what I was hoping to talk to you about. How busy are you? I could come back."

It was morning yet, but getting on for midday. She had dinner at her desk most days — too damn often, actually — but she could allow herself a treat for once. "Tell you what — we could talk over some dinner." In fact . . . . She laughed outright. "When was the last time you went on a picnic?"

Half an hour later, she'd passed the word around to tell Trudi — who she'd put in the small parlor, *not* her office — if anything needed handling, or to send someone to look for her down by the creek, near the big trees, if bad trouble blew up or blew in. She gathered the basket Cook had put together and then gathered up Jake, waiting in the kitchen and licking his lips at all of what Cook was packing. "Follow me."

Jake bowed and whisked the basket out of her hand. "Yes, m'lady. Lead the way, m'lady." She was mightily tempted to swat him, the way she once would have. But she'd need to get to know this older and different Jake before taking such liberties.

They walked down to a spot by the creek where the grass was thick and the rocks sparse. It was another scorcher, but a buckeye tree spread out its leaves to give them some shade. She waved toward a spot, and Jake obligingly set the basket down and opened it. Mamie pulled out the blanket at the top, unfolded it partway, and tossed one end to Jake. "Help me put this down." After about a second, she added, "Please."

Jake looked surprised when she pulled out plates. She stopped in the act of handing him one. "Of course, if you've got used to the crunch and flavor of ants in your dinner, I wouldn't want to deprive you."

He chuckled and reached for the plate. "I may as well try this fancified lifestyle you've got used to. And maybe a few ants will manage to join us after all."

She emptied the basket, to give them the widest choice, and helped herself to a big wedge of cheese, a corn muffin, and a bottle of beer. She left the roast chicken to Jake, who seemed ready to appreciate it. She also left it to him to start on whatever he needed to talk about, though she could guess at the gist of it.

He was in no hurry to come to the point, for all that. He made it through two drumsticks and three corn muffins, washed down with water from his canteen, before he said through a mouthful of muffin, "I went to the station to see the marshal leave town. Quite a crowd there. Was he that popular, or are people here that bored?"

"Oh, folks liked him well enough. He did his job, and he never pushed people around for the fun of it."

Jake rubbed his chin, the beard stiff enough that it barely budged. "I was wondering about that. About his job. What did he do all day? Sit on his behind with his feet on his desk? Walk around town looking up and down for anyone acting shifty? Nap?"

Mamie dabbed her lips with her napkin and lay back on the blanket, watching a breeze shove the leaves around and change the patterns of the shade. "I never troubled much about how he spent his time, so long as he wasn't giving me and my girls any trouble. Some lawmen do, you know — treat whores as if they're all thieves, out to cheat customers or pick their pockets, or to lure husbands away from wives. The marshal wasn't bad, that way. He expected free service now and then, and I'm not fool enough to have said no."

Jake frowned and muttered something under his breath, then looked her in the eye. "I wouldn't. If they offered me the job and I took it. I've no interest in cheating a businesswoman. And whatever they'd plan on paying me, my needs are few enough, so I wouldn't be needing any favors."

Mamie sat back up and rolled her eyes. "Favors, is it? That's a highfalutin' name for it."

He broke off a piece of muffin and tossed it at her. "You know that's not what I was meaning."

She caught the tidbit and popped it in her mouth, chewed it, gulped it down, and patted her stomach. "Thank you, sir. That was just what I needed to finish up."

Jake stood up with a little groan and stretched. "And after that meal, I need something else. To get moving, I'm thinking." He turned slowly around in a circle, as if looking for something to race or wrestle with, and stopped, looking at the tree.

"That'll do just fine!" He grabbed a big branch and swung himself up into the tree, climbing up hand over hand like some sort of monkey until he was halfway up. Then he leaned out and grinned at her.

She chose to take it as a dare. Grinning back as if the pair of them were nine years old again, she grabbed her skirts and and tied them in a knot. Then she walked quickly around the tree to the lowest sturdy limb, grabbed it, hoisted herself up enough to lay across it, and clasped it with her legs like a lover. That let her haul herself up to a sitting position, scoot to where the branches forked, lean back, and finally look up to see what he made of it. He was bent over laughing 'til she thought he'd fall out of the tree. She could have joined in, but instead she settled herself as sedately as if she were sipping tea, and asked, "Now what were you saying about the marshal job?"

His fit of laughing wound down, and he went back to stroking his chin again. "I just don't know as it could keep me occupied. I'm used to working hard and long. Can a marshal here do anything else along with?"

She started to shrug and decided the branch wasn't wide enough for that to be prudent. "We've only had the one marshal, so I couldn't really say. Before the council hired him, we made do with the county sheriff. Someone had to go fetch him if we needed him bad enough. Otherwise, whatever men were handy dealt with troublemakers as best they could. We've been lucky, I guess, that we never had the meanest ones, nor anything here a gang of outlaws might come for."

He looked at her and frowned. "I would think a house as fancy as yours, full of fine things and finer ladies, might be enough to bring some. Word must get around, with cowboys and the like coming and going."

Mamie hadn't thought back on that night in years. She slept better that way. "Something did happen, not long after we got started. Three men came in together, whooping and hollering, pushing behind the bar and throwing glassware at each other. It was just as well they started there, and started noisy — by the time they headed for the parlor where the girls were, the men in there knew what was happening and took care of them." She managed a smile. "Even early on, I already had enough customers for that."

Jake broke off a branch and twiddled it. "Is that when you started hiring bouncers?"

She nodded, carefully. "I should have done it sooner. It's been a nuisance, though, keeping the position filled. Either they're not as capable as they think they are, like the fellow whose job you did for him, or they get frustrated and resentful being around the girls so much and not having access to them. Which I also tried, at one point, but it tended to reduce my authority, for reasons I couldn't spell out but in some way understand."

Jake nodded, more carelessly than Mamie had, one big arm around the tree trunk. "That makes sense. They probably start out resenting that they have to take orders from you, and if they're allowed to make free with what you're selling, they feel like they're getting away with something and somehow outsmarting you."

Well, he'd never been dim-witted. And that was enough about the trickier aspects of her life and business. "What sort of other work might you want, if you agreed to be marshal but it wasn't enough for you?"

He whacked the trunk with the branch he'd been holding and threw it to the ground. "That's the trouble. I don't see any coal or copper mines hereabouts, even if I wanted to go back to that work, and you've already got a blacksmith." A crooked smile, more bitter than any smile should be, came and went on his face. "And I assume you've got a town preacher."

When she'd mentioned what she would've guessed

he'd become, she hadn't had that notion in mind. He read her expression and gave a snort of laughter no more cheerful than the smile had been. "Of course, I've got no religion, and haven't for some years. But I don't reckon a preacher really needs it. Might be better if they knew they didn't, instead of telling themselves they believed all that guff and not living up to it when it counts."

The picture of young Jake, skinny and earnest and believing everything his daddy did, floated up like she was seeing double. "So you've left it all behind? Jesus, and heaven waiting, and the flames of hell licking at us, and Bible stories?" His name, and how serious he used to take it?

He actually spat, away from her and into the tree. "All the pretty stories. And the ugly ones. Plenty of those, there were. No, I decided long since that life isn't about trying to make God love you more than your daddy could. Or reward you for letting people knock you down and trample you for the fun of it."

There'd been a time when part of her wished he could make her believe life was something better than a cheap swindle. "So now you know that life is . . . ."

He shut his eyes like something was paining him. He wasn't so far from his old self that he didn't care. "Now I know life is getting through. Not letting people hurt you when they've no right to. Not letting bullies have their own way without paying for it. Leaving a mark, even if it fades as quick as a bruise on the bully's face. And finding pleasure if you can't find joy."

* * * * *

Well, that was a whole lot more than he'd planned on

saying, even — especially — to someone who'd known him before.

At least he could change the subject by asking something he really wanted to know. "What do you like about this town? Aside from having built something to be proud of?"

Her head jerked back a little, like he'd startled her. Did she think he wouldn't count a parlor house as something to take pride in? He put his hand on hers to steady her. "Don't go falling off, now. At least not before answering my question."

She took her turn startling him by sticking her tongue out at him. She laughed to see his face and relaxed back against her branch. "Part of it's how it compares to places I was before getting here. There are people I'd like to hit with a stick, but not so many, and not as eager to remind me of their existence. There's a nice mix of folks I've had a chance to get to know — and work out ways to get along with — and new faces coming through. There are pretty places around, like this one, when I need to get away from walls and furniture." She paused, looking off into the tree like she was checking a list in her mind. "I've even made a handful of actual friends. You met two of them, Joshua and Clara Gibbs. And there's one who left town — that's a story I should tell you sometime, if you stick around long enough for me to get to it! Freida Blum, a Hebrew widow lady with a tongue that never stops and a habit of plowing through anything in the way of what she sets her mind on. You'd never have thought a smooth-talking, golden-haired medicine show pitchman would take her fancy, but when he did, off they rode in his wagon as if she was twenty years younger. This town has been a duller place since she left, though she writes me now and then, and I cherish her letters."

Mamie sounded wistful, talking about this friend from whom she could only receive letters. Just more proof, if he'd needed more, that people didn't know how to appreciate their good fortune. He might never get another letter in his life, unless his life changed course enough to surprise him. Not the way he kept moving. Though that would, in fact, change if he took the marshal job. Which was a fairly compelling reason not to take it, come to that.

Oh, he'd written letters. Once in a long while, when he'd had a few drinks and could ignore how little he had to say, he'd write to Richard, who'd lay Jake flat if he ever called him by his full name. It was one of the first things he ever said to Jake when Jake showed up, a landlubber still not far from skinny and wide-eyed to see real fighting men all round him. "You ever hear someone call me Richard, you'll know they're no friend of mine. Call me Rich. Not that I'm rich or ever will be, but got to give old Neptune something to laugh at, don't we?" And then he'd showed Jake how to tie his first knot as a sailor.

But he should keep up his end of the conversation. Mamie'd done her prying, so it was only fair if he took his turn. "Have other people left that you hoped would stick around?"

She wriggled against the branch. "I'll make you a deal. I'll answer that if you help me down out of this tree. I was always better at climbing up than getting down. I'll bet you remember that."

It was his turn to laugh. "I surely do. That time when you climbed the big oak behind my house, you caterwauled loud enough to scatter the chickens. I'd better jump down and get to it before you break my ears." He did just that, and dodged the twig she threw at him on his way down. He stopped under the tree, looked around, and started whistling like he'd decided to leave her up there, but reached on up just as she grabbed for another twig to break off. She inched down toward him to where he could just reach her hips. Hips broad enough for him to grab easy. Hips to hold onto.

She slid on into his arms, her cheeks flushed a becoming pink, and pulled herself away as soon as her feet touched the ground, moving toward the blanket and the picnic basket. He took his time following her, letting her have a minute to get over whatever that all meant. It didn't take her long to pack everything up, somehow fitting the blanket and plates and napkins and bits of food remaining. He picked up the basket and started ambling back into town, letting her go just as slowly or pick up the pace as she chose. She did the former as she took a deep breath and finally answered his question.

"There's only one to tell of — at least, who left for other parts instead of for whatever awaits us after death." She paused as if to let him interrupt with his current opinion on the matter, then went on. "She was one of my girls, a country gal who came from a town like ours, if ours had been poorer and more of the folks as shiftless as my people. She ran off with some no-good fellow and ended up making her living on her back. My place was a real step up for her, and I trained her up to suit it."

They were halfway back to town. "What happened? Where did she go?"

Mamie gave a soft snort. "Durned if I know where. She took up with a young fellow, off one of our farms, who had a gift for carving on leather — saddles, boots, anything. He'd lost part of his leg in some farm accident, but he still got it into his head to go on the road with a wagon, fancying up people's saddles and such, and she went along with him as a sort of sales assistant. After they got married, that is. That's another story you'd like to hear, the way Tom told off the preacher at a funeral. After that, we had to fetch another one out of town to wed them."

If he stuck around, that made at least two stories he could count on hearing.

They were in town proper, and attracting more than a few glances. Jake ignored them, and was preoccupied enough doing so that he almost missed Mamie's next softly spoken words. "That girl, Jenny, she had red hair. At least, after I told her to. It looked well on her."

He'd been wondering, and this seemed like an invitation to ask. "Why'd you get rid of the red in your hair?"

No soft voice now — still quiet, but hard as iron. "I didn't want anyone finding me. Anyone from home, if they were to take it into their heads to look. Nor anyone from the places I passed through, in case something went missing after I left and they decided I'd be just the person to blame it on. It's too easy to ask around about the whore — or, if I did what I hoped to do, the madam — with the strawberry-blonde hair." And then, under her breath so he could barely catch it: "It was harder than most things I left behind. But it doesn't matter."

She had no idea how well he understood. If they had still been out by the creek, sitting on the blanket or even up in the tree, he'd have tried to offer the comfort she looked to need. But she wouldn't thank him for drawing more attention than they already were.

As they reached her door with its red lamps, he stopped and looked her in the face. "Honestly, Mamie, do you think I could live here without going crazy?"

She looked back at him, just as straight. "I don't know, Jake. Not unless you found something more to do than handling drunks. I don't know what it'd be."

Chapter 5

IF THERE was a God after all, He had a mean sense of humor. Which was pretty much what Jake had figured for a while now.

Jake had hardly made it halfway down the street, heading for the hotel, when he came face to face with a man he might have known was a preacher by the pious expression he affected, even if he hadn't been dressed like it. The man looked over Jake's shoulder and frowned, as if just the chance that Jake had walked by a den of sinners had made fair to spoil his day. And yet he had to know how Jake had come to anyone's notice in this town in the first place.

Jake tipped his hat and smiled politely, just to see what would happen. The man brightened up and changed direction to walk beside him. "Good afternoon to you! Am I addressing the newcomer who some are saying should become our next marshal?"

Jake put on as bland an expression as ever he had. "Reckon so. I had the good fortune to meet some of this town's leading citizens at a very pleasant gathering the other night, and they suggested as much."

The preacher's mouth puckered like he was eating that slimy food the German sailors liked. At least, that's what happened to Jake the one time he'd been fool enough to try it. Jake held in the laugh that wanted to come out as the man cleared his throat and soldiered on. "Our old marshal was a good man, certainly! We were all sorry — that is, we were of course happy for him to find a good woman to complete his life, and we wish him all the best. But we'll miss him. There were points on which he and I had our differences, but he was always willing to let me try to lead him in a direction more pleasing to the Lord."

There was only so much mischief Jake could hold back on, and it was going to brim over. "I'll tell you what, Reverend. I'll talk with you as much as ever you like, so long as we can do it over a few glasses of beer or whiskey. Maybe at Madam Mamie's, seeing as she stocks the best to be had."

The man stopped in his tracks, his face turning red. Jake kept going without looking to see how long the preacher stood there. He whistled as he walked, a sea shanty he'd learned from the cook on his first voyage after the war, hearing the words in the old cook's voice.

The captain's wife was Charlotte
She was a natural harlot
All through the night her thighs shone white
By morning they were scarlet.

An appropriate choice, that. It brought him back to the other night, and the Indian girl — though she was a duskier color. But there were plenty of other gals there who'd fit the song better.

Not to mention Mamie, whose hips he'd only felt and not seen. But he'd wager they'd look as fine as they'd felt in his hands.

* * * * *

Trudi looked a deal less smug and more frazzled than

she had when Mamie headed out. Not that anything much had happened, from what Trudi had to say — a spat between Lucette and one of the newer girls, Rena, about who had caught a customer's eye first, and another customer claiming he'd been promised a longer visit when the saloon keeper sold him a token. At least Trudi had the sense not to buy that story, though whether she'd managed the man with the right mix of firmness and flattery was more of a question.

Mamie summoned Lucette and Rena, giving a lecture Lucette had heard before and Rena had coming, and jotted down the description of the problem customer. She'd barely made it back, and the picnic felt like a distant memory. Too bad.

She expected the knock on the door to mean more aggravation. But it was Sophie who trotted in at Mamie's command, her cheeks pink from the heat outside, holding a letter in her hand. "This came for you, ma'am."

Mamie held out her hand for it. "And what else did you pick up in town?"

The cheeks got deeper pink. "Nothing much, ma'am. Only a new ribbon and an ice cream. I had the coin."

This time, she had. If Mamie had to talk to Sophie one more time about wheedling shopkeepers for credit, she'd turn Bessie loose on her. Speaking of pink cheeks.

Sophie lingered, probably curious, until Mamie sent her on her way with a "back to work, now!" Once she'd pattered down the stairs, Mamie inspected the letter and immediately broke into a broad smile. She hadn't heard from Freida Blum in a month or more, and she could use the pick-me-up. She opened the letter and sat back.

Mamie, darling, hello from Alabama! It's all so interesting, seeing new places, and it's funny to be back to not understanding what people say, almost. They talk so differently down here, I never knew people in this country could talk so many ways. It was so nice to get your letter, I could almost hear your voice, and of course I understood every word!

It is so hot, I'm melting, you'd be surprised how much of me is still left. Jedidiah is so good to me, he brings me water to wash three times a day, and last night we stayed in a hotel that had ice! I dumped handfuls of it in the bath, it was heaven. That ice bath cooled me down enough we could make love without turning into a pair of lobsters. Which reminds me, dear Joshua took me aside one day before we left town, he was blushing like a rose he was so embarrassed, but he was worried that too much of what he called "marital exercise" might be bad for my heart. Silly boy, as though I'd live forever if I pushed Jedidiah away at night, what a waste that would be! But I did listen, that's why that ice was such a gift, I've been more careful this summer since we came south. I think hell would be cooler or at least less humid, good thing I don't believe in it like your preacher!

Mamie was laughing to the point that she had to put the letter down and wipe her eyes. What she'd pay to see Freida and the preacher debate the existence of hell and the devil!

But I was going to say, you do know more about men, do you think I should ask Jedidiah if he'd like to spend time with any of your ladies when we come through town, a nice change to be with a woman so much younger, I wouldn't mind so much.

Mamie shook her head. How many women would ask such a question? How Freida must love that man.

Well, it's time for me to stop rambling on, we're packing up for the next town, still in Alabama, but sooner or later we'll turn around. Jedidiah tells me we'll head to Tennessee, Nashville, before too long, you can send me a letter to the post office there and maybe I'll get it. I'd love to hear about you and Joshua and everyone, and whether anything has changed in Cowbird Creek, has anyone new moved in? Or just tell me you're well and happy, that'll be enough.

Love, your friend Freida who's travelling all over in a wagon, who'd have thought it!

Did she have time to respond now? She should really go downstairs instead, show herself in the parlor, walk through the halls and listen for any trouble. She'd already indulged herself more than commonly. Picnicking! Climbing trees!

The smile that took over her face felt unfamiliar.

Too many hours later, with the house finally closed for the night, Mamie settled down with her sherry, read Freida's letter again, and took up her pen to answer.

Dearest Freida —

I'm so glad to hear that you're managing, and enjoying life and your delightful husband, in spite of the heat. May I ask how soon you'll escape northward? I can't claim that it's cool and refreshing hereabouts, but it can't be as bad as Alabama, and I promise to have at least two or three of the girls fan you while you sit and talk to me. Unless you'd prefer more privacy.

As for your question about Jedidiah and my girls, your generosity humbles me. If I were to do anything so drastic as to really pair up with a man, let alone marry him, I would string him up by his thumbs — or worse — if he touched another woman. Unless I decided to be particularly wild one night, and invite another woman to join us in bed. We have two girls in the house at present who almost certainly lie with each other, and they give every sign of enjoying it.

Should she mention Jake's arrival? He hadn't moved to town, not yet and maybe never. What would be the point? What could she say about him?

I told you how it looked like the marshal's fiancée was pulling his strings and would get him to give up the job and go back east.

No surprise — that's what happened. If a man doesn't have the stomach to be a lawman, then good riddance to him. Someone passing through town came around just in time to break up a fight, and now the bigwigs are trying to get him to stay and be the new marshal. If it happens, I'll tell you more about him.

Love, your friend, Mamie

* * * * *

Jake, having nothing much to do with himself before another dinner at the mayor's house, took a walk back to the creek and then along it until it left the town behind. Which part of him was ready to do. Nobody had yet given him a good reason to stay.

But then, he didn't have a better reason to be anywhere else.

The creek took him past two farms, at one of which he saw one of the cowbirds that gave it its name, sitting on a fencepost and looking less than energetic. He tipped his hat to it as he went by. Now that he was noticing, there were robins hunting their dinner in the grass by the creek, and barn swallows swooping to somewhere or other. He rolled up his shirtsleeves, and when that didn't give him enough relief from the heat, squatted by the creek and dipped his arms in the water up to the elbow.

"You make me long for different sleeves."

Jake looked up, startled and almost toppling into the water. Standing a few feet back from the creek was one of the few people in town he knew, the doctor's wife. She was picking at her sleeves as if deciding whether she could find some way to get them out of her way. "I don't, in general, envy Madam Mamie's employees, but I strongly suspect their dresses have shorter sleeves. Not that they seem to spend much time outdoors, let alone idling by the creek."

Jake finally tipped his hat. "Good morning, Mrs. Gibbs —"

Clara shook her head. "I'm more comfortable with the name I've carried all my life than the one I've acquired as an incident of marriage. Please call me Clara, if it doesn't bother you to do so."

She seemed perfectly sincere, or something more emphatic. "Clara, then. And I'm Jacob." But her manner called for a further retreat from formality. "Or Jake, either one. And I wouldn't mind leaving the idling to others, if I had something to keep me busy."

She cocked her head. "There we may differ. I don't object to being busy as a rule, but I find only fresh air makes the heat tolerable. In a minute, I'll go back to my garden and make myself useful, if at a slower pace than I would in cooler weather. My mother is with Alice, so I can actually get something accomplished there. As for you, the word is that you have a job waiting, if you care to whistle for it."

Jake stood up and shook the water off his arms. "If you're ready for your gardening, we can walk back together, if that suits you." It seemed an insult to suggest to this particular woman that anyone would disapprove of her walking with a man neither husband nor family, or that she'd pay them any mind if they did.

Clara accepted by starting to walk toward town, slowly enough that it was plain she wasn't trying to escape his offer, and then faster as if reaching her natural pace. As they walked, Jake wiped his arms on his pants and rolled his sleeves back down, leaving the buttons for when he settled somewhere. He hadn't answered her question, if he could call it that, and he figured she wouldn't badger him about it. But after a few more steps, he said, "You must have known the marshal, and gotten some sense of what he did with himself. Do you think a man who'd rather work than wander by the creek could be satisfied taking on the job?"

She took her time answering, and finally said, "I have my doubts. To be sure, you'd have some of the kind of excitement that brought you to the town's attention. But you'd be in charge of the jail, and even though it isn't likely you'd be keeping anyone there for long, it would be hard for a man to whom physical freedom is personally important. Based on our very brief acquaintance, I'd guess you'd rather thrash a troublemaker than watch him sit in a cage."

The very idea of standing on the other side of iron bars, keeping another man locked up, made the muscles across his back go tight as a drum. He'd sooner be the man springing another man from jail, one way or another, than carrying the key.

"And you'd likely end up sweeping streets and chasing stray dogs, unless you found yourself a deputy to do it. With all the farm boys hereabouts, you might have takers, though none would be likely to stay long."

Like Mamie's bouncers.

Should he consider farming? It would tie him to one piece of land, but he'd answer to no one, and he'd end the day tired enough to sleep. And maybe starve when the weather killed the crops, or the grasshoppers blew in.

Clara seemed to have no problem with his silence. When they were back in town, she stopped and said, "This is where our paths diverge, if you're going back to the center of town — and isn't that a grand phrase for it! But I hope you'll come over one day before you go — perhaps to Sunday supper."

He tipped his hat. "I'd enjoy that." Something spurred his tongue to add, "You and your husband seem like interesting folks to get to know."

The breadth and warmth of her smile startled him, and made him realize how sparing she was of her smiles as a rule. "Give us warning before you disappear, then, and we'll arrange it."

For lack of any other urgent destination, and for the refreshing pleasure of her company, Jake walked Clara all the way to her waiting garden. Clara, assuming she had chosen what to plant, appeared to like warm colors best, with tall black-eyed Susans rising above even deeper yellow coneflowers. Flanking the flowers were rows of what he guessed were herbs. The blend of practicality with something more individual reminded him of Clara herself. He muttered something appreciative and took his leave.

Without Clara to pace him, Jake's steps slowed and dragged as he neared the hotel and contemplated, without pleasure, cleaning up for dinner. The mayor was likely to press him for an answer about the marshal job. Did he know enough about it to turn it down? That'd leave him back where he'd been too often, at a loss for what to do next.

Back to sea might be best. He'd got good at it, and he could probably find a berth readily enough. And even if he had second thoughts after leaving port, he never felt as trapped when he had all the ocean around him, even if it should make him feel more so. Jake the sailor was as good as any other Jake he'd been since he left home.

Chapter 6

OVER time, Mamie and Clara had worked out a way to spend time together and remain something close to discreet about it. Clara was hardly conventional, but there was no point in scandalizing the townsfolk — who had got used to Clara's manner and activities, and appreciated the doctoring she and Joshua provided together — to the point where it would damage the couple's medical practice. When Mamie went on one of her walks, she would pass by the Gibbs place, as used to be Freida Blum's house, and whistle "The Mulligan Guard." If Clara was home and not too busy, she would take a walk as well, bringing the baby if the baby wasn't out at the farm with Clara's family, and make her way to the creek. They could walk and talk there, and then Mamie would let Clara leave first, a blameless matron with her child.

It had rained the night before, washing some of the humidity out of the air, and Mamie's feet itched for a walk. If Fate was in a friendly mood, Clara might be free and feel the same. Mamie did her walk-and-whistle routine and hustled a little, to stay ahead of Clara should her more respectable friend be following behind.

When she reached the creek, she ambled a ways downstream, looking at the yellow and red golden tickseed in the sunny patches away from the trees, and the bushes of deep pink hibiscus blossoms near the water. She didn't pick any — she rarely picked flowers, which were more use to more people, not to mention lived longer, when left alone.

When she'd had enough of flowers, she found the tree she and Jake had climbed and leaned against it, facing toward town, until she saw Clara on the way, pushing the baby's carriage. As mother and baby drew closer, Mamie laughed to hear Clara whistling that same tune. Mamie looked around to make sure no bystanders were nearby and then joined in.

Clara and little Alice reached Mamie with a measure or so left to go, so they finished in tolerable unison, Mamie swiping the baby out of the carriage in time to whistle the final notes while hoisting her in the air. Alice giggled, at the music or the motion, and waved her hands around — hands already less chubby than the last time Mamie had seen her. Mamie ignored a momentary pang at how quickly babies grew, blew at the baby's hair to ruffle it, and then handed her back to Clara, asking, "And what new frontiers has this adventurer reached lately?"

Clara cradled Alice with effortless expertise. "She is exploring the house by means of the furniture, and casting longing glances at the freedom to be found if she releases her grip. Speaking of adventurers, I met the man who disposed of your drunken cowboy visitor. Twice, actually."

Mamie would have made a point of controlling her reaction, if she could decide what reaction she preferred to show. She let her face do whatever it would, and asked, "What did you make of him?"

Clara knelt down, barely glancing first to find a dry and clean stretch of grass, and held Alice's hands so the baby could practice standing. Mamie leaned back against the tree, the better to watch the stray breezes move the leaves. Clara kept her voice soothing and low, as if addressing the baby rather than her adult companion. "He seemed comfortable with plain speaking, which you can imagine I found refreshing. Beyond that, he struck me as restless — a man who must remain in motion, for reasons of his own." Clara tugged her hands very slightly forward, giving the baby the idea of stepping. "I don't know whether you've been hoping he'd be our marshal, but if I had to guess, I would doubt he will. I may bear some responsibility for that — he asked me whether I thought he'd care for the job, and I answered him honestly."

Mamie could hardly be surprised — either at Clara being honest, or at Clara's prediction of how Jake would like being marshal. She was, perhaps, a little taken aback at Jake's asking Clara in the first place. Was it attraction? Or did he simply find Clara easy to talk to?

She should be glad, if that was the case. And Jake would hardly question Mamie about the job she herself had suggested, quite publicly, that he should take.

Clara clapped the baby's hands together, making the baby giggle, and asked, "You may know the man better than I. Do you think he'd make a good marshal?"

Mamie reached up a hand to rest on the branch Jake had used to hoist himself up, the day of their picnic. "I don't know him that well, not now, not as a man. I knew him rather better as a boy — you may well look surprised! — and I would've said, then, that he'd be a very good marshal indeed, if he could be brought to consider such a thing."

The baby started fussing, apparently tired of being on her feet and not sure what to do about it. Clara sat back and lowered the baby to her lap, rocking a little back and forth; the baby settled down, leaning against her mother's arms, her eyes drifting closed. "If we could stay here longer, I hope you'd tell me more about your and his shared past. How much do you believe he's changed?"

And wasn't that a good question. "From what I've seen so far, I'd say he's changed in almost every obvious way. I don't know, yet, whether he's changed at the core." She let her arm drop and pushed herself upright, brushing off the back of her dress. "I gather you need to get going. Shall I leave first, this time, or will you?"

Clara looked down at the child in her arms. "I believe Alice here votes for a nap, and I'd rather not try to sit here, immobilized, while she takes it." With no further ado, she rose to her feet, most efficiently, without jostling the baby more than a little. "Until next time. And speaking of next time, Joshua and I would be very happy to have you over for dinner, and to blazes with any lifted eyebrows that might result. No one is likely to do without doctoring in order to satisfy their actual or pretended scruples."

It wasn't the first time Clara had made the suggestion. It might be time Mamie stopped brushing it aside. "Maybe. Thank you. Give my best to Joshua."

Clara didn't quite smile, but the light in her eyes could almost be called mischievous. "And give my best to your friend with the mysterious background. I'm not sure what you want him to do, but I hope he does it."

Mamie's breakfast next morning came accompanied by the weekly newspaper. She could hardly help but notice the headline, "Bold Newcomer Prevents Invasion of Departing Marshal's Farewell Festivities." A reporter had come by the next day and pestered her into giving a short interview with few specifics. The reporter, or perhaps the editor, had filled in the gaps with colorful fiction. The drunken cowboy had transformed into three fearsome ruffians, over whom Jake prevailed due to his unusual strength and admirable courage. Mamie swallowed her mouthful of coffee before she could snort it out her nose. Would people actually believe such stuff, when there were plenty of eyewitnesses to gainsay it? Though they might not want to remind the townspeople that they had been part of a gathering at her scandalous establishment.

She was somewhat surprised to see Rena come into the kitchen with the *Omaha Daily Bee*. Mamie kept it in the parlor for the occasional customer to look at while waiting. What was Rena doing with it?

Rena had folded the paper to show the personals ads, and she was too excited to apologize for disturbing Mamie's breakfast. "Look, ma'am! There's a rich gentleman looking for ladies with what he calls worldly experience, because he wants a wife as knows what's what, and —"

Mamie snatched the paper out of her hand. "Oh, of all the nonsense! Girl, if you want to work at another house, probably a place with a row of huts and a line of unwashed men waiting their ten-minute turn before the next man shoves in, and get charged so much for your cot and the slop they feed you that you just get deeper into debt and can't run off without some corrupt local lawman dragging you back, then by all means write to the *gentleman* and see how you like it. You think it over and let me know — *after* I've had breakfast. Scoot!"

Rena stood there with her lip quivering, then turned on her heel and ran out sniffling. Mamie blew out an exasperated breath and took another sip of her coffee — lukewarm. She started to thrust it toward Cook, then got ahold of herself and stood up to bring it to her. "Could you throw this away, please, and bring me hotter?"

Waiting for her coffee and scooping up some eggs, which had also got less than agreeably hot, she read the offending ad and put the paper down. She was about to look for any news of interest when another ad caught her eye.

E. in Deliverance seeks news of his brother J., not seen in many years. Please send word to . . . .

Mamie dropped the paper on the table just as Cook brought her fresh coffee. She forced a smile and thanked her, hoping she'd managed to act normal. She sipped the coffee, too hot this time, and gulped it down even though it burned her mouth.

Of course it could be anyone from Deliverance, maybe someone who'd arrived there in recent years, whose name started with E and had a brother — anywhere — whose name started with J. Why would Ethan be spending the money to put ads in who knows how many papers? How could he even afford it? It probably had nothing to do with Jake.

But . . . why had Jake left home?

Chapter 7

SOPHIE tapped on the door to Mamie's office and then shoved Bessie in through it. The pair of them were like something out of vaudeville. Mamie, amused enough not to be too irritated at yet another interruption, asked crisply, "What is it? One of you, speak up."

Bessie glanced over her shoulder in a way that suggested Sophie might be poking her. "We were just wondering, ma'am, about whether we'd have a chance to thank that strong, handsome man who helped out the other night. Not that you won't have done that, of course, but the rest of us haven't, mostly." And then, with the faint resentment many of the girls had when speaking of their Indian coworker, "I don't know as Summer Dawn would have bothered."

Mamie set down the ledger she'd been studying. "As it happens, you're not the first girls to ask that question." In fact, they were the fourth and fifth — so far. "I've already sent Mr. Flint a message, asking if he'd honor us with his company for dinner tomorrow. I might even close up for the dinner hour so you can all be there, seeing as it's rarely busy then."

Sophie squealed, and Bessie pulled her close enough to buss her cheek and pat her behind. Mamie let herself chuckle. "Now get back to work, the pair of you, and leave me to do the same."

Apparently, primping for an actual guest, one the girls wanted to see, was a whole different matter from dressing to please customers. At dinnertime the following day, if there was a ribbon in the place that wasn't in someone's hair, she'd go and kiss the preacher. And as for scent, she'd already had to send two girls to wash it off. "Do you want the man to be able to taste his food or no?"

Mamie herself was wearing her newest dress, not that Jake would know the difference. She'd wager he couldn't tell one fancy dress from another, except for how much flesh it left showing. And she had no intention of competing with the girls on that score. She reached over to yank Nancy's bodice higher.

When the knock came at the door, she sent Trudi, as one of the more level-headed girls, to let him in. Jake couldn't be traveling with many changes of clothing, but he'd taken some trouble to clean up, his waistcoat freshly brushed and his hair as slicked down as it would submit to being. His eyes went wide as he looked around at the eager crowd before singling out Mamie. "Thank you for the invitation. And the reception."

A spirit of mischief led her to curtsy to him. "Thank you for accepting, sir. This way."

* * * * *

"... So my mate Rich and I hid in the hold until the first mate got good and drunk, and once he was asleep and snoring, we crept out, tied him to a barrel, and shaved him bald!" Jake grinned as a chorus of gasps and titters rose all round the table. He'd told the tale before often enough, but always in a saloon or a bunkhouse. The audiences there sounded pretty damn different.

"What *happened*?" one of the ladies said, a young one with a round face and bright brown eyes that matched her hair.

"Well, he was pretty riled when he woke up. Started hollering and cussing, naturally. But that gave me time to round up some witnesses who'd had as much ill-treatment from him as I had, and they all had a good laugh. Well worth a stretch of bread and water — especially given what they fed us otherwise."

The brown-eyed lady clasped her hands to her breast — of which there was plenty — and looked like she wanted to get hold of him and feed him extra. The Indian girl, Summer Dawn, looked more like she admired him for paying a price, even a small one, for some revenge.

Mamie signaled the cook to bring in what proved to be dessert, a tall layer cake with thick white frosting. He did his best to do justice to it while the ladies wheedled him for more stories. Halfway through his slice, he took a break, laid down his fork, and said, "There was that time on a cattle drive when I woke up from a sound sleep to find a stampede bearing down on me. Some damfool — excuse me, ladies — " That brought more tittering. " — wore a straw hat instead of something more sensible. When one of the cows decided that hat looked mighty tasty and took hold of it, he started hollering and trying to get it away from her. She panicked, and that got the rest of 'em going. I jumped up as quick as I could and managed to get out of it with a few kicks, instead of my face trampled in."

More gasps and in-drawn breaths. The brown-eyed girl looked ready to cry. Mamie just stood up and clapped her hands. "All right, girls, that's enough lollygagging. Back to work, the lot of you. Trudi, take the Closed sign off the front door." The ladies groaned, but slowly got up and made their way out of the room — except the four or five that clustered around him instead, patting his arm or his chest, fluttering their eyelashes at him.

"Shoo!" Mamie scattered them like a flock of chickens. Once they'd let go of him and got a few steps away, she came close and said quietly, "I hope we've sufficiently demonstrated our gratitude. But to make that quite clear, I'll let you have another session on the house, if your dinner has left you able to take advantage of it."

The fried chicken and corn and cake made a good-sized lump in his stomach, but it might be a long time before he'd have a chance like this again, especially if he left town soon. And Mamie's ladies were prettier and cleaner and sweeter-smelling than he'd seen in any hookshop on his travels. He wished she didn't look a little on edge, like she'd think worse of him for accepting. Hell, if she wanted him to say no, she shouldn't have made the offer.

"That's right generous of you. Since you asked, I would enjoy the chance to spend a little time with that brown-eyed girl, the one with the brown hair."

Mamie wiped the look off her face and flashed a smile at him, a professional, practiced smile that made him more uncomfortable than before. "Of course. Nancy! Come on back. Your next client is right here. Treat him right, now." She walked away with her head held high.

Nancy took his hand and pulled him toward the stairs. He'd left himself no good alternative to going along. So he went.

* * * * *

Jake didn't stay upstairs with Nancy that long. And he came down acting fidgety and looking shamefaced, while

Nancy seemed miffed. Apparently she hadn't suited him that well. That should worry Mamie, as maybe saying something about how well Nancy was doing her job. But worry wasn't Mamie's first reaction — which was maybe something else to worry about.

Nancy flounced off toward the parlor, leaving Jake standing there and shifting from foot to foot. Mamie hadn't seen him fidgety since he'd turned up in her life again, and found she wasn't ready to see it again. She asked, "How about I get you some more coffee — or would you rather have something from the bar?"

Jake cleared his throat and said gruffly, "Either one, whatever's most handy. I don't want to put you out."

Mamie studied him and made a guess. Taking him by the arm, she said, "I'm going to plant you somewhere quiet and get us a drink."

He didn't answer, just heaved a big sigh, his shoulders relaxing. She'd been right — he'd had as much socializing as he could take, for a while at least. Rather than drag him up the stairs he'd just come down, and maybe remind him of whatever hadn't pleased him during that trip, she headed for the small room she'd fixed up as a downstairs office, the time she'd sprained her ankle and didn't want to be seen hobbling and hopping on the stairs. Good thing she'd added a second chair there, just in case.

Once she had him settled, she ordered him to stay put and hustled to the bar, grabbing a bottle of whiskey and a couple of glasses. She'd rather have had sherry, but adding another bottle to that load was asking for broken glass and wasted liquor.

Jake was more sprawled than sitting in the chair when Mamie came back in, his head resting on the curved back and his eyes closed. Did it take that much out of him, being charming to a table full of ladies? From what he'd said at dinner, he was more used to the social circles found on ships and in cattle drives.

Which reminded her of something. She put the bottle and glasses down, though she now doubted she'd be making use of them, and said, "You left a hole in one of your tales at dinner time."

Jake opened one eye. "Oh?"

Mamie moved her chair closer to his. "That trick you and your friend played on the first mate, when you were in the navy. You got nothing but bread and water for however long — which I noticed you didn't mention." Jake had closed both eyes again, but smiled a little at her having caught him out. "You didn't say what happened to — what was his name?"

Jake replied with his eyes still closed, sounding half asleep. "Rich. Short for Richard. Nothing. When I said I'd done it, the others kept the secret. Rich wasn't too happy about it. He opened his mouth to say something, but one of the others dragged him away, and the first mate was bellowing too loud for anyone to hear what Rich might've said."

Should she ask the question that came to mind? Jake went on before she'd decided. "Rich was maybe fifteen years older'n I was. I was such a young pup, I thought that much older was plenty old, too old for bread and water to be good for him. Which was a laugh, seeing as he could've swabbed the deck with me without breathing hard."

Mamie reached out to stroke his hair and pulled her hand back. "He must have meant a lot to you."

"Yup." Jake left it at that. He half-sat, half-lay there with his eyes closed for another few minutes, Mamie watching him as if she'd need to draw him later, until he finally opened his eyes, stood, stretched, and said, "Well, I guess I'd best be going. Thank you for dinner." His face might have reddened a little, under the beard. "And everything."

She stood up and followed him out of the little room, fetching his hat and handing it to him. He bowed a little as he took it. She finally found her tongue as he reached the door. "Thank you for joining us. The girls will be reminding each other of your stories for weeks to come." Why not say the rest? "And I enjoyed hearing them."

His smile, somewhere between amused and smug, had little in common with the bashful version she remembered from years ago. "More where those came from." He tipped his hat and left.

* * * * *

Jake could see clear enough that Mamie needed a better bouncer, but he'd been leery about offering to help with interviewing candidates, in case Mamie saw it it as horning in on her business or — worse yet — suggesting she didn't know how to size up men. But now Mamie had got fed up with the feckless fellow she'd had, and sent him on his way. Jake didn't care for the thought of leaving town, if he did, without knowing who'd be guarding the door.

When he made his offer, Mamie studied him long enough that he knew he'd had reason to worry. But about when he was getting seriously twitchy, she said, "All right. I'll talk to them after you do."

So there he sat in Mamie's small downstairs office, in the same chair where he'd almost fallen asleep after his dinner here, and looked the latest applicant over from shaggy head to rough-shod feet. He'd shaken the man's hand before they both sat down, the better to measure his strength and manner. That first test passed, it was time for the next, in the form of the two glasses of whiskey Jake had put on the desk where the man could see them. The last candidate's eyes had kept wandering toward them, to the point he'd had to ask Jake to repeat his third — and last — question.

This man had already mentioned his name, Mark Horn, when they shook hands. Jake asked for it again, as if he'd never heard it. Horn answered with hardly any pause, and showed no sign of irritation. So far so good. Jake took his time about moving on, to see if Horn would fidget or grit his teeth or any such. Instead, he sat back (none too easy in the hard narrow chair Jake had given him), stretched his legs a little, and smiled.

Not bad.

"How old are you, boy?"

Horn was no boy, of course, though if he'd been from a lawyer's or a council member's family, his mama might still be straightening his collars and fussing with his hair. Would he take offense? Well, if he did, he was hiding it well, simply saying, "Nineteen, Mr. Flint."

"Ever had a job your daddy didn't give you?"

Horn sat up straighter in his chair, and his face got just barely tighter. "I don't suppose you've met my pa, Mr. Flint. If you had, you wouldn't doubt that I learned to work hard and long, and to make sure the work was done right."

A good balance of spine and self-control. And only one quick glance at the whiskey, when Horn first sat down.

That was as far as talking would get them. Jake stood up, took off his waistcoat, and rolled up his sleeves, flexing the muscles of his forearms. "Let's see how you handle an uncooperative customer." Jake smiled for the first time since

Horn walked in. "You can get back at me for how I've been treating you so far. If you're up to it."

Horn's jaw dropped before he pulled it smartly back up. For just that second, he looked as young as he was, if not younger. Then he grinned, showing crooked but reasonably sound teeth. Jake headed for the yard behind the house, where a vigorous wrestling match wouldn't damage anything except maybe the wrestlers.

Ten minutes later, covered in mud and dead grass and sporting not a few bruises, the two men trooped back toward the house, stopping to brush off as much of the dirt as they could. Jake led the way up the stairs to Mamie's office, knocked on the door, and met her raised eyebrow with a grin. "Madam Mamie, meet Mark Horn. For what it's worth, I think he'll do."

As before, the food at the mayor's dinner table was ample and dull, much like the mayor himself, and the setting rather less elegant than Mamie's had been, for all the doilies under every dish and the hothouse flowers crowding the serving platters. Jake had had plenty worse, and applied himself with a will. He avoided questions about his intentions by asking questions of his own, particularly of the mayor's wife, as he guessed the mayor was sufficiently cowed not to interrupt her lengthy and rambling replies.

He had somehow failed to notice earlier that the mayor had two daughters, one about nine and the other almost grown. They must have been amusing themselves elsewhere. Now, the younger watched him out of the corner of her eye, seemingly unsure whether he was likely to break out into some frightening demonstration of masculine roughness over the roast and rolls. The older gazed at him with wide eyes, perhaps hoping for the same.

The mayor, no doubt tired of Jake's evasions, said as they all stood up from the table, "Mister, the council members and I are all hoping you're interested in the marshal position. We need to have someone in place soon, of course, and your arrival strikes us as positively providential."

Jake bit back the comment that he and Providence were not on very cozy terms. Little as he liked what Clara Gibbs had said about the job, he wasn't quite ready to turn it down flat, so he hedged, saying, "I promise you, sir, I'm giving that generous offer my attention and consideration. I know you want the people of this town to have every protection they're entitled to." And that the stout and stuffy men in charge would be useless if called upon to provide it . . . .

Jake excused himself to walk off the meal, throwing the mayor a bone by pointing out, "If I should become your marshal, you'll want me to keep fit, I'm sure." That made the older daughter flutter her eyelashes at him. He left as quick as he could without running.

Jake started out by strolling around the town square, seeing places people were working hard and half envying them, half glad he didn't have to do any heavy work just that minute. He cast an eye at Madam Mamie's as he approached, glad to see that no one was causing any obvious ruckus. Mamie was out on the small front porch, seemingly at ease in a well-made rocking chair, fanning herself with something black and lacy and foreign-looking. She used it to beckon him closer. "Good afternoon! Are you enjoying your walk in our balmy summer weather?"

He laughed. "It's this or sit somewhere letting my dinner weigh me down like a prize pig."

Mamie stood up. "Would you like company, or would you rather not remind the local citizens that your visit to town started with your setting foot in a parlor house?"

"Ma'am, the day I let people's opinions worry me, I hope someone kicks me in the rear hard enough to straighten my head out. If you don't mind leaving that shade behind, I'd be happy for you and your fan to come along."

She stepped down, light on her feet for a woman carrying those generous curves, and handed him the fan, saying, "You're taller, so you can do a better job. Where are we headed?"

"Hmm. I've already been down by the creek. What's the opposite direction?"

Mamie gave him a wry smile. "Not a whole lot. But it's pretty enough. And 'not a lot' suits me, as it happens."

Which sounded worrisome, but he could hardly say so. "I'm with you. Lead on."

That had come out a little more serious-sounding than he'd intended. He didn't look at her for a minute or two, in case she was staring at him. Finally he glanced over, to see her evidently lost in thought. He said nothing, waiting for her to get through whatever was on her mind, as they reached the edge of town and the street became a footpath running across prairie grass.

Bird calls and their own footfalls kept it from being altogether quiet. When Mamie spoke, her voice was quiet too. "I've been wanting to say something. Something I never said before I ran away."

He stopped and pivoted to look straight at her. "Ran away? I didn't see it like that, not really. You had a right to go when you wanted to. And not a whole lot to stick around for."

She looked down at her feet and then back at him. "I don't suppose you know whether my family saw it that way."

He chewed his lip a moment before saying slowly, "I can't say as I ever noticed your family paying much attention to what all happened to you. And once you were gone, I had less reason to care."

The sound she made was too bitter to call a laugh. "Can't say as I disagree with that observation. . . . Anyway, thank you. For standing up for me when no one else did. For trying to help me."

He turned away and started walking again. "Me trying didn't do you much good, did it. Just gave people more to snicker at."

She caught up and put her hand on his arm to slow him down. "It did me good that someone thought enough of me to take a chance, defending my reputation. You knew well enough you might suffer for it. You didn't have to do that, and as bad as I felt at you getting punched and knocked down, I was still grateful. I didn't even stay and make sure you were all right. Were you?"

He shrugged. "They broke my wrist." She winced, and he added quickly, "The doc set it, and it healed up fine. It was all better by the time I left town myself."

They walked a few more steps, breeze sighing in the tall grass, before she said softly, "I've wondered about that. About when you left, and about why. Did you just get tired of being pushed around?"

If only. "No, I knew it wouldn't make much difference where I was until I got strong enough to defend myself, and learned how."

She didn't ask, but he could hear the question as clear as if she'd hollered it. He'd better say something, if as little as he could manage. "It was a family thing. With my brother and my father. One of those fights there's no way back from."

Mamie made a little noise as if she'd started to say something and thought better of it. He almost asked what, but the odds were he wouldn't want to know. Fortune did him a favor, for a change, and planted a tree along their path. He stopped and pointed to it. "Care for another climb?"

Mamie looked relieved, as if she needed a distraction from their talk as much as he did. She dropped her fan on the grass and said, "All right — but I'm afraid I'll need a boost to get up to that branch."

Jake bowed. "It'll be my pleasure." It would've been more of one if he'd been bold enough to pick her up and plant her in the tree. That round bottom would fit his hands just right. But instead he knelt and used his hands for a stirrup, hoisting her up. Luck was still with him — she didn't reach high enough to throw a leg over a branch without him pushing on her seat to raise her up. He climbed up after her as soon as she was settled, packing the memory away for when it might be wanted.

He was hotter than ever after the exercise. If he'd been a praying man, as he'd been a praying boy, he'd have prayed for a cloud to sail on over and then stay a spell. He wiped sweat off his forehead, slung an arm around a sturdy branch to brace himself, and leaned this way and that, hunting for another breeze.

Mamie watched him, not even trying to keep a straight face. "Don't you know heat rises?"

He grinned. "At least the leaves block the sun some."

Then it was quiet again, with not even a bird call to break it. He heard Mamie take a breath and knew he hadn't gained anything but time, and not much of it, with this diversion. "That fight — it didn't have anything to do with me, did it?"

"Not a thing." That'd make a better memory, if he'd had the guts to speak up for her to his grandpa or pa.

Since he didn't pray, he could hope, and he hoped Mamie would leave it at that. For now, at least, she stopped asking questions. After a while, she asked, "Help me down?" and he did. He picked up the fan and fanned her as they walked, until she said, "All right, I'll take a turn." They took turns the rest of the way.

As they reached the parlor house, Mamie put a hand on the front step railing, faced him, and said, "Enough shilly-shallying. Are you taking the marshal job?"

Seemed all he needed was the plain question at the right time to know the answer. "No. I don't think it's for me. At least, I'll be moving on and see what else I find, or what else finds me. If nothing does, I might come back through after a while and see what's happened."

Mamie held the fan stiffly, as if it had gone on strike. "You mean, if you're desperate enough, you'll see if the job's still open."

That wasn't a picture he liked the look of. Instead of saying so, he reached for her hand. "It's been mighty fine seeing you again. The first unexpected thing in a while that I've been glad of."

Mamie took his hand and gave it a quick squeeze before dropping it. "I reckon I might see as many unexpected things as you, in this line of work. And some of them are amusing at least. But this has been better than typical. Safe travels, Jake." She paused before saying, "And if you do come back through, I'll be glad to see you. Now I'd better head inside and see what trouble a houseful of lively girls have got into."

With that, she stepped lightly up to the porch and through the door, leaving him with nothing to do but check out of the hotel, get Wrangler from the livery stable, and give his regrets to the mayor on his way out of town.

Chapter 8

WHAT WAS it Mamie had told Joshua, back when Freida pushed them into having supper together? Something about how it'd take a tougher, and a little meaner, man to touch her heart. She hadn't told him she was painting a picture of someone she knew, let alone a now-and-then lover. Not that Sterling Quinn was likely to touch her heart, unless she got uncommonly careless with it.

Quinn now sat on the side of her bed, pulling on his pointed-toe snakeskin boots — how did he polish boots like that? — and whistling a complicated tune that might come from an opera. Probably an opera where plenty of people got stabbed with swords. From behind. "Any doings in town lately? Fellows sent up state to be hanged, or local politicians caught with their hands too deep in each other's pockets?"

Mamie poked him in the back with her foot. "Nothing so dramatic, I'm afraid. A drunk cowboy tried to bust in during the party for the outgoing marshal, and a fellow passing through town put a stop to it. The mayor and council tried to recruit him as a replacement, but he didn't cotton to it."

Why had she mentioned that? She should have known it would catch Quinn's interest — or that her manner would, casual as she'd tried to be about it. He was, after all, an expert at seeing through people. And at asking questions, damn him. He put one booted foot on the bed and looked more intently at her. "Just where was this party?"

She suppressed a grimace. "Downstairs."

His eyebrows danced up and down. "My, my. And what did you make of this hero? Couldn't you talk him into staying and playing marshal, or didn't you want to? Would he have kept his hands off your business, or teamed up with the oh-so-holy crusaders to shut you down?"

She shoved his foot off the bed and stood up. "All right, one at a time. He wasn't here long enough for me to size him up that thoroughly. I didn't try to talk him into anything, but I figured him for too restless for the job. And he didn't strike me as the psalm-singing type. Now do you want breakfast before you go, or do you need to ride out right away?"

He got off the bed, came around it, and grabbed her by the waist, not quite too tight. "In a hurry to send me on my way?"

She peeled his fingers off her. "I'm a busy woman, and a hungry one. Now come down to breakfast or come down to leave, as you will. Are you in town for long?" Though for him, a long visit would be in the neighborhood of three days.

He smacked her on the bottom before he moved aside enough for her to leave the room. "I'll be leaving tomorrow, after I meet with the banker and the mayor. They've got a lawsuit coming up in Omaha in a month or so, and I need to put them through their paces. In fact, I'm having breakfast with them at the mayor's house, so I'd better get moving. Maybe I'll ask about the fellow they wanted for marshal while I'm at it."

What would they say about Jake? Were they miffed enough at his turning them down to be malicious? There was no way to get to them first and find out. She went to her own breakfast with an unsettled stomach.

* * * * *

HADN'T some ancient philosopher noted that the only thing constant is change? That was Jake's life, right enough. How many times had he ridden away from one place or another? A lot more than how many he'd ridden away from a person he'd miss. He'd made friends of a sort, here and there, but he didn't really collect people. The closest would be Rich, in the navy. Since then, the people he had a chance to get to know were mostly like him, rovers and roamers, no easier to track down than he liked to be.

Jake thought of heading straight east to the Mississippi River. Once he got there, he could ride along it and check at every port until he found a boat that was hiring, wasn't smuggling, and looked likely to stay afloat. And if he found no boat he liked, he could make his way to the coast and some ocean-going vessel. But he wasn't so sure he was ready for shipboard life just yet. He headed southeast instead, to have a better chance of finding some work he could stand doing before he reached the water.

Wrangler had got fat and lazy during their stay in Cowbird Creek He kept wanting to stop and graze, or just stop, period. At least keeping the gelding going gave Jake something to think about besides what he was leaving behind, the wreckage he'd left behind already, and the hollow place where a future should be.

Who'd have thought he'd find Mamie along the road! And running a parlor house. She hadn't been what people called her, back in Deliverance, so just how had she turned into a prostitute? Because he'd bet — and he knew better than to bet carelessly, by now — that a woman didn't end up running a hookshop of any kind without spending time on her back first.

And yet he'd have sworn she was proud of what she'd made of herself, or at least of what she'd built. That was one way to throw slander in people's faces, to make what they said come true and somehow end up the better for it.

They'd started out in such different places, him having a family that took care of him and had plans for him, and her having nothing but trouble at home. And look at them now. It'd make a cat laugh. Did it prove that things could turn around the other way, and somehow he'd be back on some sort of track? Not that he'd want fate to throw Mamie off of hers.

He spent two nights on the road, one trying to keep dry under a bush and getting rain-soaked notwithstanding, but by sundown the next day, he had found a place he could pay for supper and a bed. He got Wrangler settled just before the supper bell. The food made him miss Mamie's and even the mayor's, but it was more or less enough. Not having anything else to do between supper and bed, he took a stroll around the town, which was bigger than Cowbird Creek but not as well kept up. There were more horse droppings in the street, and a few drunks tottered their way from one side of the street to the other.

He backtracked the drunks to find the saloon they'd come from and stood outside getting the measure of the place. It was bigger than he'd expected, maybe big enough to have a poker game going. He could use some more coin for his travels. And he had a good chance of taking all comers.

He could barely remember how he'd felt those first

months after leaving home, not so much as touching a card — even in the navy, where that made him look even more like a green kid with no business on a boat. He had Rich to thank for getting him over it, teaching him to play poker and vingt-un and craps.

Of course, he might end up losing. But it was worth a try.

After three games and one fight, he made his way back to the hotel with a sore jaw, fat lip, and three more dollars than he'd rode in with. And he'd drunk enough that the jaw and the lip didn't hurt, or not to mention. It was what he called a good day, for the road. Any other kind of day didn't matter now.

He saddled Wrangler right after breakfast and rode off.

* * * * *

It'd been maybe a week since Jake left town, and a dull enough week it'd been, though you wouldn't know it to look at Mark Horn. Mamie's new bouncer made the rounds of the ground floor like an infantryman on patrol with his eyes darting back and forth, alert for trouble now that Jake's departure left him without backup.

None of the party guests had come in lately, but this evening two of the council members came in together, elbowing each other and making the kind of jokes they'd probably made since they were still lying about being with a woman. She sent Lucette upstairs with one and Bessie with the other, then sat down to give her feet a rest and listen to the piano player. That would've been a better plan if he were playing something suited for sitting — his bouncy tunes made her want to get up and dance. How long had it been since she danced? Some years, she reckoned.

Bessie's customer came down first. She could keep a man interested with the best of them, but she didn't always take the trouble. She might be up in her room right now with Sophie, giggling about their latest men and showing each other how much better they both were in bed. Mamie set the man up at the bar with his favorite whiskey and sat down next to him. "I hope everything was satisfactory."

"Sure was! I always say, you've got the best girls of any place I've seen. Told that lawyer feller too, when he came through town. He just gave that smile of his, like he knows everything there is to know already, and said he'd maybe stop in the next time he came through." He took a gulp of his whiskey. "By the way, what did you make of that Jacob Flint, as helped out here and then left?"

Mamie had a sinking feeling that question wasn't exactly a change of subject. "I didn't see all that much of him. He was kind of a rough sort, but acted decent enough. Why do you ask?"

The man finished the whiskey — fortunately an inexpensive brand Mamie could mark up quite a bit — and waved the empty glass at the bartender. Maybe he'd make up in whiskey what Bessie had let get away in time. "Oh, that lawyer was asking questions about him, where he came from and all. He was kind of hinting there might be something shady about him, like maybe we'd been lucky he didn't stay."

Mamie clenched a fist under the table. "That lawyer certainly seems full of himself. I doubt he knows anything at all about the fellow, but he likes to act important. Maybe it'd be just as well if he doesn't come by." She made herself smile. "Though his money should be as good as anyone's, and he's sure to have more of it."

As the man finished his second whiskey, the other council member came down with Lucette holding his hand, stroking it until he got to the bottom of the stairs. What with the besotted stare he was giving her, he'd be back before long. The first man wobbled to his feet and joined his companion, and out the door they went, none too soon. Mamie had to think. She hadn't managed much of it before her eye lit on the Omaha paper, still folded neatly on a side table near one of the easy chairs. She hesitated and then sat down in the easy chair, picking up the paper and quickly finding the personals ads.

Seeking any word of my brother J. Please send word to Ethan at Deliverance, IN. More urgent-sounding than the last one. And there was precious little question any more who was meant.

What had that fight been about, if it wasn't about her? Had he lost his religion and told his pa and grandpa so? They'd neither of them take that well, what with the big old parchment from Indiana Seminary up there on the dining room wall in their fine big house. She'd seen it when Jake snuck her in one hot summer afternoon, when the rest of the family was away, to give her a glass of lemonade.

Was the old man maybe dying, if he were still alive, and wanting to see his prodigal son one more time? Should she have told Jake about the first ad? Would he even care?

And why was Quinn sticking his nose in things and stirring them up? If he'd sniffed out that she and Jake might have a history, was he doing it just to bedevil her? Did he think he could turn it to his advantage somehow? Jake wouldn't have more'n two nickels to rub together, most likely — no point in blackmailing him.

And how had she jumped to the notion that whatever Jake had done had to be kept secret from the law? It wasn't like he had any special reason to tell her about it otherwise.

Even if she might be the closest thing he had, at the moment, to a friend.

When Quinn turned up on her doorstep only two days later, he seemed determined to rile her further by bringing up the subject. And naturally, he was clever enough to wait until he'd got what he came for, and was combing his hair in her dressing table mirror — with her comb, yet. He looked an odd sight enough sitting there, and she almost told him so. But she had the feeling any such comment would bring his mean side closer to the surface, maybe too close for comfort. She was pushing away the temptation when he spun around and said, in his citified drawl, "I was talking to a few of your townsfolk not long ago, about that big lout who took a turn as your bouncer. For men who thought about employing him, they didn't seem to know much about him. I suppose they thought an abundance of muscle sufficient qualification — hardly a compliment to your last marshal."

And he knew enough about Jake to be calling him a lout? "I suppose you think any man with muscle must be thick-headed."

Quinn turned back toward the mirror, gave his hair a last stroke, tossed the comb on the dressing table, and stood up. "They do tend to be incapable of relying on any other attribute. And to consider brute strength quite enough answer to any challenge."

Was that bitterness in his tone? Quinn was taller than Mamie, and no doubt stronger, but he might have started out as thin and weedy as Jake, and hadn't transformed nearly as much. Had Quinn been bullied as a boy? He might have developed his wits and his tongue in self-defense.

Which didn't make them any less cutting.

Quinn reached for his waistcoat, hanging from the hook on her door. "And I've heard nothing of your temporary bouncer to suggest he rises above the common herd."

Mamie had learned long ago to control her temper — to the point that when it somehow got loose, it usually surprised her. It surprised her to find herself saying, "Well, even the all-knowing Sterling Quinn doesn't hear everything there is to hear. From what I —" She managed to change course before mentioning any prior knowledge. " — saw of him, Mr. Flint was a clever man, and well-spoken."

Quinn was staring at her, his eyes narrowed. For a moment, he looked as if he'd hiss at her, like the snake that'd died to make his boots. But instead, he spoke in almost a purr. "Indeed! Well, darlin', I'd love to hear more about the unexpectedly clever Mr. Flint." He held her eyes, waiting. She shut her lips tight. "Nothing to add? Well, perhaps another time. I have more important matters to attend to." He looked her up and down as if to say that she was one of those matters less important than whatever business awaited him.

Mamie pulled herself together enough to smile and toss her head. "As do I. And you've kept me from them quite long enough. You can show yourself out." She sat down at her dressing table, resenting the warmth lingering on the chair, as he chuckled and walked out, his boots clacking on the floor.

Chapter 9

WAS IT because she'd gone and told Jake about Jenny and Tom that Mamie kept thinking about them? Because think about them she did. So she was gladder than she would have admitted, if anyone had known to ask her, when a letter showed up addressed in Jenny's uneven handwriting.

Dear Ma'am, I hope you are well, and all the girls. Are Bessie and Sophie still there? I kind of think they might be back on the road by now.

No, they were still around, for a wonder. If she'd had to guess, she might guess that Amanda Jane's death had sobered Bessie some, and got her thinking about all the things that could go wrong. Once you got thinking that way, the dangers of the road would stand out stark compared to a roof and three square meals a day, with (Mamie prided herself) a madam more reasonable and less mean-spirited than common.

And that just got her worrying more about how the road was treating these two youngsters. She went back to reading.

Me and Tom are keeping pretty well so far. We got through the winter all right, mostly being far enough south by then that we didn't freeze. The horses have worked out real well, and Tom likes having Cochise with us. He talks to him more than to the mare, but she don't know the difference.

Tom has mostly been able to find work where we stop, the

cowboys being real impressed with his boots and saddles. I'm starting to talk to the fine ladies about shoes. Times got lean enough once that I had to find some other work, but I was able to help out in a saloon without working on my back. The saloon keeper thought that'd be a fine idea, and Tom had to lay him out, which surprised him plenty along of Tom's wooden leg, and then we got out of there in a hurry. But we've been doing all right since then.

Well, none of that was any worse than she'd been picturing, and maybe better. Good thing Tom had learned how to fight one-legged. She'd have liked to see that bastard's face.

I don't know where we're going next, or I'd ask you to write to me and tell me how you are, and how Bessie and Sophie are if you know. I think of you often. I owe you a lot, and I'm not forgetting it. Tom prays sometimes, and I've heard him praying for all to be well with you.

Well, if that didn't beat all. She could just imagine the Almighty scratching his white head and wondering what the world was coming to, for someone to be bending His ear about Mamie after all this time.

Your friend, Jenny Barlow

Underneath that was a postscript in squarer script.

This is Tom. I wanted to add a word about how brave-hearted Jenny has been. She almost never gets down, or not that she lets me see. And she charms the cowboys right out of their old boots, so's they're eager for new ones. Thank you for giving Jenny that coat, it's kept her warm when she'd have been cold otherwise. — Tom Barlow

She shouldn't be surprised that Jenny had risen to the occasion. It just meant Mamie had been right to see potential in Jenny when the girl first showed up, raggedy and bruised, with paint so thick it cracked when she smiled.

Which she had enough spirit to do, even then.

And what Jenny had said about Mamie . . . .

Mamie blinked a stray drop of water out of her eye, folded up the letter, and tucked it in the back of her desk drawer before heading down to the kitchen to see what Cook planned to serve for supper.

But as she came down the stairs, who should she see but Sterling Quinn, smirking at how he'd surprised her.

She hadn't expected Quinn back through town quite this soon. Given how provoking he'd been last time, she had mixed feelings about his reappearance, and just when she'd been letting her feelings come out from where she usually kept them, feelings Quinn would laugh at or worse. But she couldn't deny that it did her good to have those snakeskin boots under her bed for a visit. She could practically feel her skin glowing as she sat at her dressing table putting her hair back up. If he ever went with one of her girls, she could ask how Quinn measured up to other customers. But that first time he'd walked in, he'd run his gaze around the parlor, looked at her coming down the stairs, and laughed out loud. He'd walked right up to her and grabbed her by the shoulders, then spun her around and walked her back up. She'd been too flabbergasted to say him nay, and by the time they reached the landing, those hard, smooth hands had made their way up and down her to the point where she'd grabbed one of them and led him to her bedroom.

And if he made a move toward one of her girls now, after all this time, she might just kick him out the door. And the girl after him.

No, just him. The girls were her investment in the future, and every one picked for the purpose. And it wouldn't be fair.

She'd been sitting long enough for him to notice, and he came and put his hands on her shoulders. "What's on that clever little mind of yours?"

She stood up against the pressure of his hands. "Just remembering your impertinent manners the first day you came here."

He ran a smooth finger up the side of her neck. "My manners got me into your bed, didn't they? I'd say they were calculated perfectly."

Calculated, yes. As so much of what he did and said was calculated. Which made him marvelous in bed, and dangerous everywhere else. She wouldn't face him in court if it cost half her savings to avoid it.

"Speaking of unusual arrivals, what happened to that fellow the mayor and council wanted for marshal? Still thinking it over?" He pinched her bottom. "Are you offering him any incentives?"

She bit back the urge to tell him it was none of his business, even though that was true a couple of different ways. "He left town. If he's planning on coming back, he didn't bother to tell me. Now let me get back to work." A mistake, that — it wasn't up to Quinn to let her do anything, and talking as if it was would only encourage him. She couldn't let him get her flustered enough to make mistakes.

Especially about Jake.

He snapped his hat off the hook and headed for the door. As he grabbed the handle, he tossed back over his shoulder, "I'll be meeting the mayor again later today. Maybe I'll see if he's heard from his wayward would-be marshal. You'd think a man with no job and no prospects — and a houseful of fine ladies grateful to him — would stick around, if he'd got no special reason to move on."

Mamie didn't come up with a snappy answer, or any, before she heard his boots clatter down the stairs.

Chapter 10

CARD-playing wasn't real work for a man. He needed work that tired him out by day's end, so he could fall asleep without thinking too much. Not to mention work less likely to get him shot by some suspicious loser.

At least now, when he lay awake at night, he had something better to think about than the mess he'd made of his life. He could remember climbing trees with Mamie, or teasing her, or her teasing him back. Or talking to her in the quiet of the little room she called her downstairs office.

How was the new bouncer, Horn, working out? He'd seemed all right — smart enough for the job but not treating it as beneath him, and tough enough to give Jake a good tussle. And Mamie had hired him, so he must have had decent manners. But maybe Jake should've stayed in town a little longer, to make sure Horn wouldn't let her down.

In the next town but one, he brought Wrangler to a livery stable with an overworked and flustered man in charge. Rather than take chances with what sort of grooming the gelding would get and when he'd get his feed, Jake took charge of matters himself. By the time Wrangler was happily crunching mouthfuls of sweet-smelling hay and had clean straw underfoot, the man was asking wearily whether by any chance the stranger was staying for a few days, and would like a job while he was around.

He'd never given much thought to working with

horses, which was strange given that he liked them better than he did most people, and could get them to trust him more than most people should. The slow times would give him too much time to think, but he might be able to get around that — find tasks to keep thoughts at bay. And it was the sort of work you could get in lots of places, though not as likely in smaller towns like Cowbird Creek. For whatever difference that made.

He told the man yes, after acting reluctant enough to make him raise his first offer. It'd save him paying the stable fee for Wrangler, at least.

He stayed longer than he'd figured, to see how he liked the work. Turned out he liked it fine. But not enough to keep him there.

He tended to forget the date when he traveled, seeing as it made no real difference to anything he was doing. But as he rode past a town so small he only stopped to refill his canteen, and wiped the sweat off his face with his sleeve, he got to wondering whether it shouldn't be getting cooler sometime soon. Then again, he was moving south. If he wanted cooler any time soon, he'd have to change direction. He'd need more reason than comfort to do that.

The stables in the next town were in such poor shape, he couldn't face the task of putting them to rights. If he'd known, he'd have counted himself lucky to spend however many days ankle-deep in filth. The kind of filth he could see and smell, and do something about.

He'd sunk low before, though never as low as right before he left home. This might be the lowest since then.

Not tending bar — he could call that downright humanitarian, helping his fellow man ease life's pains and sorrows with what the supposedly good Lord provided for the purpose. And tending bar in a casino was all right. No chance he'd be tempted to play any game he didn't know inside and out — he'd right enough taken the lifetime cure for that.

When he was told to run the faro and Mexican monte tables, he'd even thought — more fool he — that he could keep things honest, make sure none of the miners who wandered in with their pay or a sack of gold dust in their pockets would be cheated blind. That was before the owner, devils gnaw his soul, drew him aside and said with a wink that whenever a short fat man with a limp and a red waistcoat came to play, or a tall handsome one with a bright red beard and broken-down boots, Jake was to keep his observations to himself and "let the cards fall as they may."

He'd already paid half the coin he rode in with for a bed and a stall at the livery stable. He wouldn't get more until the week was out. And when he asked around, folks said it'd be three days' ride to the next town where he might find paying work. If that wasn't stuck, it was damned close. It didn't help that the look of the place made him more restless — fancy velvet wallpaper faded and scuffed, it made him think of Mamie's parlor, if the parlor'd been darker and more crowded and no one had bothered to take care of it for years.

He'd made it most of the way to payday without either of the men coming in. And he'd shortened his suspenders so his trousers wouldn't sag, eating light to hoard what coin he had left. He was setting up a faro table and daydreaming about a nice thick steak when he sensed someone looming over him. He straightened up to see a red beard, glanced down to check the man's boots, and clenched his teeth so tight his jaw hurt.

By the time the table was full up, it had mostly grizzled old miners, maybe knowing enough not to be taken in. But then in came a bright-eyed young fellow, barely old enough to go down a mine and find his way up again, with a bounce in his step and jingling pockets. All he lacked was someone writing "fleece me!" on his forehead.

The swindler would probably let his target win once or twice. Jake would wait for his moment and try to give the kid a warning.

Sure enough, the first hand went the kid's way. And the second. Which meant that by the time Jake brought the kid a drink "on the house" and whispered in his ear while setting it down, he was in no mood to listen. And when Jake straightened up, the red-bearded man gave him a narrow look, surely meant to menace him.

Too bad Jake didn't menace easy.

He grabbed the kid's arm, yanked him out of his chair, and shoved him toward the door. In a burst of inspiration, he hollered, "I saw what you tried to pull! Out you get before someone puts a hole in you!"

That confused the real cheat for maybe a second and gave Jake time to redirect his attention. When the red-beard came up out of his chair, Jake knocked him backward, the chair clattering down behind him and the man sprawling over it. That gave Jake enough of a head start that the first bullet whined its way past him. He didn't linger to see where the second one went.

He ducked this way and that through the streets, hiding in shadows and behind outhouses, until things got quiet and he could creep up to his room, pack what little he'd unpacked, grab Wrangler, and ride out of town. He'd ride through the night. Good thing he hadn't had a drink — he might stay on Wrangler's back until dawn. Then he'd look for a handy haystack or shade tree to shelter him for a nap.

Time to head for the river. Maybe it'd take him somewhere he'd never been, somewhere he actually wanted to be. Not that he could picture what a place like that would be offering.

And if he took a riverboat job, he'd have to sell Wrangler. He'd make damned sure he found a buyer who'd treat him right. Jake was too old to betray any living creature — any more living creatures — and hope to live with it. Hadn't Milton said something about the mind making a heaven of hell or a hell of heaven? No point looking for a better place to end up if his mind would just turn it into another earthly version of fire and brimstone.

How his grandpa and pa would laugh if they knew.

Jake had made it to the Mississippi, even by his winding and roundabout route, and he was broke, hungry, and pretty much out of options. He'd found a job shoveling out the livery stable in this port town, and that'd keep him in beans and bacon while he found someone to buy Wrangler and take good care of him. Except it seemed everyone stabling a horse was on his way through town, not to mention having a horse already, and he hadn't seen any folks wealthy enough to keep a choice of horses for riding. The livery stable kept extras as post horses, but after seeing what shape they were in when the riders dropped them off, he'd rather put Wrangler down that let him suffer that way. And he wasn't going to shoot Wrangler. So where did that leave the pair of them?

The stable owner interrupted his brooding, holding out coin enough for supper and a drink, or else two or three drinks. "Here you go. See you back here in the morning.

Unless, of course, I don't." He knew well enough that most men wouldn't stay at the job for longer than they had to. Liking horses, and needing a free stall for Wrangler, gave Jake more reasons to stick than most, but he wouldn't say so and give the man cause to pay him even less.

He wiped his right hand on some straw, held it out for the coins, and tucked them away in his trousers. Before he climbed on a boat, he'd best wash his clothes in the river, or the other sailors would gang up to toss him and clothes over the side to get the job done.

And he could write to Rich before he went on board. He'd never written Rich's direction down, but with only one person he ever wrote to, it was easy enough to remember. He made a quick trip to the general store for paper and pen, using up too much of his coin to do it, and crouched in the corner to get started.

Rich, it's Jake. Been on land too long — time to get back to the water. Should be able to find a boat that'll take me.

Why did he even bother, if his letters were going to be duller than the dullest small town paper ever printed? He owed Rich better than to waste his time. He'd have ripped up what he'd written, but he'd only bought the one sheet of paper.

Found a surprise in a town I passed through. An old friend — go ahead and laugh, I had one or two back in the day — turned up, doing real well for

He almost wrote "herself," but that'd likely get Rich jumping to all manner of conclusions.

someone who started out poorer'n I did.

It wasn't a lie, exactly, even if it felt like one. He'd never told even Rich that he'd come from what passed for money in Deliverance, and it was a little late to say so now.

I hope you're keeping well. If you've got kids, I hope they're growing like weeds.

Hell, by now Rich might have grandkids for all Jake knew. Rich had no way to write back, even if he'd a mind to.

And that was all he seemed to have to say. Time to wash his clothes.

As he was giving Wrangler a see-you-later scratch behind the ears, a cowboy rode in, coated in trail dust and taking swigs from a flask. He looked around, maybe for the owner, and then made do with Jake, asking, "You happen to know anyone as can ride and handle cattle? We just lost a hand to a riverboat, and we've got a cattle drive starting tomorrow. Heading to Kansas. Ellsworth."

Right back the way he'd come, almost. But it wasn't like it made much difference, and he generally got along well enough with cowhands, not to mention critters. Only — "This here's my horse, and he can go steady for a long day without falling behind or getting fractious. If I can ride him, and the pay's good enough, I might be willing."

The cowboy looked Wrangler over from fetlocks to nose to tail. "He looks sound enough, I guess. You've been on a drive before?"

"A few. And I'd guess more than anyone else you'll find hereabouts. What's the pay? And how's your cook?"

The cowboy named a sum that'd let Jake save up for the next lean times, or the start of such anyway. "And as for Cookie, I've et better and worse than what he turns out. His stew's pretty tasty. And he can turn most anything into stew."

Jake had eaten rattlesnake, rats, and what was probably horse meat. "I'm in. I'll fetch my gear." He looked around from the owner, to tell him he'd guessed right, but the man was nowhere to be seen.

The cowboy clapped him on the back, and didn't pay any mind to the cloud of dust he raised. "You do that, and I'll take you back to camp. You can have supper with us."

As he stuffed his shaving kit and change of clothes back into his knapsack, he tried to remember if he'd heard where Ellsworth was. From what he recalled, it wasn't close to Cowbird Creek — but it was a lot closer than he was now. He could keep riding, after, and visit Mamie, if he cared to. And maybe pay for his pleasures, this time through.

And never mind wondering whether Mamie ever lifted her dress, now that she ran her own house and could pick and choose.

He stopped at the front desk to tell him they could let his dark hole of a room, scribbled a quick end to his letter, and swung by the general store to drop it off. No time to change what he'd written, and it hardly mattered. He headed back to the stable, whistling for the first time since he'd got within sight of the river. Some other day, maybe, he'd be a sailor again. But not today, nor tomorrow neither.

Chapter 11

"WISH I'd got a chance to know Mr. Flint better."

Mamie froze and then turned to look at Horn, who'd just come out of the kitchen with a mug of coffee. She hadn't told him he could drink coffee on duty. Hadn't told him he couldn't, but still, he might've thought to ask.

Horn stopped in mid-sip and stood up straighter. She must be glaring at him. She closed her eyes to let her temper ebb away and opened them again. "What's that about Mr. Flint, now?"

"I liked him, that's all. And I think I could have learned a fair bit from him, if he hadn't left town. I've got plenty to learn, Lord knows."

That he did. Including when to ask permission. . . . Why was she taking offense so easy? She'd got out of sorts, somehow. She'd best go for a walk and hope it settled her down. Maybe Clara could join her. If anyone could stay unreasonable around Clara, it wasn't Mamie.

She didn't stride out quite as strong as she'd planned to, but it wasn't long until she reached the Gibbs place and whistled the usual tune. It had rained earlier, which meant dodging puddles, more of them as she left the smoother road behind. She suppressed a sudden urge to splash around in the puddles instead. Someday soon, little Alice Gibbs would probably yield to that impulse. Mamie doubted either Joshua or Clara would fret too much about what it did to her clothes. What a lucky girl Alice was.

Mamie, however, had laundry bills to think of. She'd worn her brown print dress that didn't show dirt so much, but she still refrained from sitting by the creek, instead finding a tree with smooth bark and leaning against it. Pretty soon Clara came along, her long strides eating up the distance and her firm footsteps raising little splashes from the mud. Mamie went to meet her. "No baby today?"

Clara flashed her rare, broad smile. "No, she's with her daddy, gathering herbs in the garden. If someone comes by with an emergency, he'll leave her with the neighbors and try to find me on his way." She pulled a thick wad of material out of her pocket. "Here, I brought a tarp. If we don't mind sitting close, we can sit down in spite of the mud." She spread it out and plopped down on it, letting Mamie decide whether to do the same without further urging. Mamie grinned and lowered herself a little more carefully, for all it made her feel like an old crone. She'd been having some muscle aches lately.

As Clara's smile fell away, Mamie studied her face and got the feeling she had something on her mind. It wouldn't take long for Clara to come out with it. Sure enough, Clara moved to the same tree where Mamie had been leaning and said, "I've been thinking about Jake Flint, and the way things went. His turning down the marshal job, after he and I talked about it."

Mamie leaned back on her hands and let the damp breeze cool her face. "So he introduced himself as Jake? You didn't mention that, when last we talked about him."

Clara stretched out her long legs and tapped her toes together. "I don't know if you were counting on him taking the job, given that he seemed to have no prejudice against your establishment."

Mamie shrugged. "Don't go fretting about it. I didn't

really expect him to stay in town. You could tell he wasn't exactly looking to settle down, not to mention dealing with those stuffed shirts all the time." Should she say more? She already had, the last time they talked about Jake, and Clara could keep a confidence. "We come from the same home town. Back then, he wasn't the kind to live on the road — but back then, he wouldn't have been able to handle that cowboy. Not even close."

Clara took that in and then asked, "And you? What kind were you, back then? How did you come to know each other?"

Mamie let out something between a snort and a laugh. It hurt her throat. "Not through my present trade, nor that of my girls. In fact, little as anyone in town would have credited it, I was a virgin. But my mother had a reputation, and I had a body ahead of my years, and plenty of people in town put the two together and decided I must be cut of my mother's cloth. That gave some of the boys the idea of bragging that they'd been with me, when their pizzles'd probably have shrunk down to straws if they'd got close to a girl's pussy."

"And Jake believed you?"

Mamie sighed. "Better than that — he guessed the truth somehow, though I'd given up denying the lies. Once he told me that — and he had a hard time putting tongue to it — I owed it to him to tell him he was right. We'd already ended up friends, somehow, and better friends after that. He was pretty much the only friend I had. He had a brother and they were pretty close, I think, but Ethan and I never really took to each other."

Clara picked up a river birch leaf, yellow and fallen ahead of schedule, and twiddled it. "And Jake was the settled sort then? And less physically capable?"

Mamie's arms ached enough that she lay back on the tarp, careless of her bonnet touching the ground. "His pa and grandpa were both ministers. His grandpa'd been to a college for it, away in Bloomington — we lived in Indiana, but a ways further south. They wanted Jake to become a preacher, and he seemed inclined to go along. He sure read the Bible enough — and believed it, for all I could tell, no matter how I teased him about it. Which seemed fitting for a skinny twig of a fellow, who might as well hope for help from Jesus when he couldn't help himself in case of trouble."

She swallowed the lump in her throat. That hurt too. "But he tried, one time. That is, he didn't try to help himself. He tried to help me. A few of the boys had caught up with me and surrounded me, calling me — well, you can guess the sort of names they called me — and kind of shoving me from one to the other like it was a fine new game. He came up and hollered at them to quit it, and when they ignored him, he grabbed one of the boys — and not even the smallest one, the damn fool — and tried to tug him away from me."

Clara was sitting up straighter now. "I assume that didn't end well."

"It ended with Jake sprawled on the ground with a split lip, a bloody nose, and a broken wrist. I didn't know then about the wrist, though. I left town that day."

She shut her eyes. Clara didn't say anything for maybe a minute, which left Mamie wondering what Clara was thinking about the way Mamie'd cut and run, without even seeing how heavy a price Jake had paid, let alone thanking him. But what Clara said had nothing to do with Jake or the past. "You don't look well. How are you feeling?"

Mamie opened her eyes. The sun was on her face, and it hurt her head to look anywhere near it. She rolled her head to one side and said, "Not so good. My head aches, and my throat's sore, and I have other aches here and there. And chills. I must've got some kind of fever, though I don't know how."

Silence again, and then, "You lie still. I'm going to touch the sides of your neck. I'll be as gentle as I can."

Her touch was gentle enough. It felt more strange than painful, as if Clara's fingers sank in farther than she'd have expected. She heard a click that might have been Clara's teeth coming together as her jaw set. Then Clara's hand made its way under Mamie's head. "I'm going to help you get up, and we're heading back to town, slowly. We'll go by my house, but neither of us will go in. I'll call to Joshua and tell him what I'm seeing, and find out if his thoughts run the way mine do. But first — do you know if you ever had mumps?"

Once Clara got her sitting up, she started to shake her head and stopped when that hurt too. "Not as I remember. No one around me took much notice when I got sick, and I took as little notice as I could."

Clara hoisted her to her feet. "Did you have siblings? Did you spend much time around other children?"

She'd spent more time dwelling on the past today than she had in years. Maybe that's why her head hurt this much. "I had one sister, a lot older. She was married and living away from us by the time I was maybe six years old." And that one visit to her, two towns away, had been Mamie's first hint that life could be different. "Shiftless as my folks were, there weren't many children allowed to get near us. I went to school for a year or so, but I got lice and they stopped me coming after that."

They were walking now, Clara's arm supporting her. "You must have done a great deal of study on your own, to speak and write as well as you do now."

It was swallow another lump or start crying. She swallowed. "Jake taught me some. Enough that I got the taste for it, and kept up on my own when I had the chance. Especially once I decided I was going to make something of myself, not just stay a whore in one dirty hookshop or another."

Clara replied quietly, "I don't know how much time you and Jake spent together when he came through town, but it seems highly likely that he was proud, as well as pleased, with what his old friend has accomplished."

That did it. She couldn't not cry. At least she had a handkerchief in her pocket. She held it to her face, covering up as much as she could, as they made their way into town. Clara was doing her the favor of choosing the back roads as much as possible.

When they got near the Gibbs place, Clara led her to a sturdy stone fence behind their garden. "Stay here, please. If you do have mumps, as you must have gathered I suspect, you should keep your distance from Joshua until I find out whether he's had them. And from the baby, who'll probably get them sooner or later, but later — that is, a few years later, not in adulthood — would be preferable."

Mamie slumped down and let the sun warm her, which felt good only as long as the chills lasted and then had her sweating. She waited, not even trying to identify the bird calls, only letting them hold her attention until she heard footsteps leaving the house and then stopping. She opened her eyes to see Joshua just outside the back door. He called out, "Can you hear me clearly from here?"

She smiled weakly. "So far."

He had no smile for her in return. "I'm afraid I agree with Clara that you most likely have mumps. It's quite contagious to those who've never had it. Are any of your ladies unwell?"

Mamie tried to think. "Not that I know of. But most of them would tend to keep it to themselves, rather than miss working and the pay that comes of it. There's only two or three who'd play it up as a chance to be lazy."

Joshua stroked his chin before going on. "It's largely a childhood illness, but you'd be surprised how many adults have never had it — including me, worse luck. It posed quite a problem during the war, almost as much as influenza. And while most cases come and go without any permanent effects, there can be complications. One common symptom, whose emotional impact on men I'm sure you can imagine, is swelling of the testicles."

Mamie stared and then laughed, steadying herself with both hands when laughing made her wobble. "I certainly can. I'm to keep my distance from my customers, then."

Joshua lowered his eyebrows. "I'm afraid it means more than that. Mamie, you have to close down for a while. Until we know that any of the ladies who are going to get it have done so, and gotten past the infectious stage."

Mamie's jaw dropped. "And how long is that?"

"From the time the first symptoms start — which can be fever, headache, muscle pain, or loss of appetite — until about five days after the swelling beneath the ears starts. If we assume, for the sake of caution, that you're the first to fall ill, it could take two weeks or more for the other ladies to show the first signs. We'll see what develops, but you may have to close for close to a month."

Mamie jumped to her feet, almost falling over sideways, barely catching herself on the wall in time. "I can't do that! Do you know how much money I'll lose, and all the while having the usual expenses?"

Joshua took one small step closer. She'd never before

seen him look stern, and could hardly have imagined it. If she'd known, would she have been so quick to assume he could never be the kind of man to attract her? He didn't raise his voice, but spoke slowly and clearly. "Mamie, if you don't shut down, I'll fetch the sheriff from the county seat and have him ensure that you do. I don't like to think of how that might affect your future relationship with him. Or with me. But I cannot have you spreading mumps among men who may be vulnerable to it. One of the complications can be impaired fertility or even sterility."

Mamie dropped back down onto the wall and covered her face with her hands. Clara came back over and sat down beside her. "Most men would find the swollen glands unattractive. You wouldn't want word to get around that your ladies were odd-looking."

"No, it's better they should spread the word that my girls are *diseased*. I'll be ruined."

She let her hands fall away as Clara patted her shoulder. "We'll just have to come up with a less discouraging cover story."

Joshua cleared his throat, maybe planning to object. Clara looked hard at him, and he paused before saying, "I suppose it's too late, at this point, to know which customers may have been infected. Quarantining the ladies will have to do. Though I can, and will, put the word about that mumps have been seen in the county and what symptoms should be watched for, and ask anyone with those symptoms to notify me at once. The contagion may pass short distances through the air, along with possible other routes, so Madam Mamie's will not be an obvious source."

What would Jake have said and done, if he'd stayed around? She could imagine him glowering at her if she insisted on defying the doctor's orders. What would he say about her lying instead? There was a time a lie would have dismayed him, but it seemed more than likely he'd learned to lie in the years since then.

Clara had turned to face Joshua full on, and her calm had a brittle quality to it as she spoke to him. "I'll leave messages in a jar under an overturned bucket in Mamie's back yard, some distance from the house. And I'll wash my hands before I write the messages and put them in the jar. You should be able to retrieve them safely."

Mamie stood up again, her head swimming. "I don't understand. Why would you be leaving Joshua messages anywhere?"

"I'm coming with you and staying with you. You won't all get sick, nor all at once, so you'll be able to do for each other a good deal, but there'll be times a nurse will make things much easier on sick and well both."

"But — I haven't even asked! Have *you* had mumps?"

Clara's arms were strong, for all they were thin. She was able to prop Mamie up and still speak without obvious strain. "I had it as a child. If I can't catch it, I most probably can't give it to others." She paused, and she and Joshua exchanged glances suggesting some difficult conversation. "But until all danger of my transmitting it has passed, I will keep some distance from Joshua and Alice."

Joshua nodded, slowly and with obvious reluctance, and gazed at Clara with such longing that Mamie felt like the worst of criminals. "It might be possible for someone who is himself — or herself — immune to carry the contagion in some manner. I consider the risk small enough that I would be willing to take it. But apparently Clara is not."

"No. And so I'll bid you goodbye for the present, husband." Clara stopped, bit her lip, and released it. "Call on the neighbors and my mother for anything you need. And be well, in all ways, until I'm home again."

Mamie didn't hear what Joshua said in return. She was crying again.

They finally made it back to the house, Mamie leaning heavily on Clara and Clara bearing up stoutly under the weight. Trudi came hustling up to greet them, Horn trailing behind her. "Oh! Good afternoon, Mrs. Gibbs. Oh, ma'am, we've had such a time, what with Summer Dawn refusing to get out of bed and Sophie falling into a faint right outside the parlor — but what ails you, ma'am?"

"The same thing that probably ails Summer Dawn and Sophie," Clara said grimly as she hustled Mamie to a nearby chair and set her down. "How many gentlemen are on the premises, aside from this employee?"

Trudi looked around wildly as if expecting the customers to stand and be counted. "It's our slow time of day, so I'd say two or three up in the rooms, and one at the bar."

"And how are you yourself feeling?"

Trudi looked more and more bewildered. "All at sixes and sevens, ma'am, but right enough other ways."

Clara lowered her voice and asked, just loud enough for Trudi to hear, "Have you ever had mumps? The swelling sickness?"

"Oh, yes, ma'am, but ever so long ago. I don't hardly remember it."

"Thank the Lord," Mamie managed to get out, and immediately thought what Jake would have to say about it.

Before Clara could ask Horn the same question, he said, "I'm pretty sure I had it. I remember my next youngest sister swelling up, and me teasing her about it, and my pa smacking me and saying I'd looked just as funny when it was my turn."

"Good. We probably don't have to worry about you falling ill. That leaves another question." Clara glanced at Mamie, and apparently decided there was no point involving her in the discussion. Mamie opened her mouth to protest and closed it again, along with her eyes. "What, if anything, would you be able to do, and comfortable doing, as this house turns from a provider of . . . entertainment to a sick ward?"

Mamie heard the shuffling of feet. From what she'd seen so far, it took a fair amount to make Horn nervous, but that question had. She pulled her eyes open, to see him looking down at his boots. "I don't rightly know, ma'am. I wouldn't want to be sent home until this is over — I don't figure Madam Mamie could keep paying me for doing nothing, and wouldn't want to ask it of her. I've never done much nursing, but I can help people walk, like you were just doing, and I can fetch and carry whatever's wanted."

Clara studied him and said decidedly, "All of that would be most helpful — and I'd warrant you can learn how to do more than that. Unless Mamie has any objection —" She looked over at Mamie. "You can stay on and make yourself useful. Please go and fetch the gentleman at the bar and tell him it's time to leave, before . . . ." Clara pursed her lips and then nodded to herself. "Before you start your deep hygienic cleaning, recommended by all the most up-to-date experts for hotels and other establishments frequented by numerous guests. Tell him you'll be closing until it's over. And as soon as the other gentlemen come down . . . Which ladies are they with?"

Trudi knitted up her forehead. "Rena and Nancy, ma'am."

"If they fall ill, we'll have to think about warning the gentlemen. In the meantime, tell them the same as the one at the bar, and send them on their way. If you can keep them from lingering around the other ladies on their way, so much the better."

Mamie muttered weakly to Clara, "Have to tell them all. All the girls."

"Once the men have all gone, and the door locked behind them. For now, I'll get you to your room. This lady — what's your name?"

Trudi curtsied. "Trudi, ma'am, at your service."

"And so you shall be. Once the men are gone, please ask all the ladies, except any already ill and in their beds, to meet me in the parlor. I'll explain what's happening and what will happen next."

Chapter 12

JAKE was expecting the weather to get cooler as they rode north, and looking forward to it. But he'd forgot to expect the color sneaking into the trees, when they got near any — first just a yellow leaf now and then, or a green leaf with red trim on it. The change came over the saplings first, while the taller trees just stood there pretending nothing was happening. Then, with more distance covered and more time passing, the tide of color crept higher, until there were as many trees with autumn patchwork as without it. If he stayed north a while when the drive was over, he'd see trees aflame with yellow and orange and red.

He spent a couple of days in Ellsworth, like the rest of the hands, and shared a hotel room with one. He did his bit of drinking and carrying on, but he made it back to the room well before his temporary roommate, which let him pick his preferred side of the bed. As for other beds, he might've been the only one who didn't visit the local hookshop at least once. It didn't look bad, but after Madam Mamie's, he just couldn't settle for it.

He spent much of the time just walking around, stretching his legs out and enjoying the breezes and the town bustle. And deciding whether he had any earthly reason to ride all the way to Cowbird Creek.

Not that it was all that long a ride, for a man used to riding.

Six days later, and with only a few hours to go, he came to a little town whose name he didn't bother to ask and watered Wrangler. Leaning over the trough, he studied his reflection in the water. He'd cleaned up some in Ellsworth, enough so he wasn't as grimy and smelly as the first time he and Cowbird Creek encountered each other. For all that, he looked around for anywhere to pay for a bath. All he saw was a barber shop with a barber who looked like he never got nearer water than he could help.

He did take the time to groom Wrangler, bringing the gelding's coat close to a shine. When he was done, he leaned his forehead against Wrangler's muzzle and muttered, "Between the two of us, you'll make by far the finer showing. If you knew better, you'd be embarrassed to be seen with me."

Wrangler blew at his hair and tried to snatch a lock to nibble on. Jake shoved the horse's nose aside and pulled a carrot out of the saddlebag. Once it was gone, he had nothing else to wait for.

He rode into Cowbird Creek with the sun winking through the trees. As he tied Wrangler to the hitching post outside Madam Mamie's, a man who looked familiar — the blacksmith? — called out cordially, "Sorry, stranger, the place is closed. Something about a new kind of cleaning. It always looked clean enough to me, but then I don't exactly keep up on the latest."

Jake allowed himself a little smile at being a stranger again this soon and walked up to take a closer look. Sure enough, the red lamp wasn't burning. A neatly lettered sign on the front door announced that the establishment was closed for a special kind of cleaning, the latest in modern hygiene, which would regrettably take some time, and that they looked forward to — he snorted — to serving the community again when it was over. And though evening was coming on, he could see little light through the stained glass pane beside the door.

But would a good businesswoman like Mamie really close down for cleaning, instead of tackling one set of rooms at a time during the hours she was closed anyway? It didn't smell right. And yet if it weren't the truth, she must have a good reason for posting the lie. And he wanted to know that reason, because she might be in some sort of trouble.

He started to walk off, leaving Wrangler at the post for now, and then reconsidered. Someone might wonder why a horse was tied up outside a closed parlor house. He untied the gelding and led him to the town square instead, tying him not far from the one saloon located there. He was about to go in, wash down the dust, and keep his ears open when he spotted Joshua Gibbs strolling down the street, bag in hand. He'd be hurrying, or at least walking faster, if he had a patient waiting. Jake waited for Gibbs to get closer and then stepped out to walk alongside him. "Evening, Doc."

Gibbs stopped and stared at Jake, which he somehow did without looking rude. "Mr. Flint! When did you reappear?"

Jake chuckled. "Just now. And I thought to pay my respects to the ladies yonder, but I see they're closed for cleaning." He gave the doctor a look he hoped conveyed his doubts without making him out a gossip.

Gibbs looked around and then said cordially, "I'm on my way home now. Care to come along? I'm sure Clara would be delighted to see you."

Jake tipped his hat and obliged. Was he imagining that the words came freighted with some unspoken message?

He'd find out soon enough. He fetched Wrangler and led him as they walked.

As they reached the lane leading outside the town proper, Gibbs dropped his voice and said, "What I just said to you was misleading, though not quite a falsehood. I have no doubt Clara would be very glad to see you, but she's not at home awaiting us. She's at Mamie's."

And Mamie's was closed, and Clara was a nurse. Jake forced himself to breathe evenly. "For what purpose?"

Gibbs looked around again before saying, "Mamie and some of her ladies have the mumps. Clara had it as a child and can safely nurse them. I, unfortunately, cannot. Mamie was adamant that the presence of disease be concealed if possible." He looked anything but happy at the notion. Mamie must have been very persuasive — at least enough to convince Clara.

Meanwhile, Jake had more important business than imagining those negotiations. "I've had mumps. I want to help."

Gibbs nodded to himself and said, in a tone of sudden decision, "Come home with me, then, and have some supper. Clara's mother has been staying with the baby and helping out. She'll have dished up something better than I could manage." He smiled faintly. "She's a believer in suppers more like dinners. I don't know how Clara grew up thin. And after we eat, we can figure out how you can at least make the offer without causing trouble."

By the time Clara's mother had gone home, leaving the baby gurgling in her cradle, and the two men were digging into slices of meatloaf and mashed potatoes, Jake had stumbled on the trickiest part of what he was proposing. He might be able to sneak into the house at a prearranged time, since Joshua — his host had insisted on the first name — and Clara had a setup for exchanging messages. And he might be able to stay hidden until that could happen. But what about Wrangler? If he left him at the livery stable, someone working there might well recognize him. If Jake's stints at such stables was any guide, the men working there were better at recognizing horses than people, and the good ones liked the horses better. Besides, he couldn't just leave Wrangler there, even paying in advance, without checking frequently to see if they were taking good care of him.

The baby started fussing as if sharing Jake's concern. Joshua rose from the table, picked her up, and brought her back to sit on his lap. As he fed her bits of mashed potato, Jake raised the question. Joshua studied the top of the baby's head as if some answer might be written there, and then brightened up. "You may know that Clara's family has a farm. It's not far, but far enough that it isn't very likely someone from town would see and recognize your horse, if you were to entrust the animal to them for the duration."

"You think they'd be willing?"

Joshua bounced the baby on his knee. "I'm sure of it. They've been fretting about Clara, even though I've assured them she can't catch mumps again. They'd be glad to know she'll have some more help, and that they were helping to make it happen."

The next night, Jake made his slow, sneaking way through the dark back yard at Mamie's, on up to the kitchen door. He tapped twice and then three times. A long minute later, someone cracked the door open, and to his surprise, a man's voice hissed, "In, and hurry!" In the time it took for Jake to slip inside, he recognized the voice as Horn's. Apparently Jake wouldn't be the only man on the premises.

After spending weeks with male company and nothing but, that came as something of a relief.

Clara sat at the kitchen table, chopping what looked like parsnips. She stood as he entered and came to greet him, reaching for his hands and giving them a good firm clasp. "Welcome. It was very good of you to come."

"How's Mamie? And the others?"

Clara dropped his hands and sat back down, gesturing for him to do the same. "Mamie is one of the sickest, probably because she's somewhat older than the ladies she employs. As a general rule, the disease hits harder as the patient gets older. The only one as sick, or sicker, is Summer Dawn. Indians seem to be hit hardest by the diseases common among white people."

Jake remembered Summer Dawn — the challenge in her eyes, her skin the color of reddish earth in the Oklahoma Territories, and the slow smile with which she had finally rewarded him. What a waste, for that stubborn strength to wither from a disease he'd shrugged off as a child.

And Mamie.

How he had struggled, young fool that he was, with the realization that he desired her. That the lush body inspiring other boys to torment her moved him as well, haunted him at night, left him struggling with the temptation to commit the sin of Onan. At least he'd finally given in to that temptation.

Of course she'd grown older, as he had. But the years had left her even more desirable, her curves just as voluptuous, the hunted lost look in her eyes replaced with the glint of wit and confidence and knowledge of her power.

Clara was patiently waiting for him to emerge from his brown study. He looked up at her, hoping the desperation didn't show in his eyes, and asked, "How bad off is she? Are they?"

Clara stood up again and started toward the door, Jake falling into step behind her. Horn took her place at the table and started chopping more parsnips as Clara said, "Both women have been feverish for more than two weeks, with higher fevers later in that period. Summer Dawn has been delirious at times — and I can't entirely suppress my curiosity about what she's saying, as she's speaking in her own language. I can understand Mamie, of course, and when she's speaking coherently, she mentions how much her muscles hurt — more than she would, I'm guessing, even to me, if she were fully in control of what she did and didn't say."

"What can I do?"

Clara gave him the ghost of a smile. "A good question. What *can* you do? Have you done any nursing, or anything like it?"

Jake thought back over his wartime experience. Compared to what the infantry must have seen, there were damn few injuries. Still — "I was in the war, as a sailor. I lent a hand when I needed to. Not a skillful one."

"I'll show you how to help me with changing bedding while the patient is in bed. You'll be able to clean up messes and help with laundry — all of us who are well take turns at that — and bringing the patients cool compresses. And it may well do some good to talk to them, which is not something I've asked Mr. Horn to do. Though not to Summer Dawn, most likely, unless you've picked up whatever it is she speaks along your travels."

Jake shrugged. "I know a word here and a word there in some Indian talk, but not enough to help much, even if it's the right kind of talk."

Clara stopped and turned to face him. "Would you just

as soon do your talking to Mamie, rather than the woman you don't know?"

Jake tried to keep his breathing steady. "Yes, ma'am. If that's all right."

"Ma'am, is it? As you like, but you know Clara will do. Mamie's room is this way. You can tell her you've returned and sit a while, if her linens don't need immediate changing, before I introduce you to laundry duty."

Mamie's cheeks were flushed with fever. He hadn't seen them so red since the day he'd found that pack of two-legged wolves surrounding her and knew he had to wade in, no matter how badly he was likely to come out of it. He dabbed at her forehead with the damp cloth Clara had given him, wishing it were cooler. At least the heat of high summer was past, and water left to sit could stay cooler than skin temperature.

It had been years since he'd thought of his family, except to remember the looks in their eyes on that last day home. But standing in a sickroom, he was all of a sudden taken back to his own days sick in bed as a child, and his mother stroking his cheek or kissing his forehead to check his temperature. The best times had been when he wasn't all that sick any more, not enough to be miserable. He could just lie there, weakness making the bed more comfortable than before, and enjoy being looked after, with no chores waiting and laziness a requirement instead of a sin. But Mamie was too sick to enjoy any such comforts.

At least Mamie didn't have to put up with anyone praying at her.

He couldn't rightly tell if she was awake or asleep — likely some uneasy state between the two. He pulled a chair over to her bedside, sat down, and took her hand.

"Hello, Mamie. It's Jake. I use that name a lot since you first bedeviled me with it. All my mates in the navy knew me as Jake. I had some mighty scraps with those who thought it as funny as you did, and in places like that, a scrap is as good a way as any to get to know a fellow. So you did me a favor, that way. I guess I'm paying you back, trying to help out, and jawing at you. Too bad you can't answer me back. Or can you?"

She stirred and moaned, and muttered something he couldn't catch. It wasn't his name.

"Clara Gibbs is a fine woman. I hope the two of you are friends. Different as you seem, I can see you getting on well together. And her husband the doc, he's the sort of man I'd like to hate if I could, because he's so much better a man than I've been or could be. He's even good with the baby. Christ almighty."

Mamie tossed around on the bed and pawed at her throat. Most likely it hurt — Clara had said something about that. Would it hurt more if she drank some water? Her lips were parched.

He picked up the glass at her bedside and got his left hand under her head, lifting as gently as he could. Her head weighed as heavy on his hand as a corpse's would, but he could feel the heat of her fever through the mess of tangled hair. He held the glass to her lips, trying not to spill it on her, but couldn't figure out how to get her to open her mouth. He put the glass back down, dipped his fingers in it, and dripped a few drops on her closed lips. She licked them. Encouraged, he did it again, and when she opened her mouth a little, brought the glass back and managed to pour a sip she didn't choke on. He got about a quarter of the glass into her before she turned her face away.

He should really see whether he could help with any

of the other patients. He managed to pry himself away after another few minutes, and then realized he had no idea where any of their rooms were except Summer Dawn's. He found his way there without getting lost, and found a closed door. Listening at it, he could hear nothing. Was she breathing quietly? He was coward enough to want to assume so, but opened the door and crept in.

She opened her eyes as he came through the door. The few other Indians he'd known had been like that, ready to wake up at the first sign of what might be trouble. Her black eyes followed him as he approached the bed. He could still see a trace of the defiance with which she had first looked at him. Without speaking, he picked up the glass and offered it to her. She shook her head and closed her eyes again.

He left the room and went looking for Clara. Maybe she could find something for him to do, something that would make him feel more useful than helpless.

But when he found her, she was pale and drooping over a cup of coffee, with no steam rising from it. How long had it, and she, been sitting there? He sat down next to her and picked it up. "Should I get you a refill, or just put you to bed?"

She turned her head toward him as if it had weights attached. "I'm all right. But more coffee might be a good idea."

He studied her for a few seconds and said, "No, I don't think it would be such a good idea, at that. Tell me where the patients are, and then get yourself some sleep."

He could see her struggle with temptation. "I've stayed awake longer during the war, and with far worse to do."

He took the cup to the sink and drank what was left to get rid of it. "I don't doubt it. In war, you can keep going longer than flesh and blood should be able to stand. And you pay for it afterward. I'm not such a good nurse that I want to be the only one left standing for however long this goes on. Where are you sleeping?"

She tried to glare at him. It didn't work too well, whether because she was trying not to smile or because she was too tired, he couldn't say. "What if I don't tell you?"

He stood up and smiled. "Then I'll find a room no one's using, fetch a blanket, tuck you in, and tell everyone to stay away for eight hours or so. And if you try coming out again, I'll put you back there. You can watch me and take notes for when your little girl gets old enough to try and escape nap time."

He expected either an angry reply or submission. It alarmed him to see her head drop down toward the table. She didn't even have the strength to put her arms there to cushion it. He sounded to himself like a petty officer as he barked out, "That's it. I'm going to find a place to put you."

He left the kitchen, closing the door to slow down any attempt Clara might make to evade him, and headed upstairs. Closed bedroom doors no longer meant ladies might be at work, so he knocked softly, waited for any response, and then opened the doors as quietly as he could. On the third knock, he found a room with no occupant and no signs that it usually had one. The bed was stripped, and no paint pots or scent bottles littered the little dressing table. Now he just had to find a blanket. That took longer, but when he went downstairs to the parlor, he found a few ladies talking or sewing, and one of them led him to a linen chest. He dropped two blankets and a pillow on the bed in the vacant room, not bothering about sheets, and went back to the kitchen.

Clara had lifted up her head again, but still sat at the table. He pulled back her chair and got his arms under hers to hoist her up. She tried to stand and might have made it, but that was a long way from making it upstairs on her feet. Lifting her in his arms, he held her against his chest, relieved to find that she didn't actually fight him, though she muttered a protest with a few faint cusses included.

He had laid her on the bed, tucked her in, and closed the door before he realized she hadn't told him where the other sick ladies' rooms were. Cussing louder than Clara had, he headed back to the parlor again to ask.

At least there were only four sick women, and the other two were on the mend. His guide to the linen chest turned out to be named Trudi, and she'd told him that two others had already recovered. The rest of them, like Jake, had had the disease as children.

Trudi seemed to be Clara's lieutenant commander. She'd clapped him on the back when he told her why he needed the blankets, and when he came back from making the rounds of the sickrooms, she had a big mug of hot coffee waiting. "It's not much of a thank-you, but here. I'd have been the one having to get her to bed otherwise, and she's taller and prob'ly stronger'n me. I could have maybe asked Horn, but I think he's gone to lay down his own self."

Jake chuckled. "That's the way of it, often enough. Men are usually stronger, but women may just be tougher." He'd heard stories about the endurance of camp followers, from those who'd been in the infantry. And envied them that, if little else.

Trudi raised an eyebrow at the concession and went on, "I've been helping some, but Miss Clara knows what she's doing and I don't, so she didn't let me do much. You tell me if you need me to haul water or cloths or such."

He gulped the coffee, and for a wonder it was hot

enough without burning his throat. "I will, and be glad to."

She cocked her head and fluttered her eyelashes at him. "And me and the others can do more in the way of paying you for your trouble, if you've a mind."

With Mamie so sick, and Summer Dawn that he'd lain with sick also, the thought didn't appeal. "Thank you kindly, but not just now. I wouldn't want to be too busy to hear one of the ladies calling, or miss someone trying to get in." He found a smile somewhere. "After all, that's my job along with Horn, keeping troublemakers out."

A few days after he'd first come, Summer Dawn was finally on the mend, and sending hard-to-read looks in his direction. But Mamie was worse, if anything. She pawed at her breasts as if they itched or pained her, and stared as if seeing visions, even talking to them — and not kindly, either. It quieted her to have his company or Clara's, so they took turns, leaving it to Trudi and the other healthy ladies to deal with most of the chores. Clara had written about Mamie's state in one of her messages to Joshua, and come back grim and silent from his reply.

Jake didn't know how Clara passed the time she spent at Mamie's bedside, but he'd taken to talking to Mamie about anything and nothing. He told her about the time some of his shipmates put dead fish in his boots, and how he'd got back at the ringleader by hiding a big ol' eel in his bunk. At night one time, when the house got quiet, he told her about the time he fell overboard on just such a dark night, hitting his head on a boulder and knocking himself out, and how Rich jumped in and rescued him.

And on and on, more tales of his travels, even some he hoped she wouldn't remember whenever she woke up for good. Which she'd do, if he could do anything to make it happen. He painted for her with his words the picture that brought to mind. "I'll wrestle with an angel over it, like my namesake did, but I'll make him bless you instead of me. Hell, I've wrestled damn near everything else. I won't care if he's hot as hot coals and burns me wherever I touch him, I'll outlast him anyhow. I can just see glowing white feathers flying all around, and then laying in the dirt around him. I'll bring one back for you, and you can put it in a vase in your parlor, and tell whatever tales about it you care to."

She was lying a little quieter now. Had she smiled? It was gone before he could be sure, and she went back to tossing this way and that on the pillow.

And now all he could think of was that last day, when it had been Ethan — no angel, but a damn sight closer to it than Jake — that he'd wrestled with, when Ethan jumped him, and how he'd somehow thrown him to the ground, for all Ethan was stronger then.

He'd wondered now and then, since finding Mamie here, whether he'd ever tell her. He could tell her now, and she might not really hear him, or might forget.

"You can stop looking at whatever's been haunting your bed. I've got uglier haunts to tell you about. And if you remember about them when you're well, you can toss me out like a bad penny, if you've a mind to."

She didn't quiet again, or turn to listen, or pay him any mind. He hadn't told a soul any of this, and now it came to it he wasn't sure how, nor whether he could pull the details out from wherever he'd hid them, out into the air and the dim light of the bedroom.

"You probably thought I never gambled, with how holy I was always trying to be back then. And I didn't until a few months after you left town. Maybe I was missing you, thinking about what I might have had if I'd had the nerve to tell you I desired you, and wouldn't never have now you'd gone — and all the while thinking I must be some awful sinner after all, for wanting you. But that sounds like I'm trying to blame you somehow, and even I don't sink that low. It went deeper than how I felt about any one person, except maybe myself. After all those years of Bible-reading and my family's preaching, I was starting to wonder why some people didn't believe it all, and whether they knew something I didn't, some secret my own folk had kept from me. Something that would explain all the feelings I'd been getting, as I got closer to grown, feelings Pa and Grandpa never talked about except to lump them in with sinning.

"So anyway, I gambled, but that doesn't mean I was any good at it. And any seasoned gambler could tell at a glance I was greener'n grass. Not to mention I was so scrawny back then, I'd've had no chance of making something of it if I were to get suspicious.

"I wasn't just green, I was stupid as a berry-drunk skunk. When my pockets were empty, which happened quick enough with what pocket money Pa gave me, I thought the fellows I'd been playing with were being friendly when they said I could play on credit for a hand or two. Or three, or more. You recall how I dressed back then. They knew there was money somewhere around me.

"Want to hear something really funny? On the way to the saloon, when I was nerving myself up to gamble for the first time, and almost turning around every other step, I found a penny in the street. I told myself it was lucky. Lucky! It'd make a horse laugh, with where that led me."

Now Mamie was as quiet as if she was listening. Or quieter? He bent over her to listen, couldn't tell what he heard, held his hand just above her nose and mouth. There, the faint puff that showed she was breathing. He sat back in his chair and then had to summon up the nerve to go on.

"They let me get fifty-three dollars in debt — I still remember the number — before they asked me to come out to the back of the saloon. I'd never been back there — I'd never set foot in the place until all that started, and felt more and more like a lost sinner every time, and maybe that's what I was after. Anyhow, once they had me out back and away from anyone who might stick up for me, they told me it was time to pay up, or else. There were three of them traveling together, fleecing fellows like me, and none of them had the muscle I have now, but they looked like demons out of hell to me. They told me I had until noon the next day to come up with the money."

He'd thought nothing could be worse than asking his pa for the money and confessing why he needed it — but the prospect of taking another beating, not long after the last one and sure to be worse, was almost as bad.

"I came up with the worst idea you could find if you worked day and night finding bad ideas for a week. Remember how, any time Ethan and I had a squabble or I was envious of him, you'd tease me about Jacob and Esau? You must've had second sight. I knew Ethan had been saving up his pocket money, and doing extra chores and helping out at the general store to earn more, so he could go away to school. Not preacher college like Grandpa, but a university back east, where all the swells went, and he could study all sorts of subjects Indiana Seminary wouldn't offer. And he trusted me, of course, because I was his brother, and I'd been doing what I was told and reading the Bible and all the rest for so long, and he had no notion what I would get up to behind the family's back. So he'd never made any secret of where he kept what he was saving.

"I waited until they were all at prayers in the study

after supper, and I apologized and said I needed to use the necessary real bad, and I snuck up to his room. I'd just pulled out the sock where he kept the money when Pa came in and saw me. I don't know how he knew to look. I must've had guilty written all over me, for anyone who really knew me to see."

That was all he could stand to tell. Even if Mamie wasn't looking at him and might not remember, he'd be damned — if he wasn't already — before he'd break down and cry over his past when she was lying here with maybe no future. He got up and squatted low enough to see his face in her dressing mirror, scrubbed at it with a dirty sleeve, and went out back for some air before he found Clara and asked for a job to do.

What he really wanted to do was bury his face in Wrangler's mane and breathe in the warm sweat-and-hay smell of him. But that would have to wait.

Chapter 13

MAMIE opened her eyes and looked around as much as she could while lying in bed. Her own bed, with the deep mattress just soft enough and no softer, and no holes in the blanket. Her own bedroom, with walnut paneling, and white lace curtains puffing inward with the breeze. She wasn't back in Deliverance, the wind whistling through a broken window or her pa's drunken bellow coming down the hall toward her. She wasn't in hell, with a demon poking her breasts with a red-hot pitchfork and shoving her ever closer to the pit. No ghosts swooshing by overhead, nor any cold feet of long-dead companions pressed against her legs for warmth.

She tried hoisting herself to sitting, and somehow had help doing it. Clara, at her bedside? Did that make sense? She supposed so — Clara was a nurse, as well as something like a friend. And the one thing Mamie was sure about was that she'd been sick, maybe sick enough to die of it. She could feel it, bone-deep.

"Here." Clara was holding a glass of water to her lips. She tried a sip, and it went down without hurting her throat. She put one hand on the glass to at least half help herself as she drank it down. Something about the moment brought a memory floating almost within reach. Had someone else helped her to drink, before? Clara hadn't been the only one healthy and helping, had she?

"How do you feel?" Clara took back the empty glass

and put it on the nightstand. "Are you up to getting out of bed, or would you rather rest a while longer?"

Mamie tried twisting to where she could swing her legs out of the bed. Clara, seeing what she was doing, put her hand on Mamie's back as support, but let Mamie do most of the work. She could have cried with happiness to feel her feet hit the floor.

"So far, so good." Clara bent to get an arm around Mamie's shoulders. "Ready to try for upright?"

Mamie laughed, for the first time in who knows how long. "That's me, upright all the way. Let's do it."

Her scalp still smarting from her and Clara's combined efforts to comb her hair, and her silkiest dressing gown covering her nightdress, Mamie made her way downstairs clinging to the banister, Clara one step below in case she slipped. She stopped halfway down to catch her breath and shake off being dizzy, and used the moment to ask, finally, "How long was I abed?"

Clara opened her mouth and then paused. "You know, I think I've lost count? But let me see . . . about three and a half weeks. It's almost September."

Mamie managed to hold back a gasp, or maybe a wail. Joshua had warned her how long they might have to close, but she'd held out hope for better. "Did the story hold up?"

Clara stepped down another step, leaving Mamie to follow after. "I can't say of my own knowledge, having been here right along —"

Mamie stopped again, unable to keep tears from starting in her eyes. "You didn't! What about Joshua, and your baby? And why don't you look as ragged as I feel?"

Clara put her strong hand over Mamie's. "Thank you for that charitable assessment. Joshua and my mother took care of Alice. And I had help, from your ladies and Mr. Horn, and from someone else, as you'll see. Now let's get some real food in you."

Food would make her stronger. She needed to be strong, always, and she was weak as a day-old pup. Not to mention mighty curious about Clara's extra helper, and why Clara was being so mysterious about who she might be. They made their way down the rest of the stairs, Mamie now leaning on Clara's arm, and walked into the kitchen.

Where Jake Flint was sitting, calm as you please, working his way through a heaping plate of eggs and bacon and slurping a mug of coffee.

Mamie looked around wildly, almost toppling over, for anything else out of some fever-dream. Nothing — no Amanda Jane passing by the door with the banker in tow, no long-dead sister at the stove stirring potatoes. Clara held out a chair for her, and she collapsed into it, staring at Jake. "You."

He chuckled around a mouthful of egg. "None other. Good to see you downstairs."

The smell of his plateful had her mouth watering. "And have you been seeing me upstairs, then?" Was that what she'd been trying to remember?

Clara put a plate, with a much smaller serving, in front of her and sat down with her own. "Jake came to town when you'd been laid up around two weeks. He's been of great assistance."

Mamie slid her fork under some eggs and got it to her mouth without losing any. "You're back. In town."

Jake shrugged. "I almost joined a riverboat crew, but then I got the chance at a cattle drive, and that let me hold onto my horse. The drive finished up not all that far from here, so I thought I'd come through and see how you were doing. Showed up almost as dirt-plastered and high-smelling as the last time, but I saw the sign and then got hold of Joshua, who told me what was what and gave me a chance to clean up a bit. Clara and Joshua snuck me in and I've been lending a hand."

That reminded Mamie of her unanswered question. "Do people in town still believe we've been cleaning all this time?"

Clara brought her a warm-up for her coffee. "Joshua hasn't reported any problems. I don't know what he's heard, and what he'd tell me while I have other things to think about. We've had a few knocks on the door and complaints called through it, but nothing that's needed Jake or Mark Horn to handle."

"How many of the girls are still sick?" Mamie had to wash the lump in her throat down with coffee before she could add, "Did anyone die of it?"

Jake and Clara both shook their heads, and Jake said, "Summer Dawn was the sickest aside from you, and she turned the corner a few days before you did. She's still staying in her room except for meals, but that's just her way, I reckon."

Mamie studied him and couldn't tell whether he'd been keeping Summer Dawn company there. Not that it was her business, except to figure what Jake would've owed and count it as less than he had coming. "I want to open back up as soon as possible. Tonight, if we can."

Jake looked her up and down, and she flushed. Before she could snap at him about it, Clara said, "Why don't you have a bath, and then we'll see what we can do with some paint. I'll trust Jake to tell us whether you're ready for callers."

As Mamie sat before her mirror and worked on her face, Clara sat on the bed to offer any opinions Mamie might ask for. But while she didn't want to hurt Clara's feelings, she didn't guess Clara had much expertise in such matters. Instead, she asked, "So you taught Jake how to nurse?"

Clara considered before answering. "He already knew a bit from his time in the navy. He'd dealt with injury more than illness there, so I showed him how to be most helpful. He learns quickly." Another pause; Mamie turned just soon enough to see Clara smile. "He may have been most useful in compelling me to rest when I tried to ignore my need for it. He can be quite masterful."

Mamie had to wait for a flush to subside before she could assess the amount of rouge she'd put on. "Masterful, you say."

She didn't look this time, but she could imagine how Clara's eyes might be twinkling. "Quite."

* * * * *

Jake wasn't a bit surprised to see Mamie try to do too much too soon. She bustled along until nightfall her first day back on her feet, and by next morning she had some fever again — though not much, Clara said — and could hardly sit up. He now had strict instructions from Clara, not to mention Lucette — "M'sieur, you *must* make Mamie be reasonable, yes?" — to keep Mamie in bed, or at least reclining, until supper at the very least. The most straightforward way to do that was to sit on the side of the bed and push her back down when she tried to get up. After a few rounds of that contest, he'd picked up a few cuss words he'd never heard on board ship or on a cattle drive, and he felt safe shifting to the bedside chair.

She watched him settle himself as if he'd performed some feat of magic. "You're still here."

She'd said that maybe three times by now. He wouldn't have thought the strangeness of his presence matched up to the visions she'd told him of, that she had when she was sickest. Though the one time he'd had a high fever as a child, Ethan told him later that he'd been hollering about scarecrows, and not even scarecrows doing anything peculiar like walking around.

Now that Mamie wasn't busy trying to get past him and bustle around seeing to things, he'd best think of some way to amuse her. He could ask her about where her different ladies came from, or about her strangest customers, but that would only make her more impatient about staying in her room. He was coming up dry when Mamie rescued him by saying, "There's a lot we never got round to knowing about each other, back in Deliverance. Tell me something about yourself I wouldn't know. Such as, what sort of good memories do you have, from life back then or since?"

If he'd had his druthers, he wouldn't be dwelling on his past, with the kind of memories that lived there. But he thought for a minute and answered, "Learning to read, for one. I don't know what the book was, but I can still recall the thrill when I realized the letters had turned into words and I could hear them in my head." And his pa had praised him and thanked God that his son could now read the Holy Book. He shoved that part back out of sight. Could he turn the question back on Mamie, instead of trying to add to that answer? But a glance at her face showed her still expectant. And of course everything he could bring to mind had something painful come with it. Well, he'd earned that pain and had better not kick at it. "Later, going fishing. With

Ethan. The first time, I was just thrilled I caught anything at all. The next time I caught more fish than he did." And Ethan had been happy for him, not minding he'd been beat.

Thankfully, Mamie seemed to feel it was her turn now. "It won't surprise you that things got better for me once I left Deliverance, for all no one there would believe it. Not at first, of course. But the day I bought this place, and knew it was mine and I could make something of it, that was the gladdest and proudest I'd ever felt. I've never been much for regrets, but especially since that day."

She twisted around and punched at her pillows, fluffing them, and leaned back. "But back before, in Deliverance, there's just one thing that comes to mind. Do you remember the day we met, more than just in passing?"

He was pretty sure he remembered just fine, but he asked, "Was I eating ice cream?"

Mamie nodded vigorously and then put a hand to her head. He dipped the washcloth in the basin of water at her bedside and handed it to her. When she'd applied it to her forehead and handed it back, she went on, "Yes! The ice cream parlor had just opened up the week before, and you came out of it with a cone. I didn't know much about flavors then, but I think it was vanilla."

"I guess so. I think it took a while before they had anything else."

Mamie sat up more and reached her hand out. He scooted closer and took it. She gave his hand a squeeze he could've wished had more strength behind it, let go, and flopped back. "You saw me looking at you and that cone, and you came over and offered me a lick of it. I never dreamed of that happening. If I'd of even thought about it, I'd've figured anyone from a family like yours would expect my tongue to carry dirt on it, or maybe sickness."

She talked differently when she reminisced about the past — without the higher-class accent she'd picked up since. He doubted he'd ever see a reason to tell her so. Instead he tried to remember more about an act that had apparently meant more to her than he'd ever thought. "You looked at that cone like water in the desert — which I guess was close enough to the truth, as hot as it was that day. And as I looked at you, I realized that in the few times I'd seen you, I'd never seen you smile. I wanted to see that."

"I'll guess you did see it! I smiled so wide it near to hurt my face. And I licked that cone so hard, you had to shove the ice cream back onto it."

He'd forgotten that, and laughed to remember it. "And you looked all embarrassed, until I offered you another lick."

Mamie lay quiet on her pillows for long enough that he thought she might be dropping off to sleep. He was about to move his chair back, as quiet as he could, when she said softly, "You walked me halfway home, taking turns with me on eating that cone. And when you turned back and I went on, I kept thinking how a boy from a good family, someone so different from me and mine, treated me like I was somebody. I didn't know what to make of it, except it made me happy. Really happy."

Of course that tale made Jake a far ways from happy. She'd had such a rough time when he'd had things easy. And it only got worse when she started looking like a woman before the other girls did. Though he'd had his own troubles by then, or he'd thought he did. If he could only reach back through all the years, grab young Jacob by the collar, and shake him 'til his brains rattled.

Though if he could, and his younger self had found some better way to handle his doubts and restlessness, what would he be now? Would he even recognize himself? What would it be like, to live in that other man's skin?

And how long had he been woolgathering? He looked back at Mamie, who must be wondering what the hell was wrong with him. Except she'd fallen back asleep for true, with a smile on her face.

Mamie was finally on the mend, and that wasn't just Jake's impression. Joshua Gibbs now felt safe, or Clara felt safe for him, coming to tend her, and recommended that she take short walks in the fresh air. Given the way he'd glanced at and then studied Jake, that prescription might've been intended for the both of them. Jake hadn't spent so much time indoors since he was a boy cooped up studying the Bible.

Naturally, Mamie's idea of a short walk turned out to be ambitious. "I haven't seen the creek in so long, it could've dried up for good and I wouldn't know it. I can make it, as long as we take it slow."

If Mamie had a horse, and a nice steady one at that, he'd plop her on it and get her to the creek that way. Even if he could go get Wrangler before she headed off on her own, Wrangler was too feisty for even a temporary invalid. "We'll take it slow, and we'll stop twice on the way for you to rest. If we don't find anywhere else for you to rest, I'll make myself into a stool and you sit on me."

She gave him a look somewhere between flirtatious and wicked. "If you're especially nice to me, I'll pretend you didn't suggest I sit on your . . . back."

Jake did his best to ignore the pictures that called up, and could only hope his failure to pull that off didn't come to her attention. "Which is the shortest way to go?"

Mamie pointed, and they started out, Jake taking her

arm to keep her from walking too fast. In just a few minutes, they passed a tree with a low, sturdy branch, and he pulled her to a halt. "First rest stop."

She pouted and blew out a breath that ruffled the loose hair escaping from the front of her bonnet. "Yes, nurse, whatever you say."

"Sit down before I paddle you." And that was one of the stupider things he could say, if he didn't want distracting pictures in his head.

Mamie waggled her eyebrows at him — and was that a hint of a blush? "Why, then I wouldn't be able to sit down the rest of the way, would I?"

Jake held her upper arms and lowered her to the branch. It didn't so much as creak, so he settled carefully down beside her. "How are you feeling?"

Mamie sighed. "I'd love to be able to tell you I could race you to the creek, but I'm not *that* good a liar. At least, not to you."

That last touched him more than he wanted to show. Time to change the subject. "Let's chat a bit until you're ready to go on. Except I'd better do most of the talking, so you can catch your breath. Anything you want me to go on about?"

Mamie turned to look at him head on. "Actually, I'd like to hear more about your sailor friend Rich. Like, what did he do before the war — if he ever talked about it?"

"Oh, he talked about it. Wouldn't hardly shut up about it. He was a fisherman on a schooner out of Gloucester — Massachusetts, that is. That meant salt water sailing. He'd go on about how soft we had it, sailing on rivers. To hear him tell it, he'd survived storms big enough to swallow Jonah and the whale together."

And that was enough talking. He stood up and reached

down to her. "Ready to move on?"

She answered by grabbing his hands and helping him hoist her up. She was getting her strength back at that. But he still put his arm through hers to keep her from hurrying. He was looking around for another branch, or a stump or a boulder, when the creek came into view. Among the trees lining the bank, the maple tree just ahead blazed in a red so bright it distracted him, just for a moment, from the woman at his side.

She'd kept to his pace along the way, aside from bitching about stopping to rest, so he was unprepared for her to jerk her arm loose and stride down toward the water. By the time he gathered his wits and ran after her, she had reached the bank and turned to face him, obviously preparing the right taunt. But before she found it, her foot started to slide on some loose bits of rock.

Could he reach her before she had time to feel afraid? He'd give it a damn good try. He bounded to the bank and jumped into the water, right under where she swayed and started to topple, and caught her, lifting her up in his arms.

Her eyes were wider than he'd ever seen them — he hadn't been quite quick enough to keep her from being startled, or more than startled. But it took almost no time before she wiped the shock off her face and let a slow grin take over. "Bravo, brave knight! Now that you've rescued the lady fair, if you'll allow that description, what do you propose to do with her?"

He chuckled as he sloshed to the bank and climbed back up. "Given that we're out here for anyone to see, I propose the lady put off showing her gratitude for my rescue until a more private opportunity arises."

He cussed to himself a moment after coming out with that last word, knowing what Mamie would do about it.

Sure enough, she cast her eyes downward to what was already arising before closing her eyes and lying back in his arms. Was the fright taking its toll? They could both use a place to sit down, her to rest again and him to empty out his boots, but there was nothing suitable close by. He carried her until he found a fallen maple and set her down, making sure she was steady before letting go. It maybe wasn't wide enough for him to sit without sliding forward or back once he went to take a boot off, so he plumped down on the ground beside it and pulled off the wettest one first.

Mamie was looking pale now. He'd best distract her somehow. Gratifying her curiosity might help. "I wonder sometimes whether Rich went home and had a passel of kids. He didn't have any when I knew him, I don't think, but he was older'n most of us, and he used to lecture us, and teach us, like he was our —" It wasn't a word that came easy. "Like he was our daddy. He'd have made a good father." A damned sight better than some. "I hope he is one by now."

He'd got as much water out of his boots as he'd be getting. He pulled them back on, shook off the memories and regrets, swallowed down the taste of them as best he could, and stood up. "Time to get you home. And then I'm going for Doc. He'll probably send you right back to bed."

Mamie tossed her head and sniffed. "He can do all the sending he likes. I'll go when I'm good and ready." She stood up without his help and put her hands on her hips. "Let's get back to my place before any more time's a-wasting."

Jake took her arm one more time. "Well, I suppose I'd best get my boots off soon and put them somewhere to dry. While you get your rest."

Mamie pulled her arm free, swatted his rear, and took his arm again. She leaned on him a little heavier than when they set out. He'd go get Joshua as soon as he got her home, wet boots or no.

Chapter 14

MAMIE woke up, sat up, and looked around for one of her minders, but she was alone in her room. Jake had fetched Joshua after their trip to the creek, and Joshua had given her another lecture about being sensible, but it seemed he hadn't gone so far as to set a watch on her. Though she was pretty sure Clara was still somewhere about. As for Jake, she'd just as soon not do any guessing, let alone hoping, on the subject.

She made it out of bed and into her clothes without it taking much longer than usual, and perched briefly in the chair at her dressing table to brush and arrange her hair. If she opened the house tonight, she could do a more thorough job. Just now, she had a great desire for fresh air, even more than for breakfast. She opened her window, but the sunshine, and the breeze that came through to tickle her chin, only whetted her appetite for more. She left her bedroom and found Sophie, Bessie, and Trudi all heading for the stairs. She let them fuss over her in their different ways — Sophie clapping her hands and saying how much healthier Mamie looked, Bessie giving a short satisfied nod, and Trudi inspecting Mamie as if deciding whether to send her back to bed. At the foot of the stairs, the three younger women clattered and chattered off to breakfast, leaving Mamie to make her way out the front door.

She closed her eyes and took one, another, a third deep breath, only to hear a familiar male voice say with an unfamiliar uncertain tone, "Mamie?"

She opened her eyes, to see a startled look just fading from Quinn's face, replaced by the more habitual knowing smile. He tipped his hat and asked, "Is your establishment open again? All properly . . . *hygienic*?"

She decided on the spot. "Open later today, and I'll be glad to have it so."

Quinn studied her, chewing his lip as she'd never seen him do, and said with less than his usual smoothness, "Not to be ungallant, my dear, but you're looking poorly. Have you been ill?"

A dangerous question! She'd deny it if she could, but if he already knew better, the lie would just make him suspicious, or more so. "Cook went to visit family while we were closed, and the substitute I hired didn't know a fresh chicken from one going bad. I didn't notice until I'd already had some. I threw the woman out on her ear, but I spent the next two days being most unattractively sick."

"I certainly approve of you giving this incompetent her walking papers." Quinn hesitated, also unusual, before asking in a casual tone, "Is there anything I could do to ease your recovery — run some errand, say?"

Mamie was too surprised not to show it. Quinn gave her a mocking smile and said, "One must, after all, keep people guessing, It wouldn't do to be too predictable."

She wished she had a fan to flutter. It would give her a way to fidget without being too obvious. "Well, you'll be happy to know you succeeded. And thank you, but we don't need anything done, or fetched. My people can handle such things."

"Then I'll be on my way." He looked her up and down with something like his usual greedy appreciation, but she thought she sensed some lingering concern showing through. She waited for him to get some ways down the street before she went inside to tell everyone they were opening for business.

* * * * *

Mamie had been out of bed — the second time —for three days, and the house open for two. Jake had no way of knowing how great a blow Mamie's finances had taken with the long shutdown, and little he could do to help, so he had no good reason to ask.

As for what he wanted to know more, it was only his own cowardice that stood in the way.

Something in him said that he could trust Mamie, if he could trust anyone, to know the truth and not hate him for it. Which was next to crazy, as little as he could say he knew her any more. Of course, he'd already told her most of it. But she hadn't mentioned it, and most likely she didn't remember a word.

Enough of stewing about such things! He could come and go, now, after all this time, and he may as well take a walk. They had put together a tale of how he'd just got to town and been lucky enough to be riding up when the sign came down. Wrangler was back at the livery stable — he'd go give him a visit, and a carrot.

Wrangler saw or smelled him coming and was practically dancing in the stall as Jake walked up. He buried his nose in the horse's mane, the way he'd dreamed of doing during those weeks tending Mamie, and stroked the muscled neck. "How's life here in the stable? I hope you liked farm life, but better get used to town again for a bit. We'll be hitting the trail to somewhere or other soon enough, I expect."

A stable lad came by with an armful of fresh straw. Jake stepped back to let him dump it and then grabbed a rake to help him spread it. The lad thanked him and said, nodding at Wrangler, "That's a right good animal you've got there. Doesn't give us no trouble. How long have you had him?"

"Five years now." And the best piece of luck Jake had had since his travels began, finding the gelding at auction just when he had the coin for a horse of his own. He'd been near broke not long before and not long after.

The lad looked at Wrangler with sad, greedy eyes. "I'd like me a horse of my own, sure enough. Maybe when I've worked here awhile longer. Yates pays pretty good."

"Does he, now." If Jake stayed in town for a while, he'd need some sort of work. Maybe he'd hunt up this Yates and see if he had work enough for another pair of hands.

As Jake made his way back toward the center of town, he heard footsteps behind him. He turned to see a man in an embroidered waistcoat, an unusually clean Stetson hat, and snakeskin boots, looking him over like he knew something and was making sure of it. The man tipped his hat first. "Now if I don't miss my guess, I'd say you're Mr. Jacob Flint, who the mayor and council members so hoped would become the town's new marshal."

Jake tipped his hat, barely. "That's right. And good afternoon, Mr. . . . ."

The man's smile made him think of a coyote's. "Sterling Quinn, at your service. I'm a lawyer by trade, and have had the honor of representing some of the officials I mentioned on several occasions. Though just now, I've come from chatting with my old friend Mamie, whose . . . *cleaning* project is finally completed." He kept his eyes on Jake as if he knew the secret, which Jake doubted, or more likely, suspected that Jake might and wanted to make him uneasy enough to somehow reveal it.

Jake decided on the spot to get a room at the hotel, as he should have done already, and maybe take the chance of paying extra for the manager to say he'd done it two days earlier. "Yes, I'm glad to have missed the drought the town had to put up with. The place certainly looks extra clean now."

The man's teeth practically gleamed as he showed them. "Ah, so we have another mutual acquaintance! Hmmm, that reminds me. I know Mamie takes a copy of the *Omaha Daily Bee*, to help her guests pass the time as they wait for the ladies. Did you happen to look at it, and perhaps notice this advertisement from last week? I thought the coincidence of the initial might attract your attention." The lawyer extracted a folded paper from his inside waistcoat pocket and handed it to Jake, his manicured finger pointing to a personals ad. Jake looked at it, and his blood ran cold.

Ethan F. seeks news of his brother Jacob. F., not seen in many years. Please send word.

Jake forced himself to look up. The lawyer was watching him the way a vulture watches a cow with a broken leg in the desert. Jake called on everything he'd learned about deceit over the long miles and shrugged, holding out the paper with a little smile. "I hope the fellow finds his brother, but it's nothing to do with me."

The lawyer waved the paper away. "No, you keep it. I've read it all, and I'll get the next issue soon. I wonder if the ad will still be there. I have a feeling this Ethan will keep trying until he finds what he's looking for."

And with that, the man strode on down the street. Jake waited for him to get out of sight and then made tracks for

Mamie's, cursing under his breath.

* * * * *

Jake had stomped in and insisted that Mamie follow him into the small parlor, evicting everyone else except Trudi, who insisted on staying in case Mamie needed help. Now he planted himself two paces from where Mamie stood, jabbing at the paper in his one clenched fist and demanding, "That lawyer just showed me — did you know about this?"

Trudi sidled over and tried to put herself between them. "Please, Mamie's barely out of bed! You shouldn't —"

Mamie put a hand on Trudi's arm and steered her away. "It's quite all right. This big bellowing bull of a fellow will calm down soon enough, and I'm quite able to wait until he does. Though I'd appreciate it if he lowered his voice before we have customers pressing their ears on the door, if they haven't already."

Clara had finally gone home to her husband and baby, but he could picture her standing nearby, not interfering yet but keeping a close eye on where things went from here. And she'd be thinking less of Jake for the way he was acting, no doubt. He made himself relax his fists and take three deep breaths before he found a dainty round table to drop the paper on and said to both women, "I apologize. I had no right to jump to conclusions."

Mamie regarded him steadily. "As a matter of fact, I did see a similar advertisement, and two others much like it in earlier editions. You were gone by then. You say Quinn the lawyer showed it to you?" She sat down in the nearest armchair. She still moved more slowly and carefully than usual, and he felt like the worst sort of villain for yelling at her. "He was asking about you a while after I saw the first ad, though I don't know if it really was the first. He collects information, that man does, just in case he can ever turn it to his purposes."

Jake thought back to his confessions by Mamie's bedside and felt his fists clench again. "And has he been collecting it from you?"

Mamie sat straighter and made a noise like spitting, though he saw no sign that she'd actually done it. "Not about you, Mr. Flint. Nor will he. You can believe that or not, as you like."

Jake turned to Trudi. "Would you be willing to leave Mamie and me alone for a few minutes? I promise I'll fetch you right away if she needs anything I can't do for her.:"

Trudi bit her lip. Mamie smiled at her and said, "Go on, girl. Go make some man understand how much he wants you." Trudi showed her dimples in a brief smile, curtsied, and left, with one last worried look over her shoulder.

Jake waited for her to close the door again — no eavesdroppers, he was relieved to see — and made his way to another, larger chair, collapsing into it. "Do you remember anything about my talking to you when you were sick?"

Mamie got that inward look of someone hunting an elusive memory. "I remember something. And since you're bringing it up now, I know it was about Ethan . . . ." She wrinkled up her forehead, which Jake tried not to notice looked cute. "Something about gambling? And money? Oh! — Ethan's money . . . ." She went wide-eyed for a second and then wrinkled up her forehead. "But I don't remember the end of it."

Jake felt a pain in his legs and looked down to see his hands clutching his knees, the fingers digging deep. "I never told you the rest. If you want to know, I'll tell you now."

Mamie shook her head and put her hands up as if holding something off. "That's not for me to say. You had some reason to tell me what you did. If you want to finish it, I'm listening."

He'd go all in, and then she could despise him as much as he despised himself. "You may remember my telling how Pa caught me red-handed. He looked me up and down and thundered, 'What sin and devilry is this?' Ethan and Grandpa came running in, Ethan in front. I was standing there holding that sock of money and staring at it, stupid as if I hadn't been the one to grab it in the first place. Ethan looked at me, and I'd never seen such a look on anyone's face, nor imagined it." He stopped to breathe, his hands shaking on his knees. "When Esau found out how Jacob had cheated him out of his father's blessing, he may have looked at Jacob like that. Shocked to his core, and like he'd been stabbed through the heart. And then it changed to anger, the kind of rage I'd been starting to feel those last months, thinking about my future and how it no longer seemed like I could stand to live it. I'd been ashamed to feel that way, and I could see Ethan struggling with it, like he was changing into some horrible creature and feeling sick to see it happen.

"And then he sprang at me, his eyes wild, like he didn't know what was happening or what he was doing. And I was so scared, it gave me the strength to get the better of him. And then he was on the ground, and I was still holding that damned sock."

Mamie had got up and was standing behind him, her hands on his shoulders. He wanted to shrug them off, but he just kept going.

"I couldn't stand to look at him, nor at Pa or Grandpa. I just stared at my hand and held the sock out toward him. He got to his feet, slow like he was hurt, and grabbed it." Jake hadn't let himself, made himself, remember that moment so clear in all the years since. He thought he might vomit up the memory before he could tell it, but he managed to swallow down the bile. "And then he threw it back at me, right in my face. And he said, 'You can have it, and go, and I'll know I've got no brother any more, for the rest of my life. Or you can put it down, and do your penance, and I'll pray for you.'

"I looked back at my grandpa, and he was crying. I'd never seen the like. And then at Pa, and it was just like in church, when he preached about hell and the devils waiting there. But he said, 'Our Lord tells us to forgive the repentant sinner, even unto seven times. If you'll take the whipping you have coming, and come to church and confess your sin, and show by how you live that you've been truly cleansed, you can stay in this house, and I'll still call you my son."

Mamie laid her head on his and said softly, close to his ear, "You didn't do as he said, to stay."

Jake let out the harshest sound anyone could ever call a laugh. "Oh, I took my beating, all right, but not from Pa. From the gamblers, because I went to them and told them I didn't have their money. I did have it, hidden in a bush at the edge of town, still in that devil-cursed sock. More than a hundred dollars. But I'd nothing else to live on once I left town, until I found a way to make more. And I knew my life in that town, that family, was over.

"Ethan never said another word to me before I left, nor my grandpa. My mother cried and cried, and asked me to repent. I kissed her before I left. With my father hollering behind me that I was as cursed as Cain, and would carry Cain's mark in this world and the next."

He hadn't cried about it since that day, leaving the house to hide the money and find the gamblers. But he cried now, and Mamie held his head to her breast until he finished.

He was too wrung out to talk more after that, and Mamie sent him off to lie down. He even slept, and if he had nightmares, they faded away too quick for him to remember them when he finally awoke. It was dark out, and the house sounded quiet. When his eyes adjusted to the dark, he saw someone had left a tray of supper on the table near his bed, and a glass half full of whiskey.

He wasn't so sure the hollow place inside him had anything to do with hunger, nor whether food could fill it. But he ate the supper, tossed down the whiskey, used the chamber pot, and went back to sleep.

Jake woke up bemused, morning sun slanting in at an angle that said he'd slept later than common. Why was he here? Hadn't he taken a room at the hotel? No, he'd planned to, but hadn't done it yet. What was he doing back in this small back room at Mamie's, normally used for storage and hastily made up for him weeks earlier? And why had he been drinking whiskey in bed?

Then he remembered, and fell back on the bed, covering his face with his hands.

But memory wouldn't disappear for the wishing, nor sleep come when called. He would have to face the day, and Mamie with it. He'd gone to sleep in his clothes, so he had little to do before going downstairs. He put his hand to the door and stopped in his tracks. He knew the voice drifting up from downstairs: the lawyer with the snakeskin boots. The one who was trying to find Jake's secrets, somehow knowing he had them.

Had the man come as a customer, this early in the day? Jake pressed his ear to the door and leaned hard against it, lest the man burst in on him. He listened for booted feet climbing the wide wooden stairs. Instead, he heard what sounded like cheery parting words, and the tinkle of the bell hanging on the front door. He waited another five minutes in case of ambush before he made his way downstairs, eyes darting this way and that as he went.

Summer Dawn came to meet him, a spark of possibly malicious interest in her eyes. "Mamie says come see her in her office. That man made her angry. You go now, you find out why."

The office door was shut. Jake knocked and then realized he had better identify himself, calling, "It's me. Summer Dawn sent me up."

Mamie did indeed sound aggravated. "Come in, and close the door behind you. Oh, and sit down, if you like."

He did like. He hadn't had breakfast, and was feeling shaky for what was probably more reasons than that. As he sat down, he said, "I thought I heard that lawyer downstairs a minute ago. What's he up to? If it were just a friendly visit, or a paying one, I don't guess your eyes'd be about to fly out of your head and bite someone."

At least that got a laugh out of her, if a short one, before she went back to glaring and tapping her long painted nails on the desk. "I don't suppose he mentioned that he and I have been on what you might call personal terms. Hell, I may as well speak plain about it — he's been my lover, now and then, when he's in town. It suited me . . . and I've no doubt getting what others couldn't, and for free, suited him.

If I thought he might value me as something like a friend, I'm rapidly changing my mind about that."

Meanwhile, Jake was sitting there telling himself he had no damn call to be jealous. And yet he couldn't stop himself from saying, "So that's your type? Overdressed and smooth as oil, with a tongue as snaky as his boots?"

He thought Mamie would fire back at him, but instead she got a remembering look. "I once told a friend I liked my men mean. It made me feel tough to say that, and to think it. And maybe there was a mite of truth to it, but the thrill is wearing off pretty damn quick."

That would give him plenty to think on, some time or other, but right now — "You haven't told me what he came for."

Mamie reached down into a desk drawer. Jake knew what she would pull out before she laid the newspaper down with a slap and then shoved it across the desk toward him. "I don't rightly know what he's after, but he showed me this."

He got up and bent over it. It was, of course, the same Omaha paper. And this time, the ad read:

Seeking any word of my brother Jacob F. Please send word to Ethan at the preacher's in Deliverance. Reward.

That raised new questions, which he could maybe deal with once he overcame the panic that had him wanting to leap for the door and run for the stable. The only way he could keep still was to freeze in place like a rabbit with a hawk hunting it. Mamie looked up at him and went on as if she didn't notice. "I don't suppose there's any other brothers named Jacob and Ethan in Deliverance. Though such could've been born or otherwise shown up since we both left."

Jake made himself relax enough to breathe and talk.

"Do you really think the town grew enough since then for that to be likely? And I expect no self-respecting mama in Deliverance would name her son Jacob, after the taint I left on it."

Mamie pulled the paper back and rested her hands on it. "Assuming this is about you and your brother, then, why do you think he's trying to find you?"

Did she really think Ethan was placing the ads? She couldn't be naive after years in her business, but she might be making a point of not planting ideas in his head. "I don't know that he is. A private detective could use an ad like that to try to smoke me out. He might be working for Ethan, or for my father, or for some lawman."

No, she must not have been thinking along those lines, from the way her mouth fell open and her eyes widened. But she shook her head a little and said, "Didn't you tell me Ethan said you could keep the money?"

"After I stole it!" And Pa hadn't said anything of the kind. If Pa had been around when Cain slew Abel, and there'd been a lawman around, Pa would have set the lawman on Cain the moment the last shovelful of earth hit Abel's grave.

But Mamie had more objections. "And I can't hardly believe the law would be chasing you, after all this time. It's been more than twenty years! Don't they have enough robbing and thieving and killing going on to keep them busy? Why assume this means trouble?"

All that sounded like sense, Jake supposed, or would to someone else. Someone good at heart, like Mamie, who most likely had never really done another soul any harm, or not harm that'd last. You had to know you had something rotten, running down to the core, before you could understand where the road had to go, what had to be waiting. But what he said was, "Your lawyer lover sure acted like he smelled trouble."

Mamie let out a low growl, surprisingly — or not so surprisingly — sensual. "Ex-lover. I told him years ago that he could play his games with other people, but if he played games with me I'd show him the door. Now I've done it." She tossed her head. "As for how he acted, that's probably just Quinn doing what he does best - playing games. To him, everyone's in some contest with everyone else, and he aims to win as many as he can. And he could probably tell something about that ad bothered you." He opened his mouth to protest, but before he could, she added, "And don't tell me you didn't turn a hair. Quinn makes his living, not to mention has his fun, reading signs others can't."

He couldn't prove she was wrong. He rolled his head, trying to loosen up the muscles in his neck and back, while she watched him with more sympathy than he had coming. He'd talked about all this as much as he could stand, and what she'd said earlier came back to mind. "You kicked him out?"

She let out a little laugh that almost sounded natural. "I'm not like my customers, panting for a poke to where I can't think straight or use my head. I can go without well enough if need be."

He should be thinking about where to run and how soon. He had no business letting anything distract him, or saying, instead, as he found himself saying now, "You shouldn't have to. There's better men who'd be honored to be invited to your bed." He bit his tongue to stop it flapping, but it got loose and went on. "And one man no one should call better, near at hand."

Now it was Mamie sitting stock still. But as he looked at her sitting there, her curves somehow seemed to get curvier, softer, even more enticing. And her voice, when she spoke, came from deeper in her throat. "To answer your question, I doubt Quinn's sent any word, not yet. If he means to, he'd want to play with you for a while first. And with me, now that he'll have guessed I'm interested in what becomes of you."

Just when he figured she was going to ignore what he'd blurted out, she added, "But just in case he's following an actual trail, not that it's likely, it'd be best not to give him any cause to move faster. He's as like to be jealous as any man, and maybe more, given how he relishes having the power to make people dance to his tune."

He could almost see her drifting away from him out of reach like a ship in the fog. "So whoever your next lover may be, you're thinking it shouldn't be me. Not that you would've —"

She held up her hand, palm out, her face still sober. "So we'd best take care he doesn't know you're here, or see you going." And now she smiled — no, grinned. "When I let you go."

And as he sat there staring like a damn fool, she laughed and came to him and sat on his lap. "Are you needing lessons on what to do next?"

Jake grabbed her around the waist and hung on for dear life. "I reckon I can make it up as I go along. But you tell me when you figure I need teaching, and I'll gladly learn."

* * * * *

Now she could admit to herself — and why had she bothered to ignore it? For fear of what Quinn might think or say? — that she'd been wanting Jake's big arms around her, and his broad strong body against hers and pressing her down, since he turned up all of a sudden like some magical story, her past made over and made better.

But she had to be careful, as much as it irked her to sneak around in her own place. She allowed herself one quick kiss — and quick as it was, it sure made her tingle in all the right places — and then made herself get up and slide out the office door, closing it right behind her. She went downstairs and found the most reliable girl who wasn't with a customer — Lucette, as it happened — and told her she was going to lie back down and shouldn't be disturbed unless the house was afire. She hated to worry the girls, but she could only hope the flush on her face looked like true fever instead of coming from the heat rising up from her loins.

Then it was back up the stairs to her office, slipping in, and listening for quiet in the hall before she tugged Jake at a run to her own bedroom and pushed him in ahead of her. At least she had a lock on her door, hardly ever used.

As soon as she'd locked the door and shimmied out of her clothes, before she'd even had the chance to look over at Jake, he'd picked her up and fairly dived for the bed with her in his arms. What was it Clara had said — "masterful"? Looked like Clara was right. If Mamie hadn't liked men strong enough to take charge, she'd never have let that two-faced lawyer under her skirts. And this time she knew it was a decent man showing his strength, even if he didn't know it himself with all that had happened. And he'd done her the favor of shucking his own clothes while she was getting out of hers.

She put her arms up to his hands, inviting him to grab her wrists. And when he understood and did just that, she laughed again and put her arms over her head, pulling his hands along with them.

* * * * *

It had been months since he'd been with a woman, and before Summer Dawn and Nancy, it might've been years. Summer Dawn had first laid in the bed like a statue, and then fought like a wildcat, only her teasing eyes letting him know she was testing him rather than fending him off. Neither extreme was what he'd choose if he had the choosing. And Nancy had flattered him nonstop, smiling the same smile the whole time like her face had forgotten how to do any different. And she'd been as soft as a featherbed.

Mamie never stopped moving, and she moved with him, or sometimes showed him where she wanted him to move. And every inch of her felt like he'd imagined when he was fighting not to think of her at night, all those years ago, except warmer and better and real. He hadn't known the little sounds she'd make, moans and growls and something like purring, and then, as they moved faster and harder, little cries that got louder until she tugged an arm loose and laid it over her mouth so the sound wouldn't carry.

It was the only thing that wasn't perfect, that she should have to hide her pleasure. He swore right then that if he could find a way, there would come the day when he could give her all the joy she could hold, and her free to shout it out no matter who heard.

And then he reached his own climax, and he was past thinking.

* * * * *

She'd been fifteen years old, and only twenty miles from Deliverance, when she'd first lain with a man. And it was painful and embarrassing and scary. But it was maybe the next time, or at most two times later, that she first realized and wondered at the strange way she felt after. She'd have called it maternal if that didn't feel all wrong to say, and if her mother had ever acted like she wanted to look after her and protect her. In all these years, she'd never learned the right word. And it wasn't every time, but often enough that she kind of thought other women must feel the same, some of them, some of the time. She'd even felt that way with Quinn, of all people.

She had that feeling strong, lying there with Jake. And it didn't feel wrong nor strange — even following the best joining she'd maybe ever had — but right, as she stroked his hair and wiped the sweat off his brow and cradled him in her arms.

She hadn't a clue what he was thinking, except that he wasn't like some men who acted afterward like Mamie and what they'd done together had suddenly got distasteful, turning away without another look at her, or pulling back from her like he'd been snakebit and had to run get help for it. Jake stayed right there next to her, relaxed against her with his arm across her shoulders, and now and then kissing her cheek as soft as a whisper. And when she made herself move to the edge of the bed, he made a mewing sound like the world's biggest kitten and reached for her hand as if to pull her back again. She caught his hand instead, kissed it, and slid out of bed, pulling her clothes on and sitting at the dressing table to fix her hair. She tossed Jake's clothes onto the bed, or rather on top of him, the whole pile landing on his belly. He laughed, picked up his shirt, and made as if to throw it back at her before he settled down to the business of dressing.

When they were both fully dressed and there was nothing left to do but leave the room, they reached for each other at the same instant and pulled each other close for one last long kiss. She could have pulled him back down, right then, and told him to take her, clothes and all. But she pulled away instead, unlocked the door, listened, and led him toward the stairs. They had to duck into an empty room once to avoid Sophie and a customer, and then Bessie looking where Sophie had gone. But she got Jake downstairs and into the kitchen without anyone catching them. Cook was there, but Mamie hustled over to her and swore her to secrecy. It was a good thing Cook had never cared for Quinn — all Mamie had to do was hint what they were hiding and from whom, and Cook was all smiles and handing Jake a fresh-baked biscuit for the road.

And then he was gone out the back, and Mamie left with the glow in her body almost enough to make her forget the worry in her mind. Not quite enough. Because Quinn might have heard something, after all. What did she know about how long the law kept looking for someone? Or what a marshal or sheriff would do to oblige a preacher, one with a whole town under his sway and nothing but hellfire and vengeance on his mind?

Chapter 15

THE BISCUIT didn't go far toward filling Jake up, but his first task was to get to the hotel, finally take a room, and find out if anyone had been seeking him there. The manager was at the front desk, and could reassure him that no one had asked after him or left him any message. Jake tipped him more than he could afford to answer any questions with simply the information that he had been a guest for days and remained such. Then he dropped his pack in his room, had a leisurely meal, and ambled out again, breathing easier and looking forward to seeing how Wrangler was getting on.

His mood lasted just long enough for him to set foot in the stable and see Quinn leaning against Wrangler's stall, Wrangler sniffing at him and no doubt hoping for a carrot. Which wasn't damn likely to be offered, with no one paying the man for it and no advantage to be gained.

The lawyer pulled the newspaper out of the same pocket as last time and said, with that wide, thin-lipped smile, "Mr. Jacob Flint."

Jake tried for something like a condescending tone. "Very good, Mr. Quinn. That's my name."

"It seems my prediction was correct, Mr. Flint. This Ethan is still seeking his brother." He waved the paper at Jake like a hawker selling it.

Jake cocked an eyebrow, took the paper, ran his eyes over it, and handed it back, trying to look bored. "I don't see anything special, except that plenty of people think it's worthwhile to spend their money on personals ads."

He expected something like a cross-examination, but Quinn apparently preferred to draw out the process of bedeviling him. The lawyer tossed the paper in a muck pile and inspected his fingernails, then pulled out a toothpick and started cleaning them. Without looking up, he said, "The mayor appears to have given up on recruiting you for that marshal job. Will you be moving on again?"

Jake looked at Quinn lounging so close to Wrangler and wished he had a rake in hand to shove the man away with. Which reminded him of the idea he'd had on the road. "I'm planning on checking out some local possibilities."

Quinn finally straightened up, tossing his toothpick in the straw where some horse was likely as not to step on it. "How interesting. Then perhaps we'll see each other again soon." He sauntered out, whistling. He whistled poorly, but to look at his confident air as he went out, you'd think he was good at it.

Jake stooped to pick up the toothpick and tucked it in his pocket to throw someplace safer. Then he made his hellos to Wrangler and went in search of the hostler.

Half an hour later, Jake had a job. Not much pay in it until he'd proved his worth, but he could sleep in the warmest part of the stable, which'd do until winter came, and the hostler would give him something in the way of grub. Though he might have to move on before it got close to wintertime. At least he'd be better off, somewhat, while he figured out what he was going to do about the advertisement and about whatever mischief the lawyer might have in mind.

And it would keep him near Mamie while he did his figuring.

* * * * *

Mamie still got tired easy, or maybe she was more likely to notice when she did. So she was glad to sit in the small parlor with her feet up during their slow time of day and enjoy the treasure Bessie had brought her — another Freida letter.

Darling Mamie —

Tell the buckeye and cottonwood trees to put on their brightest dresses, we're coming to town! It's too bad we're heading north when it's not so terribly hot here any more, but Jedidiah tells me we'll head south again by winter. I should enjoy a season around here for a change, but I'll be thinking of all my friends in Cowbird Creek shivering in the cold and wishing you were with me sitting on a porch with no boots on.

I don't know for sure if I get every letter people send me, but if I didn't miss any from you, that interesting man you mentioned, because I know you wouldn't have bothered mentioning him if he wasn't interesting, didn't stay and become marshal, too bad, but it's a dreary job, isn't it? Did anyone else agree to take it? Here I am asking questions when I'll be seeing you soon enough to ask them face to face! But Jedidiah tells me we'll be able to get mail in Chattanooga on our way north, I'll be sure and check just in case, such fun to have things to look forward to, isn't it? — Fondly, Freida Kennedy

Mamie read the last bit again, and then one more time. Freida could have no idea how much it spoke to her. And yet that was foolishness, because Jake might leave town any day, running from the law — or more likely, it seemed to her, from phantoms in his head. And then her bed would be empty until who knew when, now she'd sent Quinn on his way, and her conversation would be back to coaxing customers and haggling with tradesmen and managing her girls' complaints and worries. Because they had their worries, about whether they'd caught something and whether their looks were going and what they'd do then.

She tucked the letter in her bodice and let go of all such thoughts as best she could until the clatter of booted feet pulled her back to business.

Late that night, a glass of sherry on her desk and the lamplight warming its depths, she started on her reply to Freida. She'd have been discreet as to what she put in writing in any event, but knowing the letter might miss Freida on the road, she'd best be more so.

Dearest Freida —

I'm so glad we'll be seeing you and your sweet husband! Of course it won't satisfy my appetite for your company, but that's far better than letters only, glad as I always am to get them. If you can tell me when you're about to appear, I'll have Cook bake apple and pumpkin pies to help us celebrate the autumn.

Now the tricky part.

The marshal job remains unfilled, leaving us to the mercies of the sheriff, when he bothers with us, and any locals who might be on the scene should trouble blow through. But one of those locals, though in a temporary sense, is the same man I mentioned in my last. He did leave not long after I wrote about him, but he's back in town, though for who knows how long. I can tell you more about him when we meet, if he isn't here for me to actually introduce him.

Mamie read over that last paragraph and slowly lowered the pen back into the ink pot. There'd be no harm in some stranger reading what little she'd said about Jake. But what if Quinn was doing more than talking and teasing? What if he was truly investigating Jake's affairs, and that advertisement, and what connection there might be? The way he'd been acting, she didn't put it past him to get hold of a letter she left for the mail. If she sent it with one of the girls, as she normally did, it might not even make it to the store. Just the suggestion that Mamie had more to tell could encourage him to harass her further. And would also inflame his jealousy, if she'd guessed right that he was feeling it.

She blew on the letter to dry the ink, let it sit for a minute or so, and then slid it into her desk drawer. The one with a lock and key. If she could think of a safe way to send it, she would. If not, she'd write another one, with a less tantalizing ending.

* * * * *

In negotiating the terms of his employment, Jake had forgotten one detail. He might enjoy the smell of horses, but not everyone shared that pleasure, and he couldn't pretend he came away from a day in the stable with no worse odors clinging to him. He would have to pay for and spend time on a bath before he set foot in Madam Mamie's again, whether or not he made it any farther than the parlor.

Assuming he went there at all. Assuming he didn't saddle Wrangler and ride away, maybe to Mexico this time, well out of reach of whatever judgment was in store if he stayed easy to find.

But he hated to run if he didn't have to. Not now that he might, just might, have something to look forward to from one day to the next, at least until the novelty wore off and Mamie sent him packing. If he could only find out who had placed the ad and why, to really know instead of imagining . . . .

And that gave him an idea. But it meant leaving town again for a spell.

Jake was passing by Mamie's on his way to the barber shop, moving a mite slower after a long day of handling horses and pitching straw, when Lucette came out on the front step. She looked wearier than he felt, stretching her arms this way and that with her eyes closed and breathing deep of the crisp evening air. She opened her eyes slowly at first, then quicker and wider as she caught sight of him. "Welcome, Monsieur Jake! At least, I hope you are coming to pay us a visit."

Jake tipped his hat to her. "As soon as I can, you can be sure. But I'd best hire a bath first."

Lucette fluttered her eyelashes at him. "That will not be necessary, m'sieur. We have the facilities to provide for one, all modern and convenient —" At least, that was probably what she said, though it sounded more French. "Madam obtained the plumbing not long after the mayor did, and she already had the pretty enameled tub. Be assured, you will have ladies eager to help you."

How the heck had Mamie afforded that? Not his business, really. Jake grinned at Lucette. "That's a lovely picture you paint me, and I'll take that bath, with my thanks, if Mamie says it's all right. But I can scrub myself." He doubted Mamie would be standing in line with a scrub brush, and he'd no hankering to make do with her girls when he could manage without help, and daydream of Mamie the while.

The tub was as pretty as Lucette had promised, with little blue flowers painted around the rim and polished copper fixtures that must have cost plenty. The water was clear as any mountain stream, and shut off gradually when he turned the handle instead of with a sudden lurch. Mamie might not have got this kind of plumbing before the mayor, but she'd made up for it in quality. He could only imagine what that meant to her, after the trouble it must have cost her back in Deliverance even to wash in cold water.

Even the soap was fine, milled and shaped in an oval with embossed scroll work on both sides. He scrubbed himself clean, grabbed the generous towel sitting on a nearby stool, and dried off, only to see his clothes, creased and stiff with dirt, lying by the bath where he'd dropped them. No doubt they carried enough odor on them to undo half the good the bath had done. He stood there feeling stupid for a minute or so before he shook his head, grabbed the pile, and dumped it in the bathwater. Good thing he hadn't got around to pulling the plug. He got everything wet through, then pulled the garments out one at a time, wringing them out and then blotting them in the towel. They wouldn't be altogether dry, but with luck, he'd be taking them off again without having to sit on anything delicate first.

He was almost through when someone knocked. Mamie's voice came through the door, a trace of mockery in her tone. "It's a nice deep tub, I will allow, but did you get careless and drown?"

Jake chuckled. "It was a near thing, but I managed to save myself. I'll be out directly."

When he emerged, Mamie raised an eyebrow at his damp clothes, then took a sniff and smiled. "This is one of your more gentlemanly days, I see."

Jake bowed. "Your elegant bathtub inspired me. Consider me thoroughly impressed."

Mamie fairly glowed. "Glad to hear it. I got the tub first, but with needing two or more girls to fill it quick enough that the water stayed warm, and all their running back and forth, it was too expensive for many folks to pay for the girls' time, even after I'd got hot water in the kitchen. Once I'd saved up enough for more plumbing, I had to decide whether to go with baths or put in one of those mechanical water closets. Picked the bath, as you see — men don't give a hoot about where they piss, but they'll pay for extra time with a girl oohing and aahing about how well they strip down, not to mention the swank of the thing."

She reached out a long finger and touched his shirt. "And now let's get those clothes off you long enough for them to dry. Even if you do work up a sweat all over again."

When they came back downstairs, his trousers were dry enough for him to take a seat in the kitchen. She offered him tea, which reminded him how much they didn't know about each other — he considered the stuff tasteless at best. When he admitted the fact, she gave him some of the first pressing of cider she had ready and sipped her own tea as he explained the scheme he'd come up with on his way over. She listened, tapping her chin, until he got to the end and then asked, "How far did you figure on riding?"

"I haven't decided. I've just started at the livery stable and would like to have my job waiting when I get back, which may not be likely in the first place but gets less likely the longer I'm gone. On the other hand, if I'm just a town or two over, it'll be too easy to trace me from the postmark, if I send a letter, or from the telegram. I may have to chance it — I don't have enough coin to get me far." At least not without going altogether hungry for long enough that he might run out of strength for handling any trouble.

And speaking of trouble, Mamie took a deep breath as if preparing for some. "I, on the other hand, have a few more coins to spare. I'd be happy to help you find out what's going on." As he opened his mouth to protest, and pretty loudly, she added, "Not to mention keeping you from leaving for as long as you might, should you have to hide your trail better."

That took the wind out of his sails, or mostly. "I'll owe it to you. Sooner or later I'll be less thoroughly broke."

Mamie gave a brisk nod, as if to say she'd won the point, as she surely had. "All right, then. Have you picked a direction?"

He gulped down the last of the cider. "I'm trying to figure out what's the least likely way to head, according to how that lawyer thinks. Going south would look like running for it." As it would be, if it came to that. "That leaves some kind of north. I might just start riding and flip a coin now and again, to be harder to predict." And then, like rubbing a sore place, he added, "One of the coins you're lending me."

Mamie reached out and took hold of his hand. "You just make sure and bring it right back here, when you're done. I haven't hardly had my fill of your . . . *company*."

From that, it wasn't a long time or a far leap to them going back upstairs to Mamie's room, as sneaky as before and, from what he could tell, without being spotted. And as he got closer to finding out what might be awaiting him, he found it hard to care as much whether someone saw them or not.

There was part of his idea Jake hadn't told Mamie, maybe out of superstition that telling would make it less likely to work. It meant trusting Rich. But if he couldn't trust Rich, then the hell with it.

Of course, he had no way of knowing if Rich yet lived,

let alone lived where Jake had been writing to him. If nothing appeared to come of it, he'd have to ride out again, and if he were still trying to cut down on the risk, he'd have to go farther. Which would leave both Yates and Mamie unhappy with him. And either one could make it so he'd have to leave town after all.

For now, he had to get this letter written before he lost so much of the day that he'd have to wait until tomorrow. He was more than ready to be gone and back again.

Dear Rich,

This letter is going to be different from any I've sent you. I need

A favor?

Help?

to ask you to do something for me, if you can. I hate to ask, what with all I already owe you for the help you gave me more times than I've counted. If you can't do what I ask for any reason, don't let it trouble you.

Though Jake would stake his life — in fact, might be staking close enough to it — that Rich would find a way to help him, if he were still above ground and able.

I need you to send a telegram for me to Ethan Flint in Deliverance, Indiana. I've kept the text as short as I can, and I'm sending a money order that should cover the cost. It should say,

He'd thought he'd known what it should say, until it came time to write down the words. Mamie had offered him as much paper as he needed, and he'd taken one extra sheet, just in case he spoiled the first. He pulled it out and held the pen over it, a drop of ink falling on it as he pondered, and finally wrote,

May have information Ethan brother. Why looking? How much reward?

He read it over and scratched out the first question.

Too personal a question might make whoever had placed the ad uneasy.

On the other hand, wasn't that what he wanted — needed — to know? What was the point of leaving Yates in the lurch, losing some of the time he could have with Mamie, putting himself and Wrangler through days of hard riding and hiding his trail, if he didn't learn something about who was after him and why?

May have information Ethan brother. Why looking?

Asking about the reward made him sound like someone hoping to collect it. Well, why not? Whoever kept paying for those ads wouldn't have offered a reward if they didn't want answers from people eager to claim it.

May have information Ethan brother. Why looking? What reward?

But . . . if it really was Ethan or Pa, and not some lawman, would they be willing to explain a family disgrace to a stranger just out to make money off that disgrace? He scratched out the second question.

He had thought to say next, *Use ad to respond.* But no one in his family would answer the first question in an ad any stranger could read. If he wanted the best chance of getting that answer, he would have to involve Rich more than he'd planned. He copied the telegram text into the letter and went on.

You could sign your own name or some made-up one, whatever you'd rather, as long as you send the telegram from some place you can get to easily. If you hear anything back from it, you can write, or send another telegram, to me at Cowbird Creek in Nebraska.

It maybe won't surprise you if I ask you not to mention Deliverance or Cowbird Creek to anyone, nor say anything about my having a connection to Indiana or Nebraska.

Was there anything else he needed to say? Anything to change? But he could chase himself in circles all day, at this rate. Time to be done with it.

Hope all is well with you

That sounded cold, what anyone would say to a bare acquaintance. This might be his last letter to Rich.

, now and always. — Jake

He folded it up, wrote a made-up return address on the envelope, tucked it in his waistcoat pocket, and went to tell Mamie goodbye.

* * * * *

The day after Jake left town, Quinn came by and smoothly bullied his way into the house and her office, as if to heighten the contrast between her former lover and the better man she had taken since. It was time she told Horn not to let the man get past the front door. If he did any guessing as to why, given how little Quinn resembled the typical roughneck, that was Horn's affair. Maybe he'd figure Quinn liked abusing the girls — which she had no special reason to think was true, but it was no time to worry about Quinn's reputation.

She refused to offer Quinn refreshment, or to invite him to sit down — not that that stopped him. "You're looking as lovely as ever, my dear." Did he look a little relieved at her obvious good health? And then . . . she could see the idea strike him, see his eyes narrow and his jaw tighten, just barely enough for her to see. "Might I ask whether anything in particular is responsible? Or anyone?"

Mamie ignored the question, doing her best to drill a hole in him with her eyes. "How fortunate that you've appeared. I have a legal question, apparently urgent. What is the proper mechanism to prevent an unwanted caller from intruding on a residence or a place of business?"

He chuckled. "Before I could undertake to answer such a question, I would need to know the identity of the troublesome individual. In case there should be some conflict of interest, you understand."

Enough of playing his games. "Since I've told you not to expect what used to bring you, why are you here?"

Quinn took out a cigar, cut it, and lit it. When he'd been her lover, he had refrained from filling the place with smoke, but of course he wanted to make plain that she was no longer entitled to such a courtesy. Between puffs, he said, "I'm leaving town for now, and as I was getting my faithful steed ready for the journey, I noticed the absence of the livery stable's newest employee. In fact, the hostler was rather disgruntled that the man had walked out on him so soon after being hired. I wondered what you might know about this abrupt departure."

Mamie coughed and fanned the air in front of her, more energetically than necessary. Then she thought better of it and folded her hands in her lap, sitting back and relaxing as if the first breath of spring was wafting in the window. "I have no knowledge of the gentleman's destination, not that I would be inclined to share it if I did."

She had the advantage, this time, of telling the simple and complete truth. She could see him absorb the fact, and — though he quickly concealed it — his dismay that she hadn't given him some sort of evasion, as a wedge with which to work on her. But of course he stayed long enough to finish his blasted cigar. When he finally left, Mamie told Trudi to send Horn up, and said to him with no introduction, "You saw the man who just left, assuming you were on duty."

His "yes, ma'am" was convincing enough. And she hadn't yet known him to lie.

"If he shows up again, I want you to toss him back out." Should she tell him to make sure the bastard bounced? No, that would be inviting trouble. Quinn was chummy with the mayor, and for all she knew, the sheriff as well. "Make it polite, but keep him out. Just keep turning him around until he gets bored and leaves."

If he ever got bored, when he was following a trail. Which made her think of Jake, and whether he could keep Quinn from tracking him. Maybe she should have kept Quinn busy for a while, to make the trail colder.

But no. Jake wouldn't want that any more than she did. A day's head start would have to be enough.

Chapter 16

JAKE had no idea whether Quinn could track someone on horseback. But if not, the fellow could pay for someone to do it. Jake could only hope whoever might be following him wasn't as good at tracking as he was at hiding Wrangler's tracks.

The first day was the simplest. It hadn't rained for maybe a week, so it was easy to avoid mud and soft dirt. He still had to keep from breaking branches, or dismount and pick them up when he did, but he had a good enough eye for terrain that it didn't happen often. For good measure, he tied bunches of branches together and tied them to Wrangler's back legs, which took him plenty of coaxing and carrot-bribing, but did a nice job of hiding his trail. If he'd seen any carts or coaches, he'd have had to decide whether to follow close behind them, so their horses' hoofprints could disguise Wrangler's, but that close meant close enough for someone to see him and describe him later.

It rained the evening of the second day, and through half of the third. He rode on boulders when he could, the rain washing away any dust or dirt he left. But when the boulders ran out, he made more and sturdier bundles of branches, and stopped to change them more often, though he grudged the delay. Where branches were scarce, he wrapped Wrangler's hooves in burlap instead. They'd still leave marks, but not marks anyone could be sure came from a horseshoe.

Midafternoon on the third day, and after maybe five flips of the coin, he found himself at a lively river town called Plattsmouth. All the changes in direction meant he probably hadn't traveled as far as he would like, but with the return trip ahead of him, he had no stomach for going farther. He marched himself past the saloons and straight to the post office.

Standing outside the door, he took out the letter, tempted to read it over again, and went inside, handing it over before he could change his mind. Then he bought a money order for enough, by his figuring, to cover the cost of the telegram.

He made himself take just as many precautions on the return trip and approach Cowbird Creek in roundabout fashion, much as he wanted to get back. To see if he could talk his way back into the stable job, and to see Mamie again while he could, before he maybe had to ride for Mexico, or was taken up before he got the chance.

Jake was leading Wrangler to the livery stable, blinking morning sun out of his eyes, when a young man in straw-covered clothes came hurtling out and almost collided with them. Wrangler shied and came near kicking the fellow, and settling the gelding down kept Jake too busy to see where the man went. Once Wrangler was biddable again, Jake led him in and looked around for the hostler — who found him instead, limping up to him with bloody trousers and a ferocious scowl. "That young jackass lost control of a hell-bitch of a mare some city feller left. You can have your job back if you start right now so's I can go see Doc."

Jake studied the man's unsteady posture. "I'll take that offer and thank you for it, but if you like I'll go fetch Doc myself, if he's to be found, and you can stay off that leg."

Jake started with Doc's office, which looked closed up tight. He'd just got back on Wrangler, to ride as quick as a tired horse could carry him out to the Gibbs place, when Joshua came hustling up the street, his face shifting into alert inquiry on spotting Jake. "Have things taken a turn for the worse at Mamie's?"

Jake slid back down, patted Wrangler's neck, and said, "Not as I know of, but I haven't been there yet since I got back to town. It's Yates who needs doctoring — a matter of a new stable lad, a fractious mare, and both men bested by her."

Joshua looked Jake up and down. "I'll head right over, if I'm correct that there's nothing amiss with you that a wash and a good night's sleep wouldn't cure."

Jake grimaced. "It'll be a while before I take that cure. I'll head back there with you, as I'm in charge for the day." And he'd be spending that day wishing he could head straight to Mamie's.

Joshua was striding toward the stable, with Jake and Wrangler stumbling after, when a swishing skirt appeared in the corner of Jake's eye. He stopped and turned, almost toppling onto Wrangler, to see Nancy stepping lightly along. She stopped and threw up her hands. "Goodness me! You're back, and that's a mercy — but you sure look tired. Did you get sick and that's why you're following Doc?"

Jake managed to reach all the way up to his hat to tip it. "No, Miss Nancy, I'm well enough. Just trail-weary, and going back to my job at the stable, where Doc'll be treating my boss after a little matter of an unruly mare." A pretty girl had the power to bring him back to life some, seemingly, as he was able to smile at her and add, "Maybe we should fetch Mamie over, as she's so practiced at keeping fillies in line."

Too late, he wondered if she'd take that as rude, but her cheery laugh and the twinkle in her eyes suggested otherwise — or just proved her to be a good actress, which on reflection seemed likely. "I'll tell Madam Mamie you've made it to Cowbird Creek again. We'll see you later, won't we?"

Joshua had made it halfway to the stable by now, and Jake had better catch up. "I've got to go, but I'll come by at least long enough to say howdy. And maybe take a bath, if I can do it quick enough."

Nancy cocked her head at him. "It'd be quicker, I reckon, if I helped you out."

Jake chuckled. "I'm not so sure. At any rate, I'll manage on my own."

* * * * *

Mamie would have let Jake take his bath in privacy, rather than risk tongues wagging — but Nancy had told her that Jake wouldn't be able to stay long. So once she could hear he'd gotten settled in the water, she marched right in and snatched his clothes away — despite his startled protests — to be laundered properly this time, and then settled herself on the stool in the corner. "We have a selection of spare clothes for men, in case of need. You'll have your own clothes, fit for wearing, by tomorrow evening."

Jake slid lower. "When I win an argument with you, it'll be the first, I'm thinking. So thank you. But I'll need those clothes pretty quick, with Yates close to laid up and counting on me."

Mamie took him at his word, hustling out the door and flagging the first idle girl to put the clothes in the big laundry hamper, then going herself to the extra clothes chest and quickly sorting through the options. Better too big than too small, and nothing fine enough that she'd care what the dirt of the stable did to it. By the time she got back with a couple of possible outfits, Jake was already up and drying himself off. She prided herself on having good-sized towels, but they did cover up rather too much of him.

She put the clothes on the stool and held up one garment at a time. "You've a choice, though not much to choose from. What you don't pick, I'll keep for your use another time."

At least he had to put aside the towel to get dressed. And if looking him over left her wanting more, she'd take wanting, and likely having later, over neither.

Plus she finally got to see Jake's tattoos all the way around. The two of them had always stripped and fallen into bed too quick for a full inspection. As she circled him, she said, "An anchor, I'd expected. But I didn't know sailors got tattoos of horses."

"They don't, as a rule. I got that one later, in a riverside place where I went when I was missing sailor company. It's Wrangler, not that it's good enough for you to tell."

It was sad, if she let herself think about it, that he carried an image of his horse where another man might have worn his sweetheart's. At least he hadn't had them do some made-up woman falling out of her clothes or not wearing any. "And the third, is that any particular ship?"

Jake shook his head, water drops flying out of his hair. "Just a ship, to remember my sailing days. I got that in between the other two, when I knew I'd be moving on."

She made one more circle around him. "I like thinking of you as a sailor." Streaks of oil along bare muscled arms and shoulders, muscles rippling as he hauled on a line, strong legs and thighs clambering up a mast . . . .

He read the avarice in her eyes and laughed, coming close enough to stroke down her side, hand lingering on her hip. "I like a woman with a good imagination." He stepped back, grimacing. "And I'd best be getting out of here before either of our imaginations runs away with us."

She knew there was no point arguing, but did anyway. "He can't expect you to work day and night."

He stepped into a pair of trousers and reached for a shirt. "I was supposed to be sleeping there anyway, as a sort of night guard. And Yates is in no shape to deal with a horse thief, or to help someone riding in late at night, at least not without maybe doing himself harm."

"Then he should hire someone for nighttime!"

Jake was dressed except for his boots. She hadn't thought to clean them, but they'd be filthy soon enough even if she had. He sat down and pulled them on, saying, "Maybe he will, and I may push the point if he doesn't. But not tonight."

She could do nothing but walk him to the door and watch him stride down the street toward the stable. It was a fine sight, the muscles of his legs pressing against the too-large trousers with every stride, and made her even more frustrated. But it was time to show herself, to make her rounds and remind girls and customers alike that she was there and in charge.

Damn it.

* * * * *

Jake should've known whose horse the troublemaker mare was. But it hadn't occurred to him until Quinn showed up, that smug smile on his face, and came over to claim her.

Jake was almost sore that Quinn had brought the mare an apple. He'd rather the man have no redeeming qualities.

"We meet again, Mr. Flint!" the man said with obnoxious cheer. "Seen any good advertisements lately?"

Jake could stick to the truth, if he was careful. "Nope. I've been too busy for reading papers."

The man's smile broadened. "Yes, I see you've plenty to do, cleaning up this place. You and your shovel must be busy indeed."

No doubt it'd bother the man plenty, having to deal with horseshit — at least the tangible variety. "It comes with looking after animals properly. You wouldn't want that mare getting hoof trouble from standing in foul straw, would you, for all she's given to using her hooves as she shouldn't."

The lawyer stroked the mare's freshly groomed flanks. "You think so? As for me, I like a little spirit — in mares and women both. Perhaps you prefer the more . . . placid offerings in Mamie's stable. I may have the chance to see for myself, if you and I encounter each other there. Of course, you have to keep 'em on their toes, or they start thinking they're in control. I like to strike a balance."

More layers to that speech than Jake felt like dealing with, but one stood out. "Don't know as you'll have the chance, what with Mamie too riled at you to let you in the door."

The lawyer's eyes gleamed. Jake had said too much, which must've been the man's intention. "Interesting that she should have confided in you." He paused to let Jake stew before going on. "Yes, Mamie's angry with me. Furious! But Mamie's a lively gal, and she'd rather be furious than bored. You might bore her, don't you think?" And he mounted up and rode out of the stable before Jake so much as got his mouth open, kicking the mare into a gallop and almost running down the hostler limping toward the stable.

Jake tried to shake off the lawyer's parting shot. The man made his living by throwing people off balance with his words, spying out people's defenses and getting inside them. There was no point in fretting that Mamie might grow tired of him. If she did, he had no doubt she'd let him know, kindly but firmly. And if he irritated her instead of boring her, she'd skip the kindly part. The thought made him smile as he cleaned up every trace of the lawyer's horse.

Yates came up behind him as he finished. "I've gotta say, you do a better job than the stable lads I've had before. You'd think farm boys would know how to clean up after horses, and take care of 'em."

Jake leaned the shovel against the stall and stretched until his shoulders popped. The straw he'd slept on made a better bed than the dirt and rocks on the trail, but left plenty of sore places. "I reckon I've seen a sight more horses than any farm boy hereabouts. And I like their company."

Which was all he could get out before a huge yawn took over his face. The hostler stood there, watching him as if he found yawns entertaining, and finally said, "We could take turns sleeping in that shed out back. There's a cot and a piller. If I'm the one bedding down here and something comes up as I can't handle on account of my leg, I can holler for you."

That was a temptation almost up there with Mamie and all her ladies lined in a row. But — "Wouldn't it be hard for you to get to your feet in a hurry?"

"If I have too much trouble, whoever's rode in can give me a boost. And I'm mending pretty quick." His sudden leer took Jake aback. "And once I've mended a little more, you could spend your nights elsewhere, if you had a better offer."

Godalmighty, just how many people in Cowbird Creek knew his business? Or guessed it, anyhow. But he'd best not ask which. "Thank you kindly. I might do just that."

Chapter 17

MAMIE wasn't sure how Jake expected to get an answer to his telegram — or maybe he hadn't been sure himself, when he'd talked to her. But it might involve another personals ad. She couldn't think what else it could be, not with Jake being so wary of trouble that he'd ridden days away to hide where his telegram came from. Maybe he'd had some better idea she hadn't thought of, and he hadn't wanted to confide it. The thought might hurt her feelings more than she'd want him to know, but from the older, scarred, bitter Jake who'd wandered back into her life, it shouldn't surprise her.

Still, he'd been back long enough, and acting twitchy enough, that she didn't want to count on him having some private scheme, or not one that had worked. The problem was, Jake couldn't go buy a paper for the first time without someone at the general store noticing and likely commenting on it, and that comment might catch someone else's ears.

She already had the paper. It was rare that even one of the customers showed much interest, with all the girls around to look at — she could give it to Jake with no one likely to miss it, once she worked out how to do it so nobody noticed. She didn't know how long it would be, except too long, before his duties would let him come to her place; and she wasn't eager to provoke as much talk as would no doubt arise if she simply dropped by the stable to see him. She needed some other reason to go there.

Which, naturally, should have something to do with horses.

* * * * *

The shed had a decent roof, considering, and a decent night's sleep under it made a difference to a man as old as Jake was getting. Nothing much hurt when he got up in the morning, and he had a good stomach for the biscuits Yates had left for him to grab on his way into the stable. The hostler was getting around a lot better already, which meant Jake should have his evenings free almost as soon as he'd been hoping. And it was cool enough to be refreshing, without cold enough yet to stiffen his joints or chap his hands. So he was whistling when he made his way down the stalls, changing straw and saying hello to those horses who liked people well enough to care.

But he wondered if he'd dreamed the whole morning so far when he saw Mamie leaning over the front of Wrangler's stall, stroking his nose and feeding him a carrot. She and Wrangler greeted him at about the same time, Wrangler's whinny almost drowning out Mamie's "Good morning, you! Still here?"

"Still here." Jake offered Wrangler the biscuit crumbs sticking to his hand, then waved the hand at Mamie with a grin. "I guess you won't be wanting to shake hands with me just now."

Mamie laughed. "For two cents I'd take it and lick it, just to show you not to assume things about me." She knew damn well where that would send his thoughts, the minx.

Something dropping to the ground caught his eye. Had she brought a fan, to wave away the heavy stable air, and then let go of it? She wasn't the careless kind. He glanced down — and tried to hide his startle at seeing the Omaha paper. He looked back up at her to see her looking straight at him. He leaned back on the stall door and tried for a casual tone as he said, "We've got a rubbish pile over thataway. I'll toss that paper in there for you — the rubbish pile's a bit on the high-smelling side."

"Thank you kindly, sir. And now, could you tell me where I can find Mr. Yates? I'm thinking about keeping a horse, instead of hiring one when I need one, and I wanted to know what he'd charge me for its stabling and keep."

Was any of that the truth? The look in her eyes suggested otherwise, but he couldn't be sure. He hedged by saying, "He's out in the shed resting his leg, but you could wait, or seek him out there."

He'd guessed right. Mamie gave a little never-mind wave and said, "I'll just drop by again sometime. I've no horse yet, after all. And I hope we'll see you again soon." She nudged the paper with her toe, as if to remind him it was there — which he had in fact almost forgot, what with her standing so near. He tipped his hat and watched her leave, enjoying the view, before glancing around for any witnesses. No one in sight, if he didn't count the horses.

There was no special reason to expect a new ad, but maybe Mamie knew different. He squatted to pick up the paper, stood back up as quick as he was able, and looked around again. Still no one watching, and Mamie had left the paper folded to show the personals ads.

He scanned the page as quick as he could, still not really expecting to find anything. But he did.

Ethan seeking Jacob. Time to set things right. Will pay for address. Send to Ethan F. at Deliverance, Indiana or Oberlin, Ohio.

Maybe Ethan had ignored Rich's telegram, or hadn't trusted its source enough to answer it. Or maybe he had, and still thought another ad worth the expense. But it might mean Rich had decided not to get involved in Jake's mysterious troubles. Or that he'd never got Jake's letter. That would mean, at best, that he'd never gotten the ones Jake wrote earlier, at least not all of them. And at worst, that he'd died sometime in all the years since Jake had seen him last.

He shoved the fear, and the heartsickness, down as deep as it'd go and read the ad again. "Set things right." That could mean quite a range of reckonings, from a formal disinheritance or curse, or even an arrest, to "all is forgiven." Turning the other cheek notwithstanding, he wouldn't bet on his pa or grandpa choosing the latter.

There was nothing more he could do about the ads. He would do better to keep his mind on the horses, a better place for it by far. He tossed the paper onto the rubbish heap and got on with his work.

The sun was slanting in from lower to the ground, and redder in color, when the man from the telegraph office came in, blinking as he moved from daylight into the dimness of the stable. He stood a minute, probably waiting for his eyes to adjust, and then came toward Jake, waving a piece of paper. "This came for you. I asked around, and folks said I could find you here."

Jake stood stock still until the man reached him and held out the telegram. He took it, his hand unaccountably trembling, and clenched his other fist to make sure his voice didn't do the same. "Thanks for bringing it." The man nodded and turned away to head back into the sunshine.

Jake half sat, half fell onto a handy hay bale and read

the telegram.

Got back from trip, got your letter. Will do as you asked. All the best — Rich

Jake clutched the paper and tried to remember how to breathe. He'd been breathing for thirty-nine years. Why was it suddenly an unfamiliar task, like speaking another language?

Rich was alive. He was alive, and he'd got Jake's letter, and he'd answered it.

Jake sat there until his breathing steadied and his hands stopped shaking. Then he stumbled to Wrangler, leaned heavy on his side, and hid his face in the horse's rough mane.

As the sun set and Jake's belly rumbled its demands at him, he found Yates and said, "If you're up to being the only one here for a bit, I'll go grab myself some supper. I'll be back —"

The hostler shook his shaggy head, grinning. "You be back when you've a mind to. And tomorrow morning is as good a time as any. I'm not so feeble as I need more of a vacation than I've had already." And at Jake's stare, he added, "Don't you give me no backtalk, youngster. Get on with you!"

Jake grinned back. "Youngster, is it? You must have come down with fever. I'll go get Doc again, shall I?"

Yates made a gesture Jake had learned back when such things could still shock him. "Too bad that blasted mare isn't here to give you a good kick and send you on your way."

The reminder that Quinn and his nag had left town, along with the unexpected free evening, lifted Jake's spirits to the point that he headed to town whistling. He went into the first saloon he passed, sat on a stool at the counter, and ordered a beer and a plate of fried chicken and gravy. The beer came first, and he had time, now, to drink it slowly, holding each swallow in his mouth to savor it before gulping it down. When he'd drunk down half the glass, he let his attention wander to the surroundings. Two men who seemed to know each other well were near enough for him to eavesdrop, and Jake knew from long practice how to do it without them noticing.

"I'm telling you, that was one damned fine medicine show. They had a dancing girl wearing not much more than veils all over, and a cowboy doing rope tricks — he like to took one fellow off his feet with that lasso!"

The other man gulped his whiskey and asked, "Is that the one where the pitchman is real tall and skinny and has a black beard almost down to his knees?"

"Naah, the pitchman here was tall enough, but nothing skinny about him. Well-fed, and with bright gold hair and whiskers. And fancy clothes, so his wares must be worth buying."

Jake had to hide a laugh in a cough. The fellow was begging to be taken advantage of by some swell selling colored soda water. But the description rang a bell. Mamie had said something once about the pitchman who'd carried off her widow friend, and about gold hair . . . .

When the fried chicken came, he bolted it down and hurried out the door to tell Mamie. But by the time he got to the square, there was a crowd in the street and a wagon in the middle of it, with a cowboy snaking a red rope all over. He didn't see any dancing girls, who might have been yet to come. He couldn't guess whether Mamie would be irked to have a half-naked girl out front distracting potential customers, or would be just as glad to have such a show get their blood pumping and send them into her place to do something about it.

He edged around the crowd to get to the parlor house, but stopped short at the sight that met him near the front step. There was Mamie, out on the street where he rarely saw her, and half swallowed in the embrace of a big woman wearing a gigantic fur coat.

* * * * *

"Mamie, dear Mamie, I can't believe it, here you are, I finally get to see you, are you well, are you happy, tell me everything!"

Mamie's laugh was muffled in Freida's coat. Where to start? As best she could recall, Freida knew nothing about Mamie's illness, and this was hardly the time to tell her about it. As for somehow trying to explain about Jake —

But there he was, not two yards away, chuckling as he watched this reunion. Mamie pulled back, squeezing Freida's hand so the other woman would know it wasn't meant as a retreat, and waved Jake closer. As he obeyed, Jedidiah jumped down from the wagon and joined them, somehow managing to put his arms around her and Freida both. Jake stopped and waited for them to get untangled, then came closer, tipping his hat. "Howdy, folks. I'm Jake Flint, a friend of Mamie's, and I'm guessing you're Mr. and Mrs. Kennedy, that Mamie's told me of."

He took a step back when Freida and Jedidiah both advanced on him, Freida getting there first and giving him a furry hug of his own. "So good to meet a friend of Mamie's, isn't she wonderful, how did you meet, do you live right here in town?"

Jedidiah patted her on the shoulder. "Freida, my love, let the man catch his breath." As soon as Freida let go of

Jake, Jedidiah held out his hand. "As my wife so aptly said, it's always good to meet a friend of Mamie's, and I look forward to our getting to know each other."

Jake shook Jedidiah's hand, still looking a little stunned by the friendly onslaught. Mamie tried to pull her thoughts together. Freida wouldn't be diverted from her questions for long. At least Mamie could answer them somewhere other than the street. "Let's all go inside and catch up . . . unless you'd rather not."

Freida answered that hesitation by heading for the steps as fast as she was able, Jedidiah trotting behind. Mamie let the visitors go first and hung back enough to whisper in Jake's ear, "What do you want me to tell them?"

He gave her an almost shy smile, which sat oddly on his weathered face. "They're your friends. It's up to you. But for my part, there's nothing I'd ask you to hide from them."

The moment they got inside the house and she could close the door, she pulled him close and planted a kiss square on his mouth. Then she caught up with Freida and Jedidiah, pulling Jake after her, scooting around the group enough to push open the door to the small parlor. "Please sit down, and I'll get you something warm to drink. And in the meantime, you can start getting to know my man."

At which Jake pulled her close in his turn and kissed her right back.

Freida and Jedidiah and Jake stayed long enough for all four of them to be ready for another supper. Cook had gone to bed, but Mamie knew where to scrounge in the kitchen and larder. Jedidiah, affectionate and attentive, showed no sign of desiring any other woman than Freida. And Jake soon relaxed and enjoyed their company, which Mamie found deeply reassuring. Any man who could resist

Freida's warmth and unique charm would not be a man Mamie wanted to trust with her heart. She could hardly believe she was thinking in those terms, she who once would never have dreamed of it.

When Jedidiah finally tugged a yawning Freida out the door, declining Mamie's offer of a room indoors — "We have blankets aplenty, and are still enjoying the novelty of cool air" — Jake turned from waving them goodbye and took her hands. "You and your friends were gracious enough to overlook my coming straight from the stable. But now, would you like me to wash off the dirt and smell?"

Mamie pulled him closer and took a deep sniff along his neck. "You smell more like Jake than like horses. And I'm partial to both smells. But especially the first. Come to bed."

Jake was spending more than half his nights at her place now, and usually got off work in time to take a bath when he showed up. Getting clean seemed to matter more to him than to her, not as a general matter (she supposed) but as a way of proving something to them both. She'd have tried harder to talk him out of it if it didn't give her the chance to admire his body at her leisure. It did tend to mean they headed straight from the bathroom to her bedroom, but Jake had charmed Cook enough that she was cooperative about giving them supper at whatever time suited them. A few of the girls had been fools enough to make wisecracks, but she'd long since mastered a glare that said, "You can get away with that — just once . . . ." There must be plenty of gossip still going on, but if it was putting up with that knowledge or showing Jake the door for good, she'd take the former. If he hung around long enough for the chatterboxes to get tired of it, so much the better.

Had any customers got wind of it? Would it matter if they did? Business hadn't fallen off, not yet anyway. In fact, it'd been booming since the drought the locals had been through, so to speak. She was in a fair way to make back the nest egg the shutdown had cost her. For a while at least, her clientele might not care if Mamie had taken to dancing naked in the street. She had to laugh at the thought. It might be a positive inducement! — until she was locked away in some madhouse. A relatively discreet indiscretion was nothing by comparison.

Jake hadn't said anything more about the latest personals ad. She saw no good in pressing him, and would just as soon not think about what the ad or Quinn's possible meddling might mean for Jake's future. Or for hers. Aside from how the two were bound up together, she didn't entirely put it past Quinn to get her charged as an accessory to whatever crime someone might lay at Jake's door. Especially once he found out it was more or less her door, literally.

The one time she and Jake spoke of Jake's past, she provoked it without intending to. She had asked him, casually, as they stood on the front step watching the sun go down, what sort of weather he wished for on the morrow. He'd answered, "I don't hold with wishing. It's like praying without even the guts to admit it. And there's some tales sailors tell that'll put you off wishing for life."

Something in his tone suggested he meant more than he was saying. "Can you really keep from wishing, then? I doubt I could." And then, challenging him further, "Didn't you wish I'd get better, when I was so sick and you doing so much to tend me?"

He half smiled, half grimaced. "Yes, I did, and knew I

was a fool to do it. It was the closest I'd come to praying in about as many years as you'd figure. It would've been the first time since I stood outside Ethan's room, working up the nerve to take his money, and prayed that he'd someday forgive me."

Little as she credited prayer, she had the urge to say that he didn't know whether that prayer had been answered. But instead she gave him a gentle kiss on the cheek and laid her head on his shoulder as the cold wind blew in.

Neither of them had seen hide nor hair of Quinn for weeks, which just meant they were that much closer to him coming through town again. And in a neat reversal of the old saw about an ill wind doing nobody good, she was on her front step enjoying a rare warmish day and a mild breeze when he rode up on the bad-tempered mare Jake had told her about. He had on a new-looking coat, almost white so it'd need frequent cleaning, and a new hat with a band that matched his boots. It wasn't the first time he'd come to town in something new and fancified, but it was the first time she'd thought about it. Did he think the outfit would impress her, or did he just like showing off his money?

Jake was still at the stable, where he probably wouldn't know about Quinn's arrival. Horn would be a physical match for Quinn, but she hated to hurry inside and hide behind her doorman. So she waited, standing athwart her door, as Quinn marched up to her and cocked his head, saying, "Closed for business again so soon, my dear?"

She planted her fists on her hips and glared at him. "Closed to you, as you well know." But he moved so close she had to yield backward or try to shove him away. And she didn't care to entertain the passersby with a wrestling match. She stepped to the side and let him breeze through. She might not be able to keep him from barging in without help, but he couldn't use the same tactic to force her to send any of her girls upstairs with him.

Quinn slipped behind the bar and fixed himself a drink. The good whiskey, of course. Time to set Horn on him. But before she could draw breath to call for Horn, Quinn had set the drink down and grabbed her by the waist. "Why would I settle for one of your girls, darlin', when I'm used to better?"

She elbowed him in the gut, taking him off balance just long enough to push free of him. "Too good for you, you no-account shyster. Get out of my place!"

The struggle would probably have pleased him, but the insult clearly did not. The glare he shot her was nothing she'd seen, and probably well beyond even what he used to intimidate witnesses. As he loomed over her, she ducked around him to grab the glass and threw the whiskey in his eyes. Too bad he'd picked a sturdy glass, or she could have shattered it and had a real weapon.

Quinn bellowed and scrubbed at his eyes. She fled toward the kitchen and its array of knives, too out of breath now to call for Horn, hearing Quinn's heavy tread catching up behind her. And then, gladder to her ears than ever before, came Jake's low growl, and the sounds of a scuffle. She whirled around to see Jake holding Quinn in a headlock, the man cussing a blue streak but unable to break free. Horn came rushing up from the other direction, but Jake somehow got a hand free without losing hold of Quinn, and waved him off.

As Jake jerked Quinn toward the front door and kicked it open, the lawyer spat out, "I'm done playing with you, you piece of trash! I'm sending *your brother* news of your whereabouts before the day is out, and you'd better get to running!" Jake's only response was to kick Quinn squarely in the seat of his pants, sending him sprawling down the steps and into the street. Jake stood in the doorway, making a far more effective barrier than Mamie had, radiating menace as Quinn picked himself up and half stumbled, half ran down the street.

Toward the telegraph office.

It was just a little too late for Mamie to remember her guesses about Quinn's history with bullies. If anything had been lacking to turn his threats into reality, she'd just seen it happen. She came up behind Jake and put her arms around him, laying her cheek against his strong back and breathing in the scent of him. "Will you be leaving, then?"

He loosened her hands just enough that he could turn to face her and pull her against his chest, saying softly into her hair, "No need. I just came from sending a telegram to Ethan, telling him where I am."

She pulled back and stared up at him. He looked tired, as tired as if he'd been running for all the years since she'd first known him — as he had been, truly. But he seemed at peace for the first time since he'd come to Cowbird Creek, as if he'd laid his burden down.

Chapter 18

JAKE hadn't crossed paths with the preacher since he got back to town. Such good luck not being his usual portion, he was unsurprised to see the man walking his way as Jake left the saloon for Mamie's place. It was comic, really, to see the man look first at where Jake had just come from, and then at where he must know Jake was likely to be going, and frown harder each time. Jake could just about read the preacher's mind as the poor man gathered his courage to approach the heathen who might yet, with God's help, be turned toward righteousness . . . .

He stopped to save the preacher having to catch up to him and scurry alongside, the fellow's legs being considerably shorter. As the preacher caught his breath, Jake tipped his hat and said cordially, "Good evening, Reverend. I do hope you're having a blessed day."

The man's eyes went wide at what must have been an unexpected greeting. Jake suppressed a grin and went from an insincere wish to an outright lie. "Now that I'm in town for longer than I'd planned on, I've been looking forward to encountering you again."

The way the preacher's face brightened with hope made Jake feel like a worm. "And I am always glad to encounter someone who may yet become a member of my flock. The more such a man may be in need of spiritual support, the more blessed my mission, and the greater the eventual reward." He stopped talking and chewed his lip.

Gratified or not, the man seemed at a loss for how to proceed. If Jake hadn't veered so far off the path his upbringing had set before him, he could probably have been as good a preacher or better. What would he say to himself, in the preacher's shoes? He was pondering that question when the preacher found something to say instead. "It was courteous of you to stand and wait for me — and the more fortunate in that it has delayed your progress toward the den of sin and corruption I greatly fear was your destination."

Viewing the matter in general terms, and thinking back over the hookshops he'd seen on his travels, he could see how the preacher might not be altogether and reliably wrong. Jake silently applauded his own coolheadedness as he replied, "Assuredly there are men, especially those too young to have established ties and settled habits, who could be endangered by the worst of the establishments you may mean."

Back came the frown. "My son, you gravely deceive yourself, to the great peril of your soul, if you believe that the purveyor of harlots who has — despite my best efforts — been allowed to maintain her accursed business in this otherwise upright town is any exception. Indeed, with her cleverness and conniving ways, she is the more dangerous. I grieve to say that she has already turned one promising young man from the light, and set him on the road to perdition, accompanied by one of her strumpets! Indeed, she somehow prevailed upon a man of the cloth to give countenance to such a union, here in our very town! Truly among all the harlots in the Devil's coven, she is among the worst —"

At which point Jake found himself lifting the preacher up by the scruff of his neck and glaring into his face from an inch or so away. In resolving to put up with the man, and then congratulating himself for having done so, he had forgotten just what sort of filth the son of a bitch was likely to throw in Mamie's direction. And he'd had every reason to know better.

Meanwhile, the preacher had gone from sputtering to calling for help. To Jake's delight at the irony, swiftly followed by apprehension, the first to respond was Mamie herself, running up to Jake and pulling on his arm. "Get hold of yourself — and let go of the fellow! The sheriff is in town, and even if you don't care about drawing his notice, having you brawling in the street with the preacher isn't going to do me and my place any good!"

Jake dropped the preacher, not troubling to lower him down first. The fellow landed on hands and knees as Jake turned and tipped his hat. "Good evening, Miss Mamie. I'm sorry to have let my temper get the best of me. I hope you're well this fine evening?"

Mamie raised her hand as if thinking of slapping him, but instead stepped hard on his instep. Even through boots, the heel of her shoe made a sharp enough impact to make him wince. And there came a man with a tin star on his chest, and the look of a lawman that made the star unnecessary. He helped the preacher rise to his feet and asked him, "Did this man — or this woman — assault you, Reverend?"

The preacher glared at them both and then drew himself up so straight his belly stuck out, saying as stuffily as a man could under the circumstances, "As is my Lord's commandment, I forgive the assault, even unto seven times seven."

Jake cleared his throat to draw the sheriff's attention. "I'm afraid I'm the guilty party here, Sheriff. I reacted to the preacher's holy word with an unpardonable display of violence. This lady here had nothing to do with it, except to do her best to restrain me, for which I must now give her thanks." He bowed to Mamie and turned back to the sheriff. "If you consider it your duty to take me in charge, I'll offer no resistance, only my apologies to you and to the good Reverend here."

The sheriff's keen eyes raked him over. "And you would be?"

"Jacob Flint, sir. Fairly new in town, but minded to stay a while if your forbearance, and that of the townspeople, should extend so far."

The sheriff stroked his gray-brown beard. "I believe I've heard that name recently. Oh, yes — that slick lawyer fellow was bending my ear about you, saying he thought there must be a hue and cry over you someplace. Something about an ad seeking your whereabouts."

Mamie was standing close enough that Jake would have known, he thought, if she was trembling. She wasn't. His pride in her helped him say with tolerable ease, "I'm not aware of any warrant or such out against me, nor the law looking for me. I did see such an ad, which seemed to come from my brother, and I've sent word back as to where I am."

The sheriff looked back to the preacher, who was brushing off his pants and adjusting the set of his hat. "It's up to you, Reverend. If you'd like to file a complaint, I'll take this fellow with me to the county lockup until the judge next comes through."

The sudden stillness at Jake's side suggested Mamie was holding her breath. Jake folded his hands and looked off into the distance as the preacher said pompously, "I am willing to overlook the incident, assuming it is not repeated, and will hold to the hope that this sinner's ears may be opened before next we meet."

The sheriff looked faintly relieved, whether at not having to deal with a possibly fractious prisoner, or from not wanting to oblige the lawyer. "Well, then —"

Jake suddenly noticed, down the street and coming up behind their little group, the bulky figure of none other than Freida Blum, bearing down on them with the light of battle in her eye. He was trying to figure out what to do about it without interrupting the sheriff when Mamie followed his gaze and slid out around to intercept her friend. The sheriff looked a trifle taken aback at Mamie's movements but continued, "I don't see any need to make an arrest if the preacher's minded to be so forgiving. Mr. Flint, I don't want to see nor hear anything to make me regret it."

"You won't, sir. I give you my word." And he'd have to keep it, so he could only hope — or pray, if he wanted to shock the Almighty with such sudden notice — that no one tempted him beyond endurance.

He waited where he was until preacher and sheriff moved on and Mamie and Freida joined him, Freida naturally talking a mile a minute. "The nerve of that lawyer, I heard him bragging to anyone who'd listen about how he was going to set the law on you, I went right up to him and said, 'I've known lawyers like you before, all talk and bluff and throwing their weight around, and I'll have you know,' but he just turned and walked off as cool as you please, and then when I saw the sheriff and you and Mamie I was going to tell him not to let that lawyer pull the wool over his eyes, but I guess you didn't need an old woman interfering, you handled it all right without me."

Freida finally stopped to draw breath, and Mamie put an arm around her, or as far as it could reach. "You just come on back with me, dear, and I'll get you a nice tall glass of tea." They headed for Mamie's, Jake following meekly behind.

One way and another, Jake had spent plenty of time with his spine prickling, wondering who was spying on him from out of sight and what weapons they might be aiming at him. He should be man enough not to feel that way when the most the townsfolk might be aiming was curious or disapproving glances, mostly from behind windows. But he was still glad to see the Gibbs' door flung open, if confused that Freida rather than Clara stood in the doorway. She explained before they'd made it up the front step. "I know, I act like it's my house, but you know it used to be, and Clara is far too sensible to mind if I let old habits take over, come in, come in!"

Mamie hadn't said a word on the way over about who might be watching, and he'd been too bedeviled by his imagination to notice she'd tensed up, but he could feel her arm relax before she pulled it out of his and ran to give Freida a hug. Freida filled a doorway by herself, let alone when tangled up with Mamie, so he stood there whistling under his breath until Freida turned Mamie loose and reached out both hands to him. "And Jake, unless you'd rather I say Jacob when I'm pretending to be a hostess, anyway, come on in! You must be hungry, Clara and I have been cooking all morning and Jedidiah hasn't managed to steal all the food yet, you'd better hurry and join us!"

As he made it inside and took off his coat, reveling in the warmth from the fireplace, Jedidiah came in from the kitchen beaming and holding a biscuit. "Out of pure generosity of spirit, I have ventured to taste some of what smells so heavenly in yonder kitchen, and can assure you that the odors are not misleading."

All this happy sociability left him almost tongue-tied. Telling tales at a dinner table was easier, less personal somehow. Jake sought out Clara and found her just inside the kitchen, looking quietly gratified at the greetings and teasing going on in the sitting room. She cocked an eyebrow at Jake's entrance, then gave him a more sympathetic look. "Are my other guests a touch overwhelming? My more restrained husband will be home shortly. He's checking that the latest broken arm in town is healing well."

A cool draft and the creak of the front door announced Joshua's return, quickly followed by Freida's cry of welcome and Jedidiah's boisterous greeting. Jake hadn't heard much from Mamie since they arrived. Were the older couple drowning her out? He headed back into the sitting room to provide any necessary moral support. Mamie, it turned out, had met Joshua at the door, brushing a few flakes of snow off his coat. Joshua greeted Mamie with a firm clasp of her hands, prompting Jake to wonder what history they might have with each other, and then looked up at Jake with a friendly, open smile. "I'm so glad you could join us! Had you been able to come when I first suggested it, you would hardly have had such lively and merry companions."

True enough — though he'd have had a better chance of getting to know Joshua without Freida's overpowering, and Jedidiah's flamboyant, presence. And he'd have liked to get to know Joshua. Maybe he'd still have that chance, and maybe not.

* * * * *

It was hard to believe it had taken this long for Mamie to actually enter the Gibbs home. Or maybe it wasn't, but at least the warmth of her welcome eased any sting from that knowledge.

With such vibrant personalities as Freida and Jedidiah demanding attention, it was hard to spare any for noticing the surroundings. But the homey comfort of the place, with deep cushions on the sturdy chairs and sofa and large lamps shedding plenty of warm light, had her wondering. Was there a way to add any of that quality to the interiors at her establishment without diminishing its elegance? Mamie put aside the question to ponder later. She had more immediate concerns.

Clara had seated Mamie and Jake across from each other, which made it easy for her to keep an eye on him without (she hoped) making it obvious. He'd eaten plenty of the hearty dinner Freida and Clara — mostly Freida, Mamie guessed, from just how hearty it was — had cooked up. But he still looked hungry, even as he leaned back in his chair.

Or maybe it was wistful he looked. She remembered walking past his house once, back in Deliverance, and glancing up as the other boys ran pell-mell through town on their way to the swimming hole, loosening up their shirts as they ran. There he stood at his window, all buttoned up and holding a Bible, and she could tell that just this once, he'd rather have been on his way to jump in that cold, deep water and come up spouting and hollering. He looked a little like that now, except harder, and more weary.

What was he looking at? Not the food, for certain. And not any one person at the table. He seemed to be gazing now at one, now at another, according to who was talking: Jedidiah, praising the meal, and comparing it to one or another comical dish he'd encountered on his travels; Freida, blushing and giving the credit to Clara; Clara, with her quiet smile, saying that Jedidiah surely knew better; Joshua shaking his head at that, patting Clara's hand.

And then, of a sudden, he'd turned, and was looking straight at her. And he looked hungrier than ever. And more lost.

If she could have reached his hand, she'd have given it a squeeze. Instead, she put as much softness in her face as it'd hold. He blinked, maybe wondering why, and then took a visible breath and donned his devil-may-care expression, the better to hide what had shown before.

* * * * *

When Jake decided to tell Ethan — or whoever — where he could be found, he hadn't thought very far ahead. He hadn't, in particular, thought about how long it would take for anything to come of it, nor what he'd do in the meantime. He hadn't planned how he was going to take the waiting. Since he first ran away from Deliverance, waiting was just about the one thing he hadn't done. Unless he counted being in the navy and waiting for a bombardment to start, and then there were sailors all around waiting for it too, with the same mix of excitement and nerves.

He had his work at the livery stable during the day, with the horses for company, and Wrangler to visit with and talk to when he felt especially low. And he had Mamie in the evenings and most nights, plus lively visits with Freida and Jedidiah while they stayed in the region, making their shorter jaunts and coming back in between.

He'd known his new friends, for such they'd become, couldn't stick around long. It still took much of the wind out of his sails when they came to tell Mamie they'd be leaving the next morning. Jedidiah, for once, made the announcement without Freida getting a word in first. "We've done as much business hereabouts as we can, so we'll have to move on — heading back south again, now that winter is almost upon us. I'm afraid it's likely to be quite some time before there's a market for our wares again in these parts."

Mamie bit her lip and said bravely, "Then I'm so glad you came in time for supper. And in time for me to tell Cook to make something special, and serve us in the party room." She smiled at Jake, almost hiding the sadness lurking behind it. "Jake, you've seen the room before, but never with such an abundance of agreeable company."

It was a cheerful, and at times a hilarious, supper. At the end of it, he shook hands with Jedidiah, accepted Freida's inevitable hug, and left Mamie to make her own goodbyes without his watching. By the time she found him in the small parlor, her eyes were dry, and if they still showed traces of red, they neither of them mentioned it.

The next day at the stable felt longer than any before. At the end of it, he found himself too restless to be indoors, even with Mamie, who would sooner or later have the best cure for restless. And a saloon would be no better — probably worse, given the opportunities to take out his mood on some drunk and end up in even more trouble. He took a long walk instead, half hoping he'd run into one of the few other people he knew, half just as glad he wouldn't have to make conversation.

When the cold finally drove him to Mamie's door, she was busy with customers, not to mention peeved at him for showing up later than usual. As she bustled from parlor to stairs and back again, she found time to throw back over her shoulder, "I thought maybe the sheriff had finally got hold of you to send you back to Indiana. Guess not."

He couldn't answer her back with her ladies and the customers all around. And in his present frame of mind, the sort of things he might say could get him tossed out in the cold for good. He grabbed the hat he'd just hung up and headed back out the door.

This time, it didn't take long before he realized he actually had a place to go. The telegraph office was still open, though the clerk had got to the point of walking to the door to flip the sign to "closed." He pushed in, apologized for keeping the man, and assured him, "It's a short message I'm sending. I won't keep you long."

Ethan, please respond to last. Jacob.

It had got even colder, it felt like, as he left the office. And the restless had drained away, leaving a hollow space inside. He would go back to Mamie's, and hope to find her in a more forgiving mood. Now, hours too late, he thought she might have needed his company more than usual, after seeing her old friends leave town the night before.

An apology might be poor recompense, but he'd give it a try.

Chapter 19

IT HAD gotten colder since Jake took the livery stable job, and the only heat in the place came from the horses themselves. The day after he sent the second telegram, Jake found himself replacing straw too often just to keep warm from the work, which brought Yates down on him for wasting the stuff. Jake was in no mood to apologize, but managed to come close to it when he contemplated trying to find other work that would keep him in town. Not that he was likely to have much choice in where he ended up, with a federal marshal maybe on his way.

Yates didn't take offense at Jake's tone, as he'd have had a right to. Instead, he stood there chewing a piece of straw — and what about straw being in short supply? — and looking like he was chewing on something else to say along with it. Finally he spat out the straw and said, "You're a right demon for work, ain't you?"

Jake shrugged. "I've never been one to just sit around." Not even back when what he did instead was study his Bible, and what other people wrote and preached about it. He'd walked with a book in his hand as often as he'd sat on his backside. And speaking of which, there had to be something he could do instead of just standing around waiting for Yates to spit something else out. He grabbed a curry brush and looked around for the scruffiest horse. As he headed for an older mare, Yates followed him, and said as Jake got to work, "Cold gets colder as a fellow gets older."

Not a bad way of putting it. Jake started up between the mare's ears and slowly worked his way downward.

"Joints get more troublesome too."

More to look forward to. Jake would have asked the mare how her joints were doing, but not with the hostler standing there.

"I'm thinkin' I might find me somewhere warmer to spend my days. A job indoors, with a stove nearby and no fear of startin' a fire from it."

Jake kept working the brush down the mare's back and sides, but looked up at Yates. The man seemed to be expecting Jake to take part in the conversation, so he settled on, "I can see you might be wanting that, though you do a fine job right here." Which was only a little ways on the side of charitable.

The hostler brightened up, either at the praise or at Jake saying anything at all. "So I've been thinking. If someone was to buy me out, they could have this place."

Which would leave Jake exactly where? Out of a job maybe, for all the difference it would make with where he was likely headed.

"And I could maybe fix up the shed as part of the bargain. Make it more weather-tight."

The mare shoved him in the ribs with her nose. Jake must have stopped brushing her. Or maybe she was telling him to listen up. Could Yates be telling him all this for some reason other than to warn him of change coming, or pass the time?

Yates studied him closer. "Don't suppose you have a lot of money saved up. Or any way to get more, anyone back home or such."

He could have laughed at the thought, or maybe cried. He could just see explaining to the man. *Sorry, I already stole all the family had handy, and they might not leave any more where I could get at it.* He bit his lip until the craziness passed and then shook his head.

The hostler gave the mare's flank a perfunctory pat. "Well, if you hear tell of anyone who might be interested, you let 'em know."

He walked away, and Jake went back to grooming the mare. Once Yates was out of earshot, he murmured into the horse's ear, "If that don't beat all. And the craziest part is, I'd have liked to do it. Buy him out, and be the one in charge of taking care of you and the others. I've had my thoughts on how he could do things better. Think there's a stove that could be safely kept near straw? What do you think?"

The mare reached for the nearest hank of Jake's hair. Jake pulled it out of her reach. "No, that's not one of the changes I'd make. Hay for you all, and oats when enough money came in. No hair."

Over that night's supper of bacon and corn muffins, Jake told Mamie about Yates's wild notion, ending with, "I just hope nothing much changes before I have to leave town, whenever that might be."

He didn't know what Mamie would have to say, but he'd expected her to say something. When she didn't, he studied her face and didn't know just what to make of it. He'd been afraid she might be thinking about crying, but he couldn't see any sign of that. And she wasn't rolling her eyes at the thought of Jake being able to buy a heap of straw, let alone a livery stable. Instead, she had the look of someone wrestling with some notion. He let her be and concentrated on good food, better than he might be getting down the road. He'd almost forgot he was waiting for her to finish thinking when she said, "This place makes pretty good money. You've maybe figured that out, seeing as what it looks like inside, and what the girls wear, and all." He'd looked up at her by then, and saw her little smirk as she added, "And the table I set for the occasional hungry man."

He put down a half-eaten muffin and stared at her.

"I had to use up some of my savings when the mumps hit, but I'd saved a lot, and I've made much of it back with how busy we've been since. So if things turn out all right, and no one hauls you away to be jailed or hung or whatever you're picturing . . . and if you care for the notion, I could maybe, as they say, diversify my investments."

She reached across the table to take his hand. "I could do worse than be a silent partner in a livery stable. This town's growing, and likely to keep doing it. There'll be more people coming through, and more of those that live here will be able to keep horses."

He gripped her hand tight, and had no clue what to say to her.

"So you could tell Yates you might know of someone who'd be interested, and he should hold off on selling it elsewhere for a bit." She flashed one of her mischievous grins. "And some other time — so he doesn't put two and two together — you could mention kind of casual-like that if he was feeling so cold of an evening, you know a place where he could warm himself up plenty."

Jake swallowed down the piece of corn muffin, or whatever in his throat was like to choke him, and lifted up her hand to kiss it. "I'll do that. Both things. And if I do get hauled away, like I've got coming, you could still do it, if you think it'd pay. You could hire someone to look like they were running the place, as long as he'd do what you tell him."

He was afraid she'd say something making clear she

was only giving the idea a moment's thought as a way to distract him from the future, or as a handout if he were somehow to stay around. But she nodded and said, "I might, at that. I'll be thinking about it as customers come through."

She stood up and brushed crumbs off her dress. "And speaking of such, we've a ways to go before we're done with them for the night. You go and have a bath if you've a mind to. And if one of the girls offers to help you, tell her hands off."

* * * * *

The knock on the office door sounded like Trudi. Mamie had done as much paperwork as she could stomach for one afternoon, and Trudi usually had a good reason for interrupting her. She called out, "Come in!" and was mildly pleased to see she'd got right who'd knocked. Life was getting complicated enough without surprises at her office door.

Trudi didn't actually enter. She just opened the door, stood in the doorway, and said, "There's a visitor, and he says he's here for a feller, not a girl. I'm pretty sure he's joking, but I'm not sure what he really wants."

This almost had to be about Jake. "What's this visitor like?"

"Oldish. Not a lot of hair, and gray in his beard. Not exactly tall, but not short." Trudi paused and showed her dimples. "He looks strong, and kind of rough, but he flirts nice."

Jake would be back from the stable in an hour or so. She had better pump this visitor for information, and figure out if he posed any threat, before Jake turned up. "Bring him here. But first, tell Horn to follow the two of you and then hang around in the hall."

The man Trudi ushered in was almost as muscle-bound as Jake, though his arms were more wiry. His feet hit the ground hard as he walked, and he stood with his feet apart as if keeping his balance on an unsteady surface. He gave Mamie a little bow and then stood there clutching his hat with both hands. "A good evening to you, ma'am."

Mamie had a guess as to who this might be, but she feared to trust that guess when the truth might be more troublesome. "Good evening, sir, and if, as my assistant suggests, you aren't here to brighten your day with the charms of my ladies, what can I do for you?"

His smile showed good, if crooked, teeth, one front tooth missing. "I'm looking for a friend, a sight less charming than your ladies, but a friend for all that. Jake Flint. Knowing him reasonable well, I thought if anyone in town might have seen him, it'd be yourself."

Mamie didn't know whether to grin or grind her teeth. If this was, as she hoped, Jake's friend Rich, just how many riverside hookshops had they visited together? And who had led the way? But she needed to know other things first. "Before I respond to your inquiry, shall we start with your name?"

It wasn't the newcomer who answered her. "You have the dubious pleasure of beholding a certain Rich Criley." Jake came striding through the door, grabbed the man's arm, and tugged him around. Next moment, they were pounding each other's backs and making growling noises that might or might not include words.

* * * * *

When they finally let go of each other, Jake shook his head and said, "Where the hell did you spring from?"

"You mean, without a boat and a river to carry it? There's this big ol' thing they call a train — maybe you've heard of it."

Jake aimed a cuff at Rich's head, knowing Rich would duck it, and a split second later going cold with the fear that Rich had slowed down too much — but Rich dodged easily, and gave him the old lazy grin. "In case you meant to ask a sensible question, such as *why* I've turned up, I had me a restless spell — which don't come on me near as much as they did when I was a youngster, but happens now'n then. My kids have had enough of me bothering 'em, and the business runs along tolerably without my sitting on my tail in my office every day. So I thought I'd see how your tale was playing out, seeing as I had a bit of a part in it."

Jake could have asked questions enough to make his tongue tired, just based on that one speech. Kids? Business? Office, of all things? What had Rich figured out of Jake's "tale"? But all of that could wait. "Thank you, Rich. For going to the trouble of sending that telegram to Ethan — and then the second one. Not to mention keeping me from harm more times than I can count, back in the day." He put out his hand, and Rich shook it. Was the man's grip less crushing than all those years ago?

Rich let go and took out his pipe. "If you don't object, ma'am?" At Mamie's gracious wave of permission, he filled it, lit it, and said after the first puff, "You're welcome on all counts, lad. I might owe you some thanks, at that. It was keeping you and the other youngsters out of trouble that got me thinking I might want some of my own, one day. And there's been nothing better in my life than those three rascals."

Jake hadn't thought to see Rich in this lifetime, and the chances weren't good that he ever would again. He could feel all the things he'd ever wanted to tell him welling up and crowding into his chest, and yet he couldn't put words to a one. He fell back on, "You look well enough, for one of the fellows who built the Pyramids."

Rich ignored him to say to Mamie, "Ma'am, I want to thank you for what I'm sure has been much kindness to this scapegrace."

Mamie raised an eyebrow and said, in her smoothest manner, "That's most gracious of you, Mr. Criley. But you should know that Mr. Flint did me a substantial favor, almost the moment he first appeared in Cowbird Creek — and others since. I would say I'm in *his* debt."

For just a moment, Jake got to see Rich caught flat-footed. While he stood there enjoying it, Mamie added, "Do you have a place to stay? I'm afraid all your friend has to offer you is a shed behind the livery stable."

"Oh, I passed a hotel on my way here. I'll book a room. Maybe Jake here would like to come with me, and catch up over a beer or two."

Jake paused as they made it to the street. "Do you still drink any donkey piss someone calls beer? Because it'll be easier to sit and talk in one of the less popular saloons."

Rich chuckled. "I'll try anything, and if it's too foul I'll numb my tongue with some whiskey."

Jake led them to the saloon farthest off the beaten track, such as there was one, and pointed Rich toward the table in the darkest corner. "I'll get the first round." He got two beers and a whiskey and took them back to the table.

Rich took a swallow of the beer and shrugged. "Not donkey piss. Horse, at least. So what's the story with you and that luscious lady?"

Jake took a gulp of his beer, wishing it was the whiskey. What the hell should he say? Not much. "There's a story, but it's not altogether mine to tell, so I won't."

Rich gasped dramatically. "Jake Flint, gentleman! Who'd've thought it?"

"Up yours, mate." Jake toasted Rich with his beer and took another swig, hoping it would loosen his tongue enough that he could ask Rich what he needed to know. But Rich got there first, saying in an offhand way, "Haven't heard from Ethan."

Jake waited until his shoulders relaxed enough that he could shrug. "Could be plenty of reasons. Thanks for trying." One more swallow of beer. "So, kids. Tell me about 'em."

"Two boys and a girl. Here's to 'em!" Rich took a hearty drink, thunked down the beer, and licked his lips. "Girl's the youngest, so when the boys aren't pummeling each other or daring each other into mischief, they're either teasing her or taking on anyone else that gives her trouble. And wouldn't you know it, she's the one who always wants to hear my sailing tales and war stories. God knows where and what she'll end up." He looked at his mug of beer without touching it. "Oldest boy's named Jake."

Jake's mug fell out of his hand, hitting the table at an angle. Rich grabbed it and kept it from falling over, then pushed the glass of whiskey over to Jake. Jake pulled it toward him, his hand shaking, and drank a third of it. Rich sat back and grinned.

Seemed like Decembers were colder than they'd been ten or fifteen years ago. The air was almost enough to sober him up as they left the saloon. Should he go back to Mamie's or head to his shed? Mamie would still be awake, though she might be busy dealing with customers and what all . . . .

"If you need to stay ahead of trouble, I've got an extra train ticket." Rich had pulled out and lit his pipe while Jake was woolgathering. The bowl must be warming his hand better than Jake's pockets were doing for his own. "You'd be my cousin, fresh off a cattle drive and ready for something more like civilization. Between us, we could scare up some work for you."

He should've known Rich would have more in mind than just checking up on him and then leaving him to whatever was chasing him. And if he'd known, he might have something to say.

"You never asked why my brother would be hunting me down."

Rich blew a puff of smoke at him. "Let's walk to the hotel while you figure out your confession. Not that it bothers me not knowing."

He'd been thinking he drank too much tonight, but not enough for this. He listened to their footsteps on the street and the soft soughing of the wind, and to Rich's easy silence, until they'd made it about halfway to the hotel. Finally he said, "I did him wrong and left town without undoing it. I betrayed him, and he'd done nothing to deserve it except look like growing into a better man than I'll ever be."

Rich took that in with a nod and more silence. The hotel was up ahead when he said, loudly enough that Jake looked around for anyone in earshot, "Can't say what you've made of the years since we parted, but by the time that happened, seemed to me you were shaping up just fine."

They'd reached the hotel. Rich put his pipe away and said simply, "Well?"

All Jake could think to do was stall. "How long're you in town for?"

Rich smirked. "Well, I don't know as I can stay long enough for you to make up your mind, if you're determined to dither. But I can hang around for a day or two. Maybe give Madam Mamie some custom. Any girls there you'd recommend?"

Would Rich appreciate the subtle, not to say sullen, charms of Summer Dawn? He couldn't remember much about Rich's tastes, back when they'd gone whoring together. "From what I've seen, you could hardly go wrong there."

And that was long enough to keep Rich lingering on the hotel doorstep. Or waiting for his answer. He said slowly, "I'm grateful for the offer. And as you can tell, I'm not sure what to do next. But I'm thinking I'll decline."

Rich shook his head sagely. "It's the woman, isn't it."

Jake glared at him. "It's getting tired, finally, of looking over my shoulder. It's standing up to the slimy son of a bitch who's been having fun threatening me. It's knowing that whatever may be coming for me, I've got it coming. I don't need any other reasons."

Rich just laughed and slapped him on the shoulder. "Have it your way, youngster. I'm for a nice warm bed. I hope you find your way to the same. G'night!" And he sauntered inside.

Jake went down the hotel's front steps and stood on the street for a good minute, in spite of the chilling wind. Finally he muttered, "It's the woman, right enough." Then he walked as fast as he could back to Mamie's. Maybe she'd have time for him, and a place in the warm bed Rich had mentioned. He might be cold again soon enough, but tonight, he could be warm.

Chapter 20

MAMIE found Jake's friend Rich an entertaining enough fellow, and an appreciative customer. He'd made Nancy extra cheerful for hours after their time together, and Mamie thought she'd actually caught a hint of a smile on Summer Dawn's face when she followed him downstairs. But as for what effect he had on Jake, and just what they'd been up to and talking about, that was harder to tell. That first night, when the two of them went out drinking, Jake came by just before closing time, three sheets to the wind, and she might've told him to go on back to his shed for the night — if he hadn't looked so bewildered, almost pitiful. And for the rest of Rich's visit, Jake bounced around between extra talkative one minute and extra quiet the next. She might've been glad to see Rich go, two days after he came, if Jake hadn't come back from the train station with his jaw set hard and his face pale enough to make his beard stand out stark against it.

Jake was almost always an energetic sort of lover, but lately he'd been more frantic about it, as if he knew it might be the last time ever. And while she could lose herself in the moment, she didn't care for what it meant. That night had if anything been more troubling. When they got to her room, she'd gone right on inside and then realized Jake hadn't followed her. He was standing just inside the closed door, leaning against it, gazing at her and around the room and at her again as if he was drinking it all in, and leaving soon for a trek across the driest of deserts. She went back for him, taking his hand and pulling him toward her. He came readily enough, but instead of kissing her, he ran his hand slowly from the crown of her head down to her shoulder and stopped there. She was starting to feel a little snappish, but she stayed calm and asked quietly, "What would you say you're doing?"

He just barely smiled. "I'm looking at you, and feeling the warm and soft of you, and breathing the scent of you. I don't want ever to forget."

Oh, *that* didn't sound ominous. But she wasn't going to join him in this melancholy vein, even if the look of him, and the low quiet voice he spoke in, made her want to cry for the first time since she'd been sickening with the mumps. Instead, she reached up to tilt his head down and gave him a kiss she knew would stir him up. Though it took a minute, long enough for her to fear she'd fail.

If the marshal hadn't left town, she might have been able to get him talking about just how likely it was for the law to come for Jake after all this time, if the man even knew. She and the sheriff weren't close enough to friendly for her to go asking him. That left her with only one thing she could think of doing. And Jake might be way beyond riled at her for doing it, but she didn't plan to tell him. At least not anytime soon.

As Jake finally lay sleeping, Mamie ran over her best girls in her mind. She'd come to count on Trudi for holding the fort, and Bessie and Lucette for running errands. But who was best at keeping a secret?

Next morning, she lay in wait for Summer Dawn to come out of her bedroom, late as usual, and stopped her on her way downstairs. "Come see me after you have something to eat. I've a job for you, an easy one, and I'll pay you to do it, if you swear on whatever spirits you call on for favors that you won't tell a soul."

Then she went into her office, closed the door, and got to work. She had to hope the name and town would be enough to get the letter where it should go.

By the time Summer Dawn slipped in without knocking, Mamie had the letter ready for her to take to the store.

Dear Mr. Flint,

I am a friend of your brother Jacob. I've known him longer than most folks have, though of course not as long as you. And I know you've reason to condemn him and harden your heart against him, because he's told me so. He carries his shame around with him, and it's been a heavy cross to bear, the more so as he knows he deserves the pain of bearing it.

She hadn't written that Jake had had good in him all along, because she daren't let on that she'd known him back in Deliverance, let alone that he'd done her as much good as he could, and as anyone had in her whole life up to then.

He's expecting the worst of having made his whereabouts known to you. He probably thinks of you as not just the man he wronged, but as God's instrument of serving justice on him. But from everything he says, you're a godly man, and you know about love and forgiveness without my trying to preach it to you. And he's paid for his crime, every day he tears at himself about it and calls himself the worst sort of sinner.

I don't believe, like he more than half believes, that you've set the law on him. But if you have, or you're inclined to, I'm asking you to think again, and let it be. Or at least give him a chance to make things right, as much as he can after what he did to you and whatever that changed in your life. I know he'd do anything a man could do, and not spare himself in the doing, if you can keep from telling him all the while what little you think of him and how hell is gaping to take him in.

She should maybe have scratched that last part out and started over, but it'd be like lying to let him think Jake would just roll over and take that sort of treatment, even if he thought he deserved it. She couldn't have — well, cared about Jake the way she was coming to, if he'd had that degree of meekness to him.

Please don't tell him I wrote to you. He knows nothing of it, let alone asking me to take his part, and he'd take it as meddling or pity or both.

Yours very sincerely, one who wishes you and your brother well

She folded up the letter, addressed it to Ethan Flint in Deliverance, Indiana, and handed it to Summer Dawn. "Take this to be mailed. And then go to the telegraph office and send a telegram to the same place, saying, 'Letter coming from friend of Jacob, please read.' Here's the money for the telegram. And here's for your trouble." As Summer Dawn reached for it, she drew her hand back and said, "Your oath first."

She could only hope that the Great Spirit and Summer Dawn's ancestors, or at least one of those, meant something Summer Dawn actually cared about. She handed over the money and followed Summer Dawn downstairs. She'd done what she could, and now it was time to mind her actual business until her efforts did or didn't bear fruit.

* * * * *

Summer Dawn had been giving Jake odd looks the last

couple of days — smug, he'd have to call them. It wasn't likely she'd know about any lawman on his way, unless the mayor or some councilman had been informed and had confided in her in a moment of passion. Which didn't strike him as likely, given how silent and standoffish she tended to be, but maybe such a man had thought to make himself seem important to overcome her resistance.

He was drinking his morning coffee, getting ready to brave the cold and head to the stable, when Mamie came in, holding a letter — and, it looked like, holding her breath as well, until she let it out and said, "This just came for you." She laid it down on the kitchen table, and he stared at the table and the letter on it, the white of the envelope standing out against the whorls of the grain.

Mamie had made it as far as the door and was hovering there, probably wondering whether he'd want his privacy to read it. And maybe he did. But his hand set to shaking, and he couldn't wait, nor do anything but pick up the letter, open it, and read.

Brother,

I received your second telegram without having seen the first. When I received the latest one, I made inquiries and discovered that our mother had come upon the first before I knew of it, and had hidden it away. This may not have been a purposeful, let alone a malicious, act, as she has become childish in the last year and tends to make off with and hide things.

You cannot know how it gladdened my heart to hear from you.

Jake stared at the letter and let it fall to the table. Mamie came closer. "What is it? If it's trouble, tell me and I'll do whatever I can to keep it from you." She sounded not so much worried as fierce. He half looked to her to grab a knife and bar the door.

Jake just shook his head and picked the letter up again.

You may have wondered why I have been seeking you, as I assume you know, unless your contacting me was a coincidence arranged by Heaven. If you harbor any fear that I seek revenge, whether or not it wears the garments of justice, for what you took from me in our youth, you may put such concerns aside.

Jake sank back against the chair and closed his eyes. He should be feeling relief, or even joy, at a reprieve for which he had not presumed to hope. He should be feeling something other than this roiling confusion. Maybe if he kept reading, this turmoil would give way to something he could comprehend.

It is not merely Christian principle that inspires me to say so. Nor is it simply the practical difficulties, the significant investment of time and attention and the resultant distraction from my principal duties, that any attempt to pursue you or set in motion some legal action would entail. Rather, it is my grateful recognition that through the grace of God and the kindness of my friends and neighbors, the wrongful act you committed, and which I am sure we both acknowledge as such, has led to results I must call blessed.

Ethan must have abandoned his own dreams, then, and embraced the family legacy of preaching. Whatever he truly felt must be long buried under the sanctimonious sentiments he dinned into his flock. Jake started to crumple the letter in his hand, only to find Mamie's hand thrust out to protect the letter and pull it out of reach. He bristled and glared at her, but she gazed at him with a calm understanding that put him to shame. He looked away and took the letter back, setting it on the table and bending over it.

You may wonder at my words, and perhaps assume that I was compelled to abandon the thought of studying any subject beyond theology. Be not deceived, for upon hearing of what had befallen me, not only our father and grandfather but the congregation, and even those in Deliverance who worshiped elsewhere, rallied around me in the most heartening fashion. Our father could not countenance soliciting funds in church for one of his own, even if he could have put aside the shame of what had happened —

Jake ground his teeth, but forced himself to keep reading.

— but by donations in divers other places, and even fundraising events such as raffles, they not only replaced the funds that departed with you, but increased them twofold. And this effort by so many not only reconciled our family fully to my ambitions, but made my pursuit of those ambitions, and my eventual success, an ongoing project in which the community came to take pride. I attended Oberlin College only a year after I had initially planned to do so. Supplemented by the scholarship I was able to win in my second year, I was able to graduate with honors, and after an appropriate apprenticeship, become a professor at that very institution.

He thrust the letter away again, but only to keep tears from blotting the paper and making it illegible. When he had more or less got hold of himself, he pulled it toward him and read on.

It was not until the college granted me leave, to help care for our mother and to find more permanent assistance for our father in that task, that I allowed my thoughts to dwell more frequently on our family affairs, thoughts which in turn led me to begin my search for you. I did so in the hope that I could tell you how I have fared, and that should you ever desire to return to Deliverance, or to travel to Oberlin, Ohio where the college is located, I would welcome you as a beloved brother.

There was a word scratched out just after "beloved"

that looked like "prodigal."

As I have noted, our father still lives, and cares for our mother patiently and tenderly, though I have now hired a nurse to join in her care, to begin next month. I have asked him whether he would receive you in the family home, and he answered that if you came with a repentant heart, he would welcome you and bless the day. I know this may be a difficult scene to contemplate.

At least Ethan knew him that well.

But only you know whether such is indeed your feeling as you ponder the past. For your sake, I pray it is, for I know that anger, and the fear and shame it often hides, make poor companions, and I wish you far better.

For my part, I also look at the past with regret for mistakes made and opportunities missed. As you left childhood behind, I knew from having done so myself that it can be a time when new questions arise and old certainties become less clear. Yet, busy with my own plans and concerns, I paid little attention to what yours might be. And on that day when you displayed such courage in protecting an unfortunate girl, I neither stood at your side nor protected you.

He could hardly remember, it had been so long. Had he expected Ethan to speak up for Mamie, or to save Jake from the violence of those who resented his attempt to interrupt their bullying? Or had he already given up on anyone taking his part, even the brother he had loved, and who had — as Jake had tried so hard to forget — loved him in return?

The next lines made him turn toward Mamie, who deserved to read them. But she was nowhere to be seen. At some point she must have crept away, leaving him to face the letter's further revelations without a witness. He took the letter and went in search, checking first the small parlor and finding only Bessie and Sophie, sitting close together and playing some sort of childish clapping game, complete with a rhyme about ponies and horses. He smiled at the sight — and suddenly realized that he was late for work, and might be about to lose the stable job just as he had the chance to keep it. He looked at the letter and then toward the stairs, where Mamie was most likely waiting in her office. Moving forward to draw their attention, he said, "Ladies, I wonder whether I might ask one of you a great favor."

They looked at him, Sophie with eyes wide and mouth rounded in surprise, Bessie with more suspicious scrutiny.

"I find I am unexpectedly delayed and will be late getting to the livery stable. I know that Mamie has some way of sending messages, but know nothing of the details. Can you instruct me?"

Sophie giggled, maybe at the idea of teaching someone something. Bessie nudged her with an elbow and said, "Cook's little nephews live in the street behind our yard. If she has time to go fetch one, they'll run messages for a penny."

Jake fumbled in his waistcoat pocket with his free hand and pulled out the penny. "If you will, please ask Cook to do so, and to have one of the boys tell Yates at the livery stable that I'll be there soon, and may be able to bring news he'll want to hear. If it can't be done for any reason, please find me and tell me so. I'll be up in Mamie's office, I expect."

Bessie mouthed the words over twice, then reached out and neatly snatched the coin. "Up you go, then."

Thanking both ladies profusely, he ran up the steps and then slowed down as he approached the office. The door was ajar, and he tapped on it. "It's Jake."

Mamie was at the door so fast she must have been standing, or pacing, rather than sitting at her desk. He looked down at her pale face and reached out to stroke the worry away. "It's well. No one's coming for me. He says he forgives me, even. Things have gone well for him in spite of what I did. And there's more. You're free to read all of it, if you've a mind, but there's one bit in particular I want to show you."

Mamie leaned her cheek into his free hand, and then took that hand and pulled him close, giving him a kiss that would have distracted him from any lesser mission. When he could pull himself away, he held out the letter. "Read here, and here."

Mamie leaned against the front of her desk, reached out, and then pulled her hand back. "Would you read it to me? It'll seem more real, somehow."

Did he still sound anything like Ethan? He might have the chance, now, to find out. Jake drew a deep breath and read, his voice hoarse and low.

And on that day when you displayed such courage in protecting an unfortunate girl, I neither stood at your side nor protected you.

For that sin of omission, that failure of the charity and courage our Lord demands of his followers, and my failure as a brother that came before your own, I ask your forgiveness, as I have long since forgiven you. And if the girl has survived unto this day, and Divine Providence should allow you to meet her again, I ask that you convey to her my prayer that she will forgive me as well.

He looked up at Mamie, to see her looking off into the distance, or into nothing. Apparently feeling his gaze on her, she said almost too quietly for him to hear, "I never thought of it. Of him helping me. I didn't expect it of anyone — except I thought you might. And you did."

He pulled her into a hug that for once was more about comfort, and comforting her, than anything else — though the softness of her breasts against his chest got his mind turning elsewhere quick enough. But he gave her one more squeeze and pulled back. "I've got to get to work. Read the rest of the letter if you'd like. And . . . we have to decide, now, or near enough. Now that I can stay in town if I want, and if you want me to. Are you really minded to buy the stable?"

Mamie had been blinking back tears, but the question transformed her. Her eyes narrowed, and she tapped her fingers together like a gambler with a winning hand and not enough craft to hide it. "Depends. You find out what he's wanting for it. And then tell him nicely that he's plumb crazy, and no one would pay that much. We'll see."

Jake made for the livery stable as quick as he could without actually running and drawing attention. As he got close, he could hear a confusion of voices — Yates's, and a high voice that might be the boy messenger, and a lower, smooth one that set his teeth on edge. Quinn was standing close to Yates, closer than Jake would've wanted any man standing, and smirking at him as a half-grown boy tried to get in between, protesting, "But he's coming, real soon! And he'll have some sort of news to tell you, like I said!"

The lawyer gripped the boy's shoulder and turned him around, the boy stumbling to keep from falling. "On your way, sonny. I can tell you the news, right enough. Mr. Jacob Flint is riding for the border, as quick as that scrubby horse can carry him, and he won't be back."

Jake laughed outright. The damn fool couldn't even tell one horse from another. Jake strode up and around him, fishing a carrot out of his pocket and feeding it to Wrangler. The boy looked at him agog, and the two men did pretty much the same thing as he said, grinning, "Hate to disappoint you, mister, but I'm still here. And I'll be staying. And Mr. Yates and I have some business to discuss, so I hope you'll excuse us." He gave the boy another penny. "You run on and tell Madam Mamie I'll see her for supper."

Chapter 21

MAMIE didn't have to tell Jake about her letter to Ethan. It might not have made any difference. And that last bit in Ethan's letter was probably a coincidence, not a message back to her. She hadn't somehow given him clues that let him guess who she might be.

Right, and Santa might come down her chimney and say she'd been a good girl this year. She snorted, drawing Cook's curious attention. That fantasy got even less likely if she kept secrets from her man. She stood up and stiffened her spine as Jake came clattering down the stairs. The noise made her smile — she could imagine him making that kind of racket as a youngster, not that even his house had had a stair like what she had here. Strange how things could turn around.

She let him drink most of his coffee and gobble half his eggs before sitting down and saying, "I need to tell you something."

"Thought you might, the way you were wearing a path in the floor. Expecting me to mind it, whatever it is?"

He sounded mild enough. Best seize the moment. "I might've written your brother, when you were fretting and looking over your shoulder."

He took another sip of coffee. "You might've."

Sterner, now. She'd never known his pa or grandpa well, but she'd bet that look came straight from them. "I did. Your worry got me to worrying." Not enough. She had better confess what came harder. "I didn't want to lose you."

The frown faded into a slow smile, and he reached across to cover her hand with his. "And I didn't want to lose either of us. So I'm glad you did what you could. For all either of us knows, it might've tipped the balance."

She shook her head. "I think he'd made up his mind long since, before he ever tried to find you." She bit her tongue not to go on and say she'd figured as much right along. This wasn't the time, and besides, she hadn't been too sure to fret.

Jake had nothing else to say, it seemed, and she let him finish eating before she asked as she took his plate, "Will you write him back?"

He stood up, patted his belly, and buttoned up his waistcoat. "I'd better, hadn't I. Wouldn't want him changing his mind." And then, more reluctantly, "Guess I owe him that much. And more, but God or the devil knows when I'll be able to pay it."

She came close enough to frame his face in her hands and kiss him before saying, "Let's see how our investment goes. There's time, now."

He kissed her back, started to leave, and stopped in the doorway. "Speaking of which, I'd best get that letter written first thing when I get back, or I'll put it off."

She came up behind him and hugged him round the waist. "I'll keep my hands off you, then, when you show up this evening." She kissed the back of his neck. "So write fast."

* * * * *

It turned out to help, having a reason not to take too long about it. Without Mamie's warm arms — not to mention the rest of her — waiting for him, he'd likely have dithered and crossed out and started over until halfway to dawn. But when he bounded up the stairs to find her, he'd finished what he figured he'd send.

Brother,

I've a deal to thank you for. For not sending the law after me, back then — I'm guessing you could've talked Pa into it, or maybe had to talk him out of it. For not doing it since. For forgiving me, when I didn't deserve it, for all you were spared the worst consequences of what I did. For apologizing, even though you did nothing different than all the others who did no better.

I don't know as I'll ever come back to Deliverance, or even write to Pa, though I'm thinking about that. You can tell him, though, that I do repent of what I did, and have all these years, and flayed myself over it worse than he'd have done, if not with a scourge anyone could see. As for Ma, I'd be grateful if you could tell her, in any moment where she might be able to understand it at all, that I love her and that I'm sorry about leaving the way I did.

You didn't say whether you've got yourself a wife and children to glad your heart. I hope so. You deserve that happiness more than most. If you've a mind to tell me about them, I'd like to hear.

Jacob

Lying in bed after, Mamie already asleep and not quite snoring, he thought of what he hadn't said, and wouldn't say, except maybe to Mamie, or to Joshua Gibbs if he came to know him better. Namely, that sometime since he first rode into Cowbird Creek and found Mamie again, and then finally knew himself out of danger from the law, he'd stopped being so angry at God. It never made much sense in the first place, to clutch tight to that anger against a being he told himself he didn't even believe in. But he'd managed it, and now, somehow, he'd let it go, and only then seen how it was burning at the heart of him.

He laughed a little and then stopped, not wanting to wake the woman at his side. Maybe he could get past believing for good and all, now he'd no need to fight that battle. Or maybe some other sort of believing would creep in while he wasn't looking for it. He could wait and see.

* * * * *

Mamie should be walking on air. Her lover was safe from the law, and had put a spoke in Quinn's wheel for good measure. She was likely to have a new investment, once Yates stopped dithering, and Jake would be a good man to run it. So why was she feeling so unsettled, and why had she snapped at Jake over breakfast, and been short with her girls when they'd been more or less well behaved lately?

Maybe it was knowing Jake was staying, backwards as that sounded. After all, she'd never in her life — which had featured fewer lovers than anyone would guess — had a man stick around instead of just passing through now and then. Whether he lived out by the stable or roomed at her place full time — and what would customers make of that? — they'd be tripping over each other in a way she wasn't used to. And what if they got tired of each other, and Mamie still Jake's silent partner in the stable and having to deal with him whenever something came up?

Who would get tired of the other first?

Would Jake want to *marry* her? If it turned out a trap, how could she get free of it?

Could a married woman run a business like hers? Was Jake trying to get her to close Madam Mamie's? Where did he think her girls would go if she did? How dare he! . . .

Mamie forced herself to unclench her fists, take a deep breath, and look in the mirror — literally and figuratively. Jake had said nothing about closing the business, or about marrying her for that matter. Why was she blaming him for what he hadn't done?

Hadn't done yet.

But if she gave up her business, and then things didn't work out, she could end up on the street with nothing — especially if he left town and there was no one to run the stable, or run it properly. Could she end up where she'd been so many years ago, except too old to even keep herself alive that way?

She needed to talk to someone. To a friend, a woman, who'd understand. Except the closest to that would be one of her girls, and she couldn't tell them any of this. She couldn't trust a one of them to keep it to herself, not if they were worried about the place going under.

That left one woman she could trust who was still in town.

She could see from the window that this was one of Joshua's days in his office, which meant Clara was most likely there too. Would it compromise Joshua to have the town's notorious madam walk in? No, not with so many people knowing he looked after her girls. She could be coming to fetch him between regular visits because one of them had got sick or hurt. She'd done that a time or three.

Joshua looked up from a list he was making and smiled, until he got a good look at her. "Are you unwell? I wouldn't expect a relapse, unless there are things I don't know about mumps and should know. Is your digestion troubling you?"

Clara came out of the back room, a box of some sort of supplies in her hands, and put it down next to Joshua. "Put these on your order list — we're running low. Mamie, are you here on your own behalf or because one of your ladies needs our assistance?"

Now that she was here, Mamie didn't know where to start, or how. And she had the ridiculous and annoying desire to burst into tears. Clara studied her face and said, "Mamie and I are going for a walk. I'm not sure when I'll be back." Joshua nodded, looking stuck somewhere between puzzled and concerned as Clara grabbed her coat and whisked them out the door.

Clara steered them toward the creek, notwithstanding the wind that grew stronger as they left the shelter of buildings behind. When Mamie had spilled out, in fits and starts, what a shrew she'd been lately and what worries had been crowding in on her, Clara slowed them down and said, "Remember you can send him on his way. Yates hasn't agreed to your terms yet, has he? Jake can simply tell him he's changed his mind. You can go on as you did before Jake burst through your door and manhandled that drunken cowboy."

Of course. Clara was absolutely right. If not for the fact that just hearing the word "manhandled" had Mamie thinking of how Jake had looked wrestling that cowboy. And how he looked other times, and using those muscles in other ways. But Mamie had put carnal needs aside before Jake showed up, except for Quinn's visits. She could do so again, whether or not she found someone else to bed from time to time.

The occasional lay had been enough before, or if it hadn't, she'd told herself it had, and not looked deeper. The thought that came to her made her laugh out loud. "It's too late, Clara. I've gone and et of the tree of the knowledge of — well, not good and evil, which I finished up and swallowed long since, but something about as hard to forget."

Clara took her hand. "Something like love?"

That was Clara, always going to the heart of the matter, so to speak. Mamie took a deep breath and said, her voice less steady than she'd have liked, "I haven't talked about love — well, ever. Not in my life."

They'd slowed all the way to a stop. "That's a sad statement, and a sad state of affairs. Whatever you do about Jake, I hope it changes. What would it take for you to decide whether you love him, or could?"

Mamie pulled her hand away. "I don't even know if he feels something special for me!"

Clara's look was a challenge. "If he loves you. That's what we're discussing. So that's two things you have to figure out." She turned back toward town and started walking again, leaving Mamie to stand there with her jaw hanging open and then scurry to catch up with her.

They were approaching the town square when Mamie sighed and said, "I don't know how to do that. But one way or another, I guess I've got to talk to Jake."

* * * * *

"And you're telling me you can pay what you're offering." Yates spat out his latest chewed-up piece of straw. "And just how does a drifter who needed a job shoveling horse droppings suddenly end up able to buy me out, even at that pitiful price?"

Jake finished inspecting a mare's hoof and straightened up, stretching his back. "I heard from my family after being out of touch for quite a spell. My brother's done right well for himself, and he's anxious to be a good brother to me." All true, if not to the purpose.

A gust of wind pushed its way into the stable, startling the horse nearest the crack it came from. Yates pulled his coat tighter around him. He chewed his lip for a long minute and then said abruptly, "All right, then. If you get the money and have it here within the week, it's a deal."

As far as Jake knew, it should take considerably less time than that. He stuck out his hand, and they shook on it.

He came whistling through the door only twenty minutes after he'd finished up at the stable. He probably should have waited to do his celebrating with Mamie, but she'd been acting peculiar lately, and he never knew quite what to expect when he showed up. A short whiskey had settled his nerves.

He didn't see Mamie in the front hall, or the parlor, or the small parlor. He finally tracked her down in the kitchen. She had apparently banished the cook and was sitting at the table. The food smells were faint enough that he gave up on getting any supper in the near future. He told his grumbling stomach to lie quiet and said, "Deal's done, if you're still game. All it takes now is paying him."

Mamie just looked at him, long enough to set him to shifting from foot to foot. Finally she said simply, "What now?"

He pulled out the chair across from her and sat down. Now or never. He reached for her hand, mouth dry, and answered her. "If I was to offer myself as a husband, would you have me?"

She looked him up and down and then stood up, her chair squeaking on the floor. "Wait here."

She left the room, and left him wondering what in tarnation she was going out to get or to do. The girls, to vote on whether to keep him around? Horn, to shove Jake out the door, or try?

She came back in with her hands full, pushing the door wider open with her bountiful behind, carrying two glasses of beer. She put one down in front of him and said, "You sound thirsty." She didn't sit back down right away, just stood holding the other glass. He took a gulp of his, saw she still wasn't drinking, and put the glass down with a thump that sloshed what remained.

Mamie studied him some more and said, the words coming slow, "We could take turns saying what might go wrong with that notion, and not run out for quite a while."

Jake made himself look at her, in spite of fearing what he might read in her face. "So we could. Is that what you want?"

Another pause, and his stomach cramped from what surely wasn't hunger. Then, finally, she smiled, impish, a smile that yanked him back hundreds of miles and too many years — to a little girl not so little any more, but still teasing the life out of him. He could just about see that girl with her hands on her hips, smirking as she said "Gotcha!" What the real Mamie, the grown and womanly Mamie, said instead was, "I reckon I'd rather take what's offered."

He jumped out of his chair and half ran around the table. Taking the glass out of her hand, he put it on the table and pulled her to him, holding on so tight he could feel every breath she took pressing against him. He wasn't sure who kissed who first, but it took a while before she could say, eyebrow arched, "That is, so long as you weren't expecting I'll promise to obey you, let alone actually do it."

Jake let out a belly laugh, shaking both of them.

"Darling Mamie, I wouldn't ask you to marry such a fool."

They stood together until Cook came back in, beaming. "All right, ma'am, now can I get to work on feeding this hungry fellow?"

Mamie gave Jake one more kiss and let go of him, saying to Cook, "You do that. And I won't let him talk 'til he's done eating, or he'll never get fed. We've a deal of talking to do yet. And time to do it."

* * * * *

As things went, and she should've known it, they didn't do much talking that night. The next day was Sunday, though, and until Yates actually up and left town, he was giving Jake Sundays off. They slept together in her bed, and slept late enough that Mamie started to get antsy — she wasn't a slug-a-bed by nature. She poked him, and when that got him to crack one eye open, she tickled him until he pounced on her and held her against the bed. Which delayed them getting up a while longer. As they lay panting, after, she drew a line around his face with a finger and said, "Still here?"

He grabbed the finger and kissed it. "Still here. Better get used to it."

They finally had themselves a late and lazy breakfast, and then went for another walk along the creek, though by now it was too cold for climbing trees. They'd been walking a while, neither one saying more than a word here and there, when Mamie started things up by saying, "I've been asking myself lately what it would take for me to love a man. Seeing as what I used to think turned out to be wide of the mark."

Jake hadn't been talking, but he somehow went quieter. She put her arm through his, as she hadn't on the way out of town. "And I decided that since I hadn't done so good a job before you waltzed back into my life —"

He snorted. "You mean stumbled back in, with my hands full of cowboy."

"Whatever, and hush now. I decided I'd better just make myself a list of why I was on the way to loving you."

Jake stopped in his tracks and pulled her close without bothering to look whether anyone was watching. When he stopped kissing her long enough to breathe, she tugged him back to walking and got herself back to talking. "I figure it'll take me a while, with you hanging around, to know what all should go on the list, but I've made a start. You caring what happened to me back when, and still doing it. And you jumping in to help me and my girls, before you even knew whose place it was. And treating my girls right since then."

Jake did something halfway between shrugging and wriggling.

"You not worrying much about what folks in town thought of you being seen with me. You thinking about more than just your next meal and your next woman and your next dollar. You smelling good, even when you come in from the stable and your clothes don't."

He pinched his shirt to lift the fabric up and sniffed at it, then offered it to her, smirking. "Smells all right today. Enjoy it while you can."

She shook her head at him, but bent to smell anyway. "You being strong enough to deal with folks that want to push you around, or do the same to me. You having lived through and done all sorts of things, so you and I both know you can." She pursed her lips and counted on her fingers. "I'm bound to be forgetting some, but that'll do for a start."

Jake grabbed her hand as it swung at her side and brought it up to kiss it. He kept holding it after, but didn't speak right away. She was starting to expect disappointment when he finally said, "My turn, I reckon. And I'll start with where you ended — how strong you are, and were from a girl. I couldn't — couldn't love a woman who didn't stand up for herself, and for those she cared about. Especially as some find other ways to get what they want, less honest ones. Sneakier ones."

Mamie thought back to how the marshal came to leave town and put in, "That they do."

"Next, I'd list the way you look after your ladies. That's two things at once — that you're smart enough to know they'll stay longer and work better if you treat them right, and that you'd do it anyway. Because as far as I can tell, knowing you from a girl and knowing you still, you don't have much mean in you."

Mamie gripped his hand harder. "Whereas you have just enough. Not too much, like that lawyer I made do with before, nor too little, like the doc, glad as I am to have him for a friend."

"Moving on, but not too far, is the way you've helped me and stood up for me — investing in the stable, when you'd no need to, and writing to Ethan. Even though you knew I might be angry about it, and how that might've changed things, or so you may have thought."

They'd about run out of creek to walk along without having to deal with farms and fences. They were about to turn around when the sun came out behind the clouds, hitting the water just right to make it sparkle. She had to stand still and just watch it. It only took a moment for Jake to see why, and watch it with her. Beauty looked like another thing they got to share.

When a cloud came over, they turned around, still holding hands. Jake picked up where he'd left off. "And there's how good you feel to squeeze. Can't help but like that plenty. And how much better you smell than I do, whether it's first thing in the morning or at night after I've got you all sweaty."

She used her free hand to pat his backside. "That's another one for my list, that you've got such a peculiar sense of smell." She let him snicker a while before she said, "That's enough of making lists. If we're really planning on marrying, what then? There'll be plenty of gossip, and it could keep some folks away from the stable."

"Maybe a few. But one thing I know is horse people. They'll care a lot more about their horses staying healthy and contented than about how the two-footed critters looking after them live their lives. I'm wondering about your own business, your true one, a little more. Will it bother customers any, a married madam?"

"I'll allow that troubled me at first. But I thought better of it. I haven't noticed much of a crowd coming to my place just to swoon over me. It's been a long time since a customer even flirted with me more'n just to be pleasant — and I can tell the difference, right enough. Any as it'd bother, the idea of a parlor house would bother them more. So I don't see it lowering the chances of the preacher dropping by. I have been thinking, though, about whether you'd feel any less of a man if you were to move in, seeing as I run the place and people'll keep knowing as much."

He pulled her to a stop again, just before the lane turned into a street. "Men swooning down to the floor or no, I'd say I come off as more of a man than most if I can keep a madam satisfied. And some folks'll think I've got my pick of your other ladies, though I'll give a good strong answer to any as says it."

He picked her up, swung her around, and planted her

back down. "And here's my answer now, for you, in case you were wondering."

But after that next kiss, she had little mind left for wondering or worry.

Epilogue

MAMIE and Jake sat close together on the love seat in the small parlor, Jake fresh from his bath. It was the time of evening when Trudi and Lucette minded the place for a while, to save the couple from having to wait until the wee hours for some time together. Mamie had a letter in her hands, and another waiting on the table. Jake had his arm around her shoulders and his head back, not quite napping while she read.

My darling Mamie, whose letter made me so happy, you can't imagine —

Thank you for sending me so many details about the wedding, you knew I'd want to picture every minute. I'd have loved to be there and give both of you the biggest hug, but it is nice to be down south for the winter, like a bluebird or a goose, a big migrating bird I'd make!

You two take care of each other until spring, we plan to come north again and see the new leaves and the flowers and the apple and pear blossoms. And of course the two of you, that matters more than all the rest of it! There, I just kissed the letter, at least I can do that without waiting months. Keep well, and Jedidiah sends his congratulations and best wishes to you both, drink a toast from him and another from me!

Mamie gave the letter her own kiss and turned to see whether Jake was still awake, though she figured she'd have heard snoring otherwise. He read her face, grinned, and said, "From Freida?"

She kissed his cheek this time and handed him the letter. "Here, you can read it while I start the other one." She'd known what to expect from Freida, but Jenny wrote so seldom that hers was harder to predict.

Thank you so much for writing us and telling us everything that's happened. We was lucky to get the letter, seeing as you had to guess where to send it, and it was clever of you to guess we might be visiting that leather worker Jedidiah knows some time or other.

I'm so glad for you, and for Mr. Jake of course! As good as marrying Tom has turned out, I'm thinking awfully well of the notion these days, and you lived without for longer than I did.

Mamie chuckled. "Good of her not to say just how much longer." Jake made a noise something like a grunt; she held up the letter to explain, and went back to reading it.

It's good you were able to get hold of the preacher who married us, and got to see him again. I hope he's keeping well. And getting married in the parlor must've been more comfortable and cheerful than outdoors over Amanda Jane's grave like we did, not that I wish we'd done any different.

I'd never have thought Summer Dawn would take the trouble to make a beaded headband for Mr. Jake. I bet he looks real fine in it, for all he didn't wear it at the wedding.

Mamie had bit her tongue about that, but if she wasn't too old and sensible to be jealous of one of her own girls, she could at least act that way.

I got something to say that I hope you don't take as me presuming. It's just that your marrying Mr. Jake, from all you've said about him, makes me feel a little like I've got a step-pa, and a good one, so much better a man than my own pa was.

Mamie put the letter down on the table, her lip quivering. Jake must've felt or heard something, because he turned his head and then pulled her over close against him, stroking her hair. In a minute or so, she got ahold of herself enough to say, "It's just that . . . I did let myself think of Jenny a little different from the others, though I never told her so. Almost like . . . and it turns out she felt like . . . It's almost like having . . . ."

For a miracle, Jake seemed to know what she was trying to say. He put a gentle hand on her cheek and said, "That's good to hear. I hope I get to meet her someday."

Mamie leaned back against his chest and picked up the letter, to read what little was left.

Tom wants to see his folks again, and I owe it to him to have the courage to come back for that. It'd be in the spring, most likely, for easier traveling. I don't think we'd come all the way into town, at least I won't, but you and Mr. Jake could come out to the farm so we could both see you. I'd surely like that. I'll write again when we're on the way.

Thank you for everything you did for us, and for me. — love, your Jenny

The words blurred as Mamie finished. She blinked her eyes hard, twice and a third time, before she laid the letter on Jake's lap. "You should read this. You'll see why."

He kept his arm around her as he read it through, chuckling at the part about Summer Dawn's headband and then going quiet. When he was through, he pulled her into his lap and said, "Sometime soon, I'd like you to tell me more about Jenny. And about Amanda Jane, and how she died, and how Jenny came to marry where she was buried. And any other tales you carry with you that might get lighter with sharing."

She held a finger to her lips and listened. She could hear the cheery tinkle of the piano in the main parlor, and a couple of men singing along out of key. She heard two pairs of footsteps, lighter and heavier, going up the stairs, and then two more going down. Everything seemed to be going just fine without her riding herd on the girls or the customers. She squirmed around to give Jake a kiss and hoisted herself up. "Let me tell Trudi and Lucette they're in charge for a while longer. And then, let's go upstairs. I'll tell you some of those stories. But I've got something else in mind first. You can get yourself a bite to eat in the meantime, to strengthen you for it. There should be sufficient in the pantry."

Jake gave her backside a hearty pat before she swayed out of reach. "I like how you think, Mamie, ma'am. Along with a whole lot else about you. I can tell you what else as we go upstairs."

Mamie turned back to wink at him before heading out to give orders. It was going to be a good evening. Another one. She hadn't thought to have so many.

Life wasn't easy, nor kind to those who expected it to be. But sometimes, it was good.

THE END

Author Interview

NOTE: this interview contains spoilers for *What Shows the Heart*. If spoilers bother you, or enrage you, please save this interview for after you've finished the story!

Q. Do you read many romances? If so, did they inspire you to write this series?

A. Most of my reading life, the novels I chose were science fiction or historical fiction. In recent years, I branched out — to fantasy, detective mysteries, and historical romance. I also read the occasional contemporary romance. I wouldn't say they inspired me — I found the idea of tackling either historical fiction or any kind of romance intimidating — but somehow, as I approached the start of National Novel Writing Month (NaNoWriMo) in 2018, the idea of a mutual matchmaker historical romance bubbled up. As readers of the series know, I ended up retaining the mutual matchmaker theme, but dialing it back somewhat.

Q. Will there be a fourth Cowbird Creek book?

A. I don't know! I never did have an overall series plan. It might depend, in part, on how the third book does, and how the first two continue to do (hint, hint). But to be truthful, I write what I'm in the mood to write as each November approaches.

Q. November?

A. I've written the (very) rough drafts of all my novels during NaNoWriMo, which takes place every November — except one novel whose rough draft I wrote during the similar Camp Nano, held usually in the spring or summer and somewhat looser in format.

Q. Who else in Cowbird Creek might get their own story?

A. The more I think about it, the more possibilities I see! There's the barber; the blacksmith; Tom Barlow's younger brother and sister (his sister would be particularly fun to write about); the preacher from out of town who married Jenny and Tom and then Mamie and Jake; any new marshal who eventually arrives; Clara Gibbs' brother; the telegraph clerk, rejected by Freida and still available; Mark Horn, the bouncer Mamie hires with Jake's help; even the obnoxious preacher, if he isn't married already as would have been typical. And no, I probably won't yield to the temptation to match him up with one of Mamie's employees . . . .

Q. Will you ever deal with the grasshopper invasions in the 1870s in more depth?

A. I do have an itch in my imagination about the devastating effects of the "grasshopper plague." It would make for a pretty serious tone, but I've already dealt with war, post-traumatic stress syndrome and other mental illness, racism, amputation, class distinctions, and the fate of prostitutes, so that would hardly be new. I don't think I have the heart to let the grasshoppers eat Cowbird Creek down to the dirt, so it would probably have to be the backstory of one or both main characters in a new book. It would be very hard to lose everything and then find the courage to start over . . . .

Q. Who is your favorite character in this series?

A. I'm not good at picking favorites in any area, so this is a somewhat evasive answer.

Freida is an absolute delight to write. I feel a familial and ethnic connection to her, as I'm a first-generation American Jew, and my parents' and grandparents' generations came from Poland and Germany. I have a quasi-maternal fondness for Dr. Joshua Gibbs, because he's such a thoroughly kind and decent fellow. (Freida would call him a "mensch," a Yiddish word literally meaning "man" and idiomatically meaning fundamentally good, serious about the right things, someone you know will do what's right.) But I care quite a lot about all the main characters in the series to date.

Q. What historical sources do you consult?

A. The long answer may be found in my Acknowledgments sections. Summing up the categories, I do online searches to find articles, blog posts, and books; read newspaper archives; pose questions to knowledgeable friends and beta readers; and post on the NaNoWriMo "Reference Desk" community forum. I haven't actually gone to Nebraska, but I'd like to. It was a relief to discover — though I still expect to call down some amorphous wrath by admitting — that I could do extensive research on a historical location *without* going there in person. Still, those of us who write any genre of historical fiction don't (yet . . .) have the option of visiting the time period about which we write, so using the same research techniques for place as for time makes sense.

Q. You deal more extensively with religion in *WSTH* than in the first two books. What concerns did you have about doing so?

A. My greatest concern was misleading my readers as to where the book was heading. I don't believe in breaking promises to the reader, and I was afraid my early references to Jake's former faith, and my use of the Jacob-and-Esau theme, might lead readers to expect that Jake would find his faith again by the end. That would have been hard for this agnostic to write, and didn't feel true to the character — not to mention that it might well have complicated his and Mamie's HEA. I took one step in the direction of clarifying this point by including (though late in the book) the scene where Jake muses about how he's become less angry at God, and wonders whether that change will make him even less of a believer or have the opposite effect.

On this topic as on others, like reflecting the language and attitudes of the time on subjects like race and gender, I spend some effort on calibrating my writing so as to offend readers as little as possible without avoiding difficult subjects altogether.

Q. Now that you've written historical romance, are you planning to branch out into other historical fiction? Or contemporary romance?

A. Actually, I've already dabbled a bit in one subgenre of romance , science fiction romance, though I've never made that the clear focus of a novel. I might tackle historical fiction someday, now that I've gotten past being so intimidated by the idea of historical research. I don't see contemporary romance as likely — but I think I'm learning never to say never.

Author's Note

The idea for this story took a while to settle into shape. Initially, I thought Jake, or the character with his role in the story, would be a circuit-riding lawyer or judge. At this point, Jake and Mamie had no shared past. When my research suggested problems with the circuit-riding notion, I came up with having Jake ride in and save the day, and being offered the marshal job in consequence. In fact, I thought he'd take it — but he made clear he wasn't so inclined . . . . I believe it was not long after this point that I discovered Jake's and Mamie's childhood friendship.

The cover story Clara Gibbs invents for the closure of Madam Mamie's fit in well with a broad national interest in hygiene and public health, and a desire that Americans demonstrate themselves to be a progressive and "modern" people. Many people investing the time and trouble to have indoor plumbing installed did so as part of that national movement.

What Jake thought of as wallpaper "scrolled with velvet" would in fact have been flock (or flocked) wallpaper, which added flock, a waste product of the woolen cloth industry, to an adhesive-coated cloth.

For some hints about how details came and went as I wrote this book, see the Acknowledgments section.

Acknowledgments

Once again, I have a long list of sources I consulted — but I'll start out, this time, by thanking my diligent and indispensable beta readers. This time around, they were Gwen Allerton-Gower, Steven, Karel, Susan Koutiel, Linda Lizenby, Glenda Morris, Harsh Kumar Rajani, and Wendy Teller.

A general note: I consulted some of the many sources listed below in order to check on some detail that no longer appears in the book — often because of what these sources showed me. I found these sources via Google.

I have done my best not to stretch the historical truth very far out of shape. When my sources conflicted, however, I chose the result most convenient to my purposes, and occasionally settled for a lack of information as sufficient basis for doing what I wanted . . . .

Sources I consulted repeatedly included:
— For language usage, *Google Ngram Viewer* and *Online Etymological Dictionary*. (I also, at least once, looked at an archived version of Brewer's Dictionary of Phrase and Fable, 1870 edition.) I also checked *The Phrase Finder*'s "Phrases and Sayings Discussion Forum" to check on the starting point for the phrase, "three squares a day" (which, as a result, I *didn't* use, quite). Absent for a similar reason: the expression "waiting for the other shoe to drop," which, I learned from these two sources, originated in New York City tenements after my time period:

— *Inc.*'s post, written by Melanie Curtin, titled "How Well Do You Know English? The Origin of 'Bite the Bullet' and 15 Other Common Expressions in English."
— Jen Carlson's May 18, 2013 article on *Gothamist*, "The Phrase 'Waiting For The Other Shoe To Drop' Was Born In NYC."

I read entries on Wikipedia for almost every topic listed below.

The remaining sources are largely, but not entirely, listed in order of where in the book I had occasion to consult them.

For an overview of events in Nebraska in 1877, I consulted:
— *History Nebraska*'s "Nebraska Timeline Columns."
— *FamilySearch*'s "Nebraska History."

For the history of perfume bottles: *Fragrance X Library*, "The History and Evolution of Perfume Bottles."

On the subject of hair dye packaging (including bottles):
— Post mentioning bottle of hair dye from near this period (though bottled dyes may have been scarce, in general) on *Digging195*'s section on "hair products and accessories."
— *Smithsonian Magazine SmartNews*, "Archaeologists Find Hair Dye Bottles Used by Self-Conscious Civil War Soldiers Posing for Portraits."
(A caveat: *Atlas Obscura*, "Found: Bottles of Hair Dye From a Civil War Photography Studio," opines that virtually all dyes available during the Civil War years darkened the hair.)
— MadisonReed *Love is in the Hair* blog, "The Colorful History of Hair Dye."

On the history of scrambled eggs: *Food Timeline*'s "eggs" FAQ.

On eating crumpets in 19th century America, I consulted an article, which has unfortunately vanished, on the blog *A Taste of History with Joyce White*. For teatime customs, I consulted *Food Timeline*'s entry on American tea.

For the roles of various lawmen in the Old West, I consulted:
— *Legends of America*'s post, "Lawmen of the Old West."
— *TrueWest* magazine's March 29, 2011 article by Marshall Trimble, "What's the difference between a marshal and a sheriff?"
— *Reddit*'s AskHistorian's forum discussion, "In the old west what were the roles of Marshals and Sheriffs?" My thanks to all participants!

I learned about wallpaper that looked like velvet at:
— *Designer Wallpaper Covering*'s article on "Flocked Velvet Velour."
— Jude Stewart's (appropriately dated) April 1, 2016 article in *The Atlantic*, "A History of Wallpaper's Deception."
— The Victoria and Albert Museum's entry on flock wallpaper.

Who knew baby carriages and strollers were relatively rare in America in the 1870s? I found out from the following sources (as well as Wikipedia):
— *ThoughtCo.*, "The History of Baby Carriages."
— *phil&teds*, "The history of the stroller — from then to now."
— *5 Minute History*, two now-vanished pages on strollers and baby carriages.

I checked on the history of whistle stops and found the page for a history course, History 3716, "The History of Technology," for which the first research topic was "The Railroad and the Rise of the Whistle-Stop Tour."

I checked on some sailor terminology at the nps.gov website's middle school lesson plan for *Island of the Blue Dolphins*, which had a section on "Sailors' Knots."

The USDA Agricultural Research Service's article on "Poisonous Plant Research: Logan, UT" helped me out with where locoweed grows.

To make sure Mamie and Jake climbed trees appropriate for climbing, I checked *Trees Unlimited L.L.C.*'s blog article, "A Great Part of Being a Kid — Climbing Trees." As for the contents of their picnic, I nixed sandwiches after consulting the following:
— The November 3, 2017 post, "A Complete History Of The American Sandwich," on *Patch*.
— *Food Timeline*'s FAQ on sandwiches.
— Joan Russell's September 20, 2005 article, "A little bread, meat, and a slice of history," in *The Christian Science Monitor*.
— *The Oxford University Press*'s English Language Teaching article, "The history of the sandwich."

I skimmed Sharon Marie Risko's scholarly 2015 article about 19th century sea shanties, "19th Century Sea Shanties: from the Capstan to the Classroom," in Cleveland State University's MSL Academic Endeavors, via the ETD Archive. I found examples of bawdy sea shanties at the blog *Everything2* in a post titled "Frigging in the Rigging."

I checked on when and where ice was available (other than in nature) in an article, "The Surprisingly Cool History of Ice," which, if I didn't mix things up in my notes, was then (if no longer) at *The Alcohol Professor*.

I read up on the histories of southern cities at *Britannica*'s online article on Memphis, Tennessee and Wikipedia's history of Nashville, Tennessee.

Various members of Facebook's NaNoWriMo group were generous enough to answer my questions about 19th century "paint" (makeup). I also glanced at several websites to which they directed me, including:
— *Kate Tatersall Adventures'* article, "Early Victorian Era Make-Up; cosmetics and embellishments," by R.S. Fleming, posted November 30, 2012;
— The May 28, 2014 post, "Makeup & Hair in the 1800's (Victorian times/Romantic era)" on CreagAaroStacy's *Makeup & Life Blog*;
— *Vintage Dancer*'s May 30, 2018 post, "Victorian Makeup Guide & Beauty History."

I confirmed that one could call for mail at the post office as early as the18th century in Publication 100 of the U.S. Postal Service.

It took a while to find the right Omaha newspaper to carry Ethan's personals ad. I consulted the Omaha Public Library's list of historical Omaha newspapers, the Library of Congress entry on the *Omaha Daily Republican*, an entry in the University of Nebraska Lincoln's "Nebraska Newspapers" site, and both Library of Congress and

Wikipedia articles about the *Omaha Daily Bee*. Also consulted on personals ads in general: an article on *Timeline*, unfortunately no longer showing up.

The following provided plot-pertinent information about Civil War naval discipline:
— *The Navy and Marine Living History Association*, Chuck Veit's article, "Naval Discipline in the Old Navy."
— *The American Civil War Society* (UK)'s article, "Discipline" (covering all U.S. military branches of the period).
— *Shotgun's Home of the American Civil War*, "Discipline in the Civil War Armies."
— *Naval History and Heritage Command*'s article, "Brief History of Punishment by Flogging in the US Navy," and the U.S. Naval Institute's September 28, 2010 post, "Flogging Outlawed 160 Years Ago Today." (Jake was going to take a flogging for his prank before I found out that flogging had been abolished in the navy some years before.)
— "Crime and Punishment in the Civil War," by Robert Bateman in the November 4, 2013 issue of *Esquire*.
— Dave Philipps' December 25, 2018 article in the *New York Times*, "No More Bread and Water: U.S. Navy Scraps an Age-Old Penalty."
— *Stars and Stripes'* December 27, 2018 article by Scott Wyland, "Navy to scrap bread-and-water confinement."

I consulted these sources about the history of doilies:
— Johanne Yakula's January 7, 2013 article, "Why Are They Called Doilies," on her website *From Times Past*.
— A May 21, 2014 post, "History of the Crocheted Doily," on the blog *Junkbox Treasures Antiques and Collectibles*.

I checked on the availability of hothouse flowers by reading the "Hothouse" entry on the website for the National Gallery of Art, Center for Advanced Study in the Visual Arts, History of Early Landscape Design.

I read up a bit on street sweeping and related topics in "Nineteenth Century Street Sanitation: A Study of Filth and Frustration," *The Wisconsin Magazine of History* Vol. 52, No. 3 (Spring, 1969), pp. 239-247.

For where prairie grass grew, I checked in the "A Complex Prairie Ecosystem" entry on the National Park Services' website.

I studied up on gambling, and specifically card games, by reading the following:
— Professor I. Nelson Rose's article, "19th Century Games, 21st Century Players," at his trademarked website *Gambling and the Law*.
— *GamblingSites.net*'s blog post from October 1, 2018, by Joey Richardson, titled, "What Was It Like to Gamble in the Wild West?"
— *HistoryNet*'s post, "Gambling in the Old West."

My sources on horse feed used at the time were:
— The *BioStar* blog's August 8, 2016 article, "Looking Back: Feeding Horses in the 1800s," which quotes at length from William Youatt's bok *The History, Treatment, and Diseases of the Horse*, first published in 1831 and updated in 1861.
— Marshall Trimble's May 3, 2017 article in *True West* magazine, "Livery Stables in the West."

PinProsPlus's June 11, 2020 article saved me from giving Jake a belt instead of suspenders. (Fun fact, which I learned from several sources including Wikipedia: Samuel Clemens, aka Mark Twain, patented a type of adjustable suspenders, though he called them "adjustable and detachable straps for garments.")

I learned much important detail that shaped Sterling Quinn's career, and helped me abandon the idea of making a major character a judge, at:
— Willard King's February 1955 article in *American Heritage*, "Riding the Circuit with Lincoln."
— *Life of the Law*'s post, "Justice on the Move," by Emily Gadek.
— The article, "Bench and Bar," by O.H. Travers, on the Springfield-Greene County Library District website.
    I also learned about the first federal district court in Nebraska from *Echo of its Time: The History of the Federal District Court of Nebraska, 1867-1993* by John R. Wunder and Mark R. Scherer.

I estimated how far Jake and Wrangler could travel in a day by checking *Worldbuilder*'s forum thread, "Possible distance travelled by horse over 6 weeks?" Thanks to all who weighed in!
    I also learned various details of horseback riding from "Pony 101: Riding for Non-Riders" on the website *Of Foxes and Boots*. And my thanks to the many helpful users of the NaNoWriMo "Reference Desk" forum for their tips on how to groom a horse.

I tracked the routes of 19th century cattle drives via the following. (I kept looking for a cattle drive ending closer to where Cowbird Creek would be, without success.)
— *Trips Into History*'s April 23, 2012 post, "Cattle Drives and Cowboys/What It Was Really Like."
— The Kansas Historical Society's *kansapedia* post, "Chisholm Trail."
— The Kansas Historical Society, again, specifically an article they digitized, by F. B. Streeter in November 1935, titled "Ellsworth as a Texas Cattle Market."
— *HistoryNet*'s post by Bob Stinson, "Five Kansas Cow Towns."
— *History Nebraska*'s blog post, "When cowboys shot up Niobrara."
— *Nebraskastudies.org*'s post, "Cattle Drives."
— The same site's "Beef Moves to Nebraska."
— *Wessels Living History Farm*'s post, "The Rise and Fall of the Omaha Stockyards."

I checked some details of the history of my county and town, Monroe County and Bloomington, at *Visit Bloomington*'s article "History and Heritage."

To find the right contagious illness for my purposes, and then to collect the details of mumps, I checked:
— George Groh's April 1963 article, "Doctors of the Frontier," on *American Heritage*.
— *Encyclopedia.com*'s "Disease and Westward Expansion."
— Rebecca Onion's February 3, 2015 article, "Late 19th-Century Maps Show Measles Mortality Before Vaccine," on *Slate*.
— An article by David M. Morens and Jeffery K. Taubenberger, "A forgotten epidemic that changed

medicine: measles in the US Army, 1917-1918," originally published in the *Lancet*, on the website of the U.S. National Library of Medicine, National Institutes of Health.
— *News Medical / Life Sciences'* "Measles History."
— *Branches of our family's* June 27, 2013 post, "Disease and remedies of the 1800s."
— The CDC's *Epidemiology and Prevention of Vaccine-Preventable Diseases* online entry for Mumps, including "Signs & Symptoms of Mumps" and "Complications of Mumps."
— Immunization Action Coalition's "Mumps: Questions and Answers."
— *Digital History's* "Overview of the First Americans."
— *MedicineNet's* "How to Cure Mumps: Vaccine."
— *Healthline's* "Mumps: Prevention, Symptoms, and Treatment."
— *KidsHealth's* Mumps page.
— The UK's National Health Services' page for Mumps/Complications.

I had a momentary doubt about how long there had been cradles, so I checked *Britannica's* "Cradle" entry.

Birds used to get drunk on berries outside one of my childhood homes, in Palo Alto, California, but to see whether this was a more widespread phenomenon, I checked Alisa Opar's March 2, 2011 article, "Spring Is In The Air — And So Are Intoxicated Birds," on the *Britannica* website.

I found (but can no longer find) a page on Northwood Custom Jewelry's website about the history of walnut wood, to confirm its suitability for wall paneling. I also consulted an October 2019 post, "The History of Panelling," on the *Artichoke* site.

Of course horses can have muscular necks — can't they? I double-checked at the *Equisense* blog, on which Camille Saute posted the reassuring "Building Neck Muscles? Piece of Cake!" on December 18, 2018.

I learned about coyote habitats by reading Dan Flores' article, "Coyote: An American Original," on *HistoryNet*.

I checked the history of milled soap in a November 19, 2015 post on the Australian Natural Soap Blog, and embossed soap in the October 12, 2011 article, "A Little History about Yardley London's Soaps," on the Yardley London website.

I confirmed my impression that letters already went inside envelopes by reading Michael Kernan's October 1997 article, "Pushing the Envelope," in the Smithsonian Magazine. I checked on how long state postal abbreviations have been around by reading the U.S. Postal Service's post about, no surprise, "State Abbreviations."

To learn about ranks in the Union navy during the Civil War, I consulted "A history of sea service ranks & titles," published on June 27, 2001 on the U.S. Department of Defense website.

To learn more about how telegrams worked, I checked *Paper Truly*'s "Telegrams - Stop - A Brief History."

I confirmed that sheriffs indeed wore tin stars as badges in Christopher Kuch's February 2, 2016 article, "The Sheriff's,

Constable's, and Marshal Star Badges," on *Law Enforcement Today*.

Jake needed to demonstrate knowledge of how not to be tracked on horseback. I obtained it from many helpful posts on the NaNoWriMo Reference Desk forum. Thanks, all!

I considered including details from Jake's navy experience. I could have gotten them from (Wikipedia and) the article, "Naval Actions of the Civil War," on the American Battlefield Trust's website. I ultimately decided that after having dealt at length with Joshua's and Clara's wartime experiences and resultant PTSD in *What Heals the Heart*, I didn't really want to retread that territory in this book.

To confirm that Jake would have been likely to encounter reddish earth somewhere, and just where that might have been, I consulted:
— Juliana Keeping's March 2, 2015 article, "Oklahoma Observed: Red dirt holds deeper meaning for tribes," at *The Oklahoman*.
— The (U.S.) *National Archives*' entry, "Oklahoma Statehood, November 16, 1907."
— The *U.S. Department of Agriculture*'s "The Twelve Orders of Soil Taxonomy," in their site's section on "Natural Resources Conservation Service/Soils."

I checked on Nebraska's deciduous trees at the Nebraska Forest Service's page for the same.

I didn't manage to find out just which predators' attacks are triggered by the movement of their prey (and went with my hunch that hawks are in that group), but I did confirm that some prey animals "freeze" when in danger, at Indiana Public Media's *Moment of Science* page, where the February 15, 2012 episode "Freeze!" is available.

Concerning the etiquette of the time and place as far as smoking indoors around ladies, I consulted:
— "Smoke, Smoke, Smoke that Cigarette," posted August 14, 2010 on *Victorian History*.
— "Smoking Etiquette," posted January 21, 2010 on *Edwardian Promenade*.

Jake fetched bed linens from a chest rather than a closet due to what I learned from Tera Harmon's February 1, 2018 article at *Birdie Brennan's Custom Closets & Organizing, LLC*, "Closets Through the Ages: The History of Closets in Residential Homes," as well as Shannon Mattern's July 2017 article, "Closet Archive," at the *Places Journal*.

I did a fair amount of research on the history of indoor plumbing, from sources including:
— *P & M* magazine's "The History of Plumbing in America," published in July 1987 and reprinted at plumbingsupply.com.
— "Lest We Forget, A Short History of Housing in the United States," by James D. Lutz of Lawrence Berkeley National Laboratory.
— "Indoor Plumbing in Victorian America," by Kristin Holt, posted to her website on June 11, 2016.
— Stephanie Pappas' post, "Flushed with Pride: 1860s Bathroom Boasts Early Plumbing Technology," on *LiveScience*.
— The overall history of Natchez, Mississippi at natcheztracetravel.com.

And last but *definitely* not least,
— Maureen Ogle's PhD thesis, "All the modern conveniences: American household plumbing, 1840-1870," an extremely thorough and helpful resource on the subject.

I picked Oberlin College as Ethan's alma mater and employer after consulting:
— "Alma Mater: The History of American Colleges and Universities" on Columbia University's *Edblogs*.
— Oberlin College & Conservatory's "Oberlin History."
On the related topic of sabbaticals, I consulted "The Origin and Early History of Sabbatical Leave," by Walter Crosby Eells, in the AAUP Bulletin, Vol. 48, No. 3 (Sept. 1962)
On the also-related question of what college tuition might have been when Ethan was saving up for college, I consulted:
— "History of Higher Education from 1785 to 1860," by Courtney Robinson and Donavan Johnson, on *Sutori*.
— The Decenber 22, 2015 article, "Harvard's Tuition in 1840 Was $75," on *Forbes*.
— The January 31, 2015 article, "History of College Tuition: The Cost of College Tuition In the Late 1800s," on *HubPages*.

And last but not least, I confirmed that Santa was a well known figure at the time, and already came down chimneys, at these sites:
— *Lewith & Freeman Real Estate, Inc.*'s December 4, 2017 blog post, "Why Does Santa Use the Chimney And Not The Front Door?"; and
— *History Today*'s December 12, 1995 article, "Christmas in 19th Century America."

About the Author

Karen A. Wyle was born a Connecticut Yankee, but eventually settled in Bloomington, Indiana, home of Indiana University. She now considers herself a Hoosier. She and her husband have two wildly creative daughters. (Return readers may notice that I no longer claim to have a sweet though neurotic dog. She left us in June 2019. We miss her.)

In addition to writing fiction (science fiction, afterlife fantasy, and now historical romance), Wyle is an appellate attorney, photographer, and politics junkie. Her voice is the product of almost five decades of reading both literary and genre fiction. It is no doubt also influenced, although she hopes not fatally tainted, by her years of law practice. Her personal history has led her to focus on often-intertwined themes of family, communication, personal identity, the impossibility of controlling events, and the persistence of unfinished business.

Connect with the Author

Learn more about Karen A. Wyle by looking her up on
her author website (http://www.KarenAWyle.com),
Twitter (@KarenAWyle),
Facebook (https://www.facebook.com/KarenAWyle),
Goodreads (https://www.goodreads.com/kawyle),
or her (rarely updated) blog, Looking Around
(http://looking-around.blogspot.com/).

Like the book? Please tell readers!
Online book reviews are enormously helpful —
and old-fashioned word of mouth is terrific as well!

You can sign up for Wyle's monthly newsletter, which
includes information about upcoming releases, insights
into her writing process, and occasional extras (e.g. cover
reveals, character art), and other book news at the
newsletter sign-up link on Wyle's author website
(see above).

Looking into the Mirror

Messages from the Authentic Self to the Inauthentic Self

GARNET THOMPSON

Published 2022 by Your Book Angel

Printed in the United States
Edited by Keidi Keating
Layout by Rochelle Mensidor

ISBN: 979-8-9876155-0-8

To Nadine, Jasmine, and Anthony, I have truly benefited from your presence and your unique personalities in my life. Thank you for your continued support and for being your real selves.

To the throngs of people who need to read this book. Behind the developing crack in your mask, your authentic self secretly resides and is starving for some much-needed oxygen.

Introduction

This book is a compilation of personal messages from the authentic self to the inauthentic self. It offers you, the reader, a unique opportunity to internalize or feed on each message, to extract the single theme or flavour that is the main seasoning in each message or, as I will often refer to them, "thought-food."

There is a single theme and key message that runs through each morsel of thought-food presented. These are messages to the inauthentic self. The self that we put on display while our authentic selves stay hidden behind our public masks.

As You Like It by Shakespeare speaks about the many parts a person plays while living on "stage."

As You Like It, Act II, Scene VII, Lines 138-141
<u>William Shakespeare</u>

"All the world's a stage,
And all the men and women merely players;
They have their exits and their entrances,
And one man in his time plays many parts…"

However, the part we humans will benefit from the most is the part of being our real selves.

These morsels of thought-food are messages to society about simply showing up as our real selves. This is one of the hardest things most people, including myself, will ever do during our life spans.

The human mind is an insatiable factory or machine, or perhaps it is best described as a separate creature living within one's skull. This creature possesses a voracious appetite and feeds on two things. Once you stand back and observe yourself or the throngs of people on our planet, you may become aware of the two types of foods to which I'm referring. The first food, which is necessary for functioning at a physical level, is "energy." The second type of food is "thought."

Our brains are like the Cookie Monster. He has an insatiable appetite for cookies, which are like the thoughts and ideas we seek out and consume with insatiable appetites. Once our bodies' energy requirement has been satisfied either via sleep or via the consumption of nutrients, we become singularly focused on ingesting as much "thought-food" as we can find. Our brains, "the creatures," graze on the thoughts from other humans who have lived in the past, or who are living in the present. We then digest, metabolize, and reform the incoming thought-food and create new, never-before-existing thoughts. Some newly created thoughts closely resemble the material that was put into our mental factories. However, the real gems, which are often rare, look nothing like the creature's feed and are immediately recognized by other humans as being highly valuable.

By digesting and then reflecting on these powerful messages, you will begin to unmask yourself and slowly start to reveal your real self to yourself and to the people in your life. This will be a liberating experience that will unlock all your desires in five key areas of life:

(1) Relationships
(2) Goals
(3) Choices
(4) Actions
(5) Freedom, the most coveted of all

I designed the experience in this book for you to commence the process of destroying your current mindset, which has kept your authentic voice hidden and jailed over the years. Acknowledging the pattern of behaviour that is not serving you well is the first step toward developing a new mindset. Destroy your old way of thinking and nurture more effective thought patterns. That will set your mind up for strategic action and efficient results.

Value your voice and free your authentic self.

Garnet Thompson

How Much?

How much of your life will you spend being the fake you? How much of your life will you spend being the real you? The real shame is wasting time thinking you are fooling anyone. Keeping up your fake appearance will make your life not worth examining. That's a pity!

Self-Reflection

What thoughts spring to mind?

____

____

____

____

____

____

____

Regrets

Lies, deceitful thoughts, intentions to mislead, and devious thoughts occur to most people. Taking action or not taking action on these thoughts is a choice we must each make. Deceitful actions and truthful actions both have consequences. Act wisely or live a life filled with regrets!

Self-Reflection

What thoughts spring to mind?

Self-Serving

You believing your thoughts and actions are saintly doesn't make them saintly. You knowing your thoughts and actions are self-serving doesn't make you a bad person. Saintly or not, you be you and that will serve everyone best.

Self-Reflection

What thoughts spring to mind?

You Don't Truly Know

You don't truly know other people. You don't truly know yourself. You falsely believe other people know you. You falsely believe you know yourself. It's truly a falsehood that your thoughts and actions are selfless. Your selfish thoughts and actions are the true you. That's no lie!

Self-Reflection

What thoughts spring to mind?

Dividends

The thoughts which enter our minds originate from an unknown source. Are they ours to keep, collect, and stash away? Are they intended to be used or returned unopened to the unknown source? Decide how you will use these invaluable deposits of thoughts which are free and available to everyone. Make them pay dividends or pay them back.

Self-Reflection

What thoughts spring to mind?

Temporary

I'm not my body, I'm not my thoughts, and I'm not my feelings. I'm an observer of my body, my thoughts, and my feelings, all of which are temporary and constantly changing. Everyone and everything around me is temporary and constantly changing. Who am I? And, who are you?

Self-Reflection

What thoughts spring to mind?

Guided

We are being guided each day by our Lord Jesus Christ. When we decide to take our eyes off our guiding star to look back on the people and problems in our lives, we meet with numerous collisions and near misses. Keep your eyes fixed forward on Him and stop driving using your rear-view mirror. Now you are headed toward a brilliant future.

Self-Reflection

What thoughts spring to mind?

Surrounded

Every day we are surrounded by both truth and lies. Truth and lies are told to us by people we know and by people we don't know. Every day we ourselves have the choice to tell truth, lies, or both. Stay true to your real self and tell people your truth. Stop lying to yourself.

Self-Reflection

What thoughts spring to mind?

Moving Forward

When you experience your greatest highs and deepest lows in the same year, stop and thank yourself for your persistence to keep moving forward. The depth of your resilience greatly depends on how much you value your own thoughts.

Self-Reflection

What thoughts spring to mind?

Emotions

When you are tempted to act on your emotions, remember that every reaction driven by emotion is unbalanced. Instead, take action on your logical thoughts to create balance. I see that you have reached a whole new level of awareness. I saw that coming.

Self-Reflection

What thoughts spring to mind?

Our Job

The solution for every problem resides in our collective human consciousness. Our job is to figure out which solution goes with which problem. Focus on finding your problems to make clever use of your solutions. Now that's less puzzling.

Self-Reflection

What thoughts spring to mind?

Wasting Fuel

Stop wasting fuel and time on unproductive thoughts, situations, and people. Look back momentarily to extract valuable lessons and start burning fuel to achieve forward momentum. Strap in for the ride of your life. Three, two, one, zero, now go!

Self-Reflection

What thoughts spring to mind?

____

____

____

____

____

____

____

The Antidote

Being your inauthentic self is toxic to yourself and everyone around you. Being your real self is the antidote for your toxic tendencies. Drink up and let come whatever may. Cheers!

Self-Reflection

What thoughts spring to mind?

____

____

____

____

____

____

____

____

Grave Situation

Self-sabotage is a habit based in fear and unworthiness. Self-empowerment is a habit based in love and acceptance. Decide which of these old habits need to die a hard death. Now that's a grave situation.

Self-Reflection

What thoughts spring to mind?

Inauthentic Words

Falling rain soaks everyone who remains unprotected. The words that fall from your lips cover everyone. Once the sun comes out, every drop of rain that has not been absorbed will evaporate. So will the inauthentic words that fell carelessly from your lips, since they had no value.

Self-Reflection

What thoughts spring to mind?

Disruptive Weeds

Some flowers from afar appear pleasant to the eye. However, when viewed up close, they are actually disruptive weeds. Gently remove all weeds from your garden to avoid disturbing any nearby flowers. That will cultivate a green garden.

Self-Reflection

What thoughts spring to mind?

Flame On

Being real and speaking truth will lead to heated reactions and fiery backlash. Staying hidden and protected behind your mask of inauthenticity will prevent you from being singed on the field of life. Flame on!

Self-Reflection

What thoughts spring to mind?

Spit Out the Bait

Whenever someone attempts to bait you or press your buttons, disconnect the buttons and watch them press them in futility. Spit out the bait to avoid being lured into a tempting trap. Focusing on freedom is never futile.

Self-Reflection

What thoughts spring to mind?

Backlash

Being your authentic self means becoming extremely comfortable with backlash. Rest assured that the degree of backlash you experience is directly correlated with the degree to which you are being authentic. No backlash means nobody knows the real you.

Self-Reflection

What thoughts spring to mind?

Happy

If you are counting on a holiday season to make you happy, you might as well have ten fingers on each hand. Get a grip on yourself and decide to be you. Choose to be happy and take a holiday from your inauthentic self. Stuff the turkey instead of stuffing your real self.

Self-Reflection

What thoughts spring to mind?

Self-Awareness

When your speech is a mishmash of famous quotes and other people's thoughts, your need to embark on a journey of self-awareness is overdue. Think your own thoughts, use your own voice, and begin to quote yourself. Otherwise, enjoy your box of crackers, little bird.

Self-Reflection

What thoughts spring to mind?

Powerless

Take responsibility for your thoughts, take responsibility for your actions, and take responsibility for your physical health. Blaming other people for your ill thoughts, ill actions, and ill health is not only irresponsible, it renders you completely powerless and ineffective.

Self-Reflection

What thoughts spring to mind?

One Hundred Percent

There is nothing more powerful or potent than your real self. There is nothing more under powered and impotent than your fake self. Focus on harnessing your power and potential by being one hundred percent you. Three, two, one, and we have liftoff!

Self-Reflection

What thoughts spring to mind?

Growing Up

Our thoughts are like children growing up. First, the thought is born, then we nourish and play with the thought. Next, the thought begins to move and turns into behaviours—good or bad. Along the path to maturity, the thought continues developing and constantly changing, eventually giving birth to newborn thoughts. It's solely your decision to starve or nourish your thoughts.

Self-Reflection

What thoughts spring to mind?

Fuel

Air, food, and water all serve as fuel for your life. Stop wasting the limited and precious fuel on non-peaceful, non-productive, and no-value-added people or activities. Make the choice to start using your fuel to travel along the most efficient trajectory for your life. The buffet line will close without warning!

Self-Reflection

What thoughts spring to mind?

Cry

Open the flask of your mind and tap into the energies of the people around you. Replenish your content and continue to pour into your life. The contents of a closed flask or mind will slowly go rancid. Now that's something to cry over!

Self-Reflection

What thoughts spring to mind?

Traffic Jam

Comparing yourself to others is like driving down a dead-end road. At the end of that road, you will be stuck in a deadly traffic jam. There you will sit for eternity, comparing with others who is trapped the best. No fuel for you!

Self-Reflection

What thoughts spring to mind?

Freedom

Relationships, goals, choices, action, and freedom are the categories around which most thoughts are focused. The achievement of any of them solely depends on you being you. It's your choice to set goals and take the necessary actions to build relationships, which will lead you to your desired freedom. Focus your thoughts!

Self-Reflection

What thoughts spring to mind?

Embrace the World and It Will Embrace You

Becoming a father myself was initially a little intimidating. Having grown up without the example and influence of open affection from a mother and father made it challenging to be sure I would do right by my own children.

But I didn't let those concerns stop me.

I went out of my way to show my children affection from birth. To spend active time playing with them, cuddling them, reading to them, and tucking them into bed. I wanted to ensure they wouldn't grow up feeling the way I did, as though they have no value and don't belong in the world.

It took me a long time to understand those feelings were horrible little lies, that I did have a place in the world and had value in and of myself, that I could offer value to those around me. And it's not an experience I'd wish on my own children. Perhaps it means I overcompensated, but is there really such a thing as loving one's family too much? Provided children learn about boundaries, right and wrong, respect, and kindness, I don't believe one can truly overdo an offer of genuine affection and affirmation.

When I was young, I overheard conversations between the adults in my life. They were worried I'd end up on the streets and involved with the wrong people. A concern I, now, can understand. But at the time, I was so determined to prove them wrong, to prove the world wrong, I internalized those discussions as fuel to ensure I never ended up the ways they expected. Perhaps that drove me to overperform sometimes, to overwork, to try too hard to do things for others instead of doing them for myself. But ultimately, I learned how to work hard through the experience.

I want my children to be motivated as well, but I want what fuels them to be their passions and desires, their goals and dreams, not determination—nor the need—to prove themselves to anyone except for themselves. And I feel as though my efforts in showing them open affection and guiding them into a path of positive goal setting and accomplishing processes has achieved that.

No one should feel unwelcome in the world.

Clocked Out

A dead person can take no more action. A person who is alive and still waiting is waiting in vain. You can take action while the clock is going or wait until you have clocked out. Either way your timecard will eventually be punched!

Self-Reflection

What thoughts spring to mind?

The First Step

Acknowledging the pattern of behaviour that is not serving you well is the first step toward developing a new mindset. Destroy your old way of thinking and nurture more effective thought patterns. Now that will set your mind up for strategic action and efficient results.

Self-Reflection

What thoughts spring to mind?

Slow Down Your Speech

Slow down your speech, slow down your actions, and slow down your thoughts. Focus on your breath, speak your truth, and take decisive action. Then picture yourself crossing the finish line in slow motion.

Self-Reflection

What thoughts spring to mind?

Start Approving of Yourself

Stop proving yourself to people you know, and stop proving yourself to people you don't know. Start approving of yourself, and start walking into your greatness. Your end results will be startling.

Self-Reflection

What thoughts spring to mind?

Support Yourself

Your family may not support you, your friends may not support you, and your body may feel like quitting. Quit waiting for other people to support you, and demand of yourself the courage to take action on your ideas. Support yourself and rise up.

Self-Reflection

What thoughts spring to mind?

Kneel

If you don't have butterflies in your stomach, your goals aren't big enough. If your knees aren't knocking, your goals aren't big enough. Keep setting bigger and bigger goals that make you feel nervous. Kneel, slow down, and take a deep breath, then get up and step into your future with courage.

Self-Reflection

What thoughts spring to mind?

Your Costume

Focusing your efforts on creating a brand for your public image is like dressing up for Halloween. You may gather a stash of candy, but your costume is only useful one day per year. Your image to the public the rest of the year is truly frightful. Now that's scary.

Self-Reflection

What thoughts spring to mind?

Stop

Stop presenting and start speaking. Stop reacting and start living. Stop worrying and start being. Stop hesitating and start doing. Stop showing the world the inauthentic you and start feeling free to be authentically human.

Self-Reflection

What thoughts spring to mind?

Autopilot

Sit at the steering wheel of your mind and direct your thoughts toward your purpose. Leaving your mind to drive on autopilot will generate numerous accidents and near misses. You have full control of whether you arrive at your life's destination as yourself or not.

Self-Reflection

What thoughts spring to mind?

Your Mortal Self

Your mistaken attitude about your permanent human existence is robbing you of peace. Embrace the transient nature of your mortal self and immerse your wave back into the ocean of life. Now that's a priceless existence.

Self-Reflection

What thoughts spring to mind?

Your Unconditioned Mind

Your conditioned mind is subconsciously thinking as programmed. Your unconditioned mind is waiting to be birthed, after the demolition of your programming. Bury your previous way of thinking and experience your newly-birthed, mature consciousness.

Self-Reflection

What thoughts spring to mind?

____

____

____

____

____

____

____

____

Appreciate Yourself

Between the day you took your first breath and the day you permanently close your eyes is a period represented by a dash. Be sure to slow down, and don't dash through the period called your life. Take the time to genuinely appreciate yourself and the people in your life.

Self-Reflection

What thoughts spring to mind?

____

____

____

____

____

____

____

False Relationships

When you look in the mirror and the person looking back at you looks like a stranger, it's time to introduce your inauthentic self to your authentic self. That will make a true difference in your false relationships.

Self-Reflection

What thoughts spring to mind?

Tired of Pretending

When you are tired of acting like someone else... when you are tired of speaking like someone else... when you are tired of pretending to be someone else, rejuvenate your body, mind, and soul by acting like yourself, speaking like yourself, and simply being yourself.

Self-Reflection

What thoughts spring to mind?

Think Real

Think your own thoughts, speak your own words, and take actions that match your thoughts and words. Think real, speak real, act real, and just be yourself.

Self-Reflection

What thoughts spring to mind?

Averting Their Gaze

You are not an automobile, stop dimming your lights to avoid blinding bystanders in life. Turn up your lights to full brightness and experience the greatness inside of you. Let others worry about wearing sunglasses, averting their gaze, and sitting alone in jealousy.

Self-Reflection

What thoughts spring to mind?

Start Biting Your Tongue

Every single word you speak creates something in your world. Look around to see the evidence of your past thoughts and words. I hope you are benefiting from what you created and are now experiencing. If not, start biting your tongue.

Self-Reflection

What thoughts spring to mind?

Adjust Your View

When quitting looks like your only option, opt to look at the situation quietly from all angles. Adjust your view and the outcome will start to take shape. It's obtuse to think otherwise.

Self-Reflection

What thoughts spring to mind?

Fertilize Your Soil

Not all roses are red and called by a different name they would be a different flower. Fertilize your soil and grow into a one-of-a-kind flower classified by your name. Blossom into the real you.

Self-Reflection

What thoughts spring to mind?

____

____

____

____

____

____

____

You Decide

You can let the obstacle block you, or you can use the obstacle as a building block. You can let people's words burn you, or you can burn people's words as fuel. I'll let you decide how best to flip the script.

Self-Reflection

What thoughts spring to mind?

Stew Over It

You can overthink it, or you can let it go. You can ruminate over it, or you can let it go. You can stew over it, or you can let it go. I'll let you decide, while I let you go.

Self-Reflection

What thoughts spring to mind?

What's Right for Me

You might be right; I might be wrong. I might be right; you might be wrong. I'll do what's right for me, and you do the same.

Self-Reflection

What thoughts spring to mind?

Only One Slice

You can create your own content and fulfill your purpose for living. Alternatively, you can use other people's creations and live a tiny fraction of your full potential. Express your own voice to have your cake and eat it, unless you are willing to settle for only one slice.

Self-Reflection

What thoughts spring to mind?

Gems of Wisdom

Embrace the silence. Block out the noise. Gems of wisdom are hidden deep in the silent river of your thoughts. Gather your gems and deposit those fleeting, high-valued thoughts into your "Silence Bank" to fund your purpose for living.

Self-Reflection

What thoughts spring to mind?

Pay No Attention

Pay no attention to people who put you down, and pay no attention to people who pump you up. Focus your attention on putting down your negative self-talk and building yourself up. It pays dividends to invest in yourself.

Self-Reflection

What thoughts spring to mind?

Strangers

Your family may not support you, your family may desert you, and your family may disown you. However, there are strangers who will support you, strangers who will stick with you, and strangers who will stand by you. It's incredible how strangers will support you while your family will leave you. May this bring your heart peace. God bless you.

Self-Reflection

What thoughts spring to mind?

Every Second

The only thing time waits for is for each second to pass without delay. Take a second to think about it. Make every second count.

Self-Reflection

What thoughts spring to mind?

____

____

____

____

____

____

____

____

Forget About Waiting

Forget about waiting for that special someone to come into your life. Remember you are special, so go step into your greatest life without waiting.

Self-Reflection

What thoughts spring to mind?

You're Never Alone

They say, "It takes a village to raise a child." I'm inclined to agree.

With my own upbringing, I relied on my grandparents and our local church community. And through raising my own children, the influence and support of blood family and found family (made up of friends and our own church community) were vital. We always had someone we could lean on, friends to turn to for advice or assistance, our children knew who and where were safe havens to turn to in times of need. Our community also helped our children socialize and learn how to empathize with others.

And helped me maintain and strengthen my connection with God.

I love my family, my grandmother. I love my friends and colleagues. But I wouldn't have any of them if it weren't for the love and guidance of God. He protected me in my youth, welcomed me time and time again despite my struggles with anger and feeling lost in the world. He brought me to my father. He embraced my relationship with my wife and blessed us with children. He allowed me opportunities to bond with the voice of a brother, without even knowing who he was.

All the relationships I've formed and will continue to form are loved and valued and bring meaning into my life. But my relationship with God is the keystone to it all. I haven't always been the most devout, but there's sweet memories in the time my grandmother and I spent playing gospel records together, growing closer to one another and God simultaneously. The book of Proverbs speaks to my heart, and I still turn to it today to soothe my soul and reflect on and honour my relationships, both with God and with all those who matter to me.

It does indeed take a village to raise a child. And God ensured I'd always have a community to support and strengthen me—us—each step of the way. I have much to be grateful for. Much to pray for. Much to look forward to. Trust is not deserved, it's earned. And though sometimes I struggle to offer it to others, with God, there's no question that the trust I have in his love and guidance is bulletproof.

Odyssey 19341

It began with a thought.

Then a decision was made.

Next the idea was shared.

The thought was entertained.

Another decision was made.

Information was gathered.

Expert advice was sought.

The plan was prepared.

Plan execution commenced.

The anticipated start date arrived.

The team commenced the journey.

Joy and nervousness were felt.

Problems arose and were faced. Doubt started to creep in. The internal struggle was real. The tight-knit team persevered. Persistence and levity abounded. Mission accomplished in the end.

Tears and celebrating flowed.

Everyone's life changed forever. Reflections of awe filled minds. The initial thought became reality.

Self-Reflection
What thoughts spring to mind?

Do Your Job

Problems are puzzle pieces of assorted sizes in our lives. Each problem has a specific solution that fits exactly right. Our job is to think independently or think collaboratively to find the right combination of actions to solve each problem. Relax, think clearly, and do your job!

Self-Reflection

What thoughts spring to mind?

The Ugly Truth

You don't need praise from people to feel good about yourself. You don't need insults from people to feel bad about yourself. Whether you feel good, bad, or ugly about yourself is something you alone decide. That's the ugly truth.

Self-Reflection

What thoughts spring to mind?

Pick Any Route

Taking the shorter route will get you there quickly. Taking the scenic route will get you there eventually. However, sitting there fearful and thinking endlessly about which route to take will get you nowhere. Pick any route and go, there is a line of fear-filled people behind you waiting for that chair.

Self-Reflection

What thoughts spring to mind?

Criticizing and Complaining

Persistently pursue your purpose with passion. Consistently avoid criticizing and complaining about your progress. Deliberately take the next steps with precision and commitment. Now that's worth talking about.

Self-Reflection

What thoughts spring to mind?

Avalanche of Garbage

When people try to manipulate you by shovelling guilt, blame, or anger toward you, step aside and allow them to bury themselves in an avalanche of their own garbage. You are responsible for your own actions, and they are responsible for their own reactions.

Self-Reflection

What thoughts spring to mind?

Nothing to Do with You

People liking you has nothing to do with you and has everything to do with them getting what they want from you. People disliking you has nothing to do with you and has everything to do with them not being able to manipulate you. Like it or dislike it, that's life and there is nothing you can do to be liked by everybody.

Self-Reflection

What thoughts spring to mind?

Faint or Fight

Is it fair for you to be afraid of fears? Is it fair for you to live with fears? I'm afraid to tell you that your fear of failure and fear of success are both fantasies. These are fairly common falsehoods that paralyze many people. It's your choice to faint or fight fear with fierceness.

Self-Reflection

What thoughts spring to mind?

Time

How much time can you afford to waste during your limited lifespan? How much time should you put to effective use? How much time do you have before you die?

Until you determine the right answers to these questions, use your time efficiently. Take some time to think about your use of time.

Self-Reflection

What thoughts spring to mind?

Polish Your Lantern

If everyone needs to like you for you to like yourself, you have likely stopped looking in the mirror to appreciate your uniqueness and value. Polish your lantern until it shines and then ignite your own flame. Light the way for yourself and others. It's unnecessary for everyone to click your "like" button.

Self-Reflection

What thoughts spring to mind?

Your Superpower

Imagine harnessing that special superpower within yourself to fully use the talents already inside you. Whether your superpower is willpower, hope, courage, persistence, or something else. Picture yourself at the top of your game, and demand of yourself the courage to rise to your own vision.

Self-Reflection

What thoughts spring to mind?

The Clock Is Running

You can be a passive spectator or an active player in the game of life. The choices you make will determine your level of fulfillment and legacy. It's solely your choice to watch from afar or to get dirty on the field. Your time will expire whether you win, lose, draw, get disqualified, or don't show up. Any way, the clock is running!

Self-Reflection

What thoughts spring to mind?

____

____

____

____

____

____

____

Fear and Fascination

When you feel frustrated with your life for a prolonged period, figure out what the specific problem is and then determine practical options. Select the option you think is the best one and start taking immediate action. The frustration will be replaced with fear and fascination as new experiences begin to unfold before your eyes. Keep looking forward!

Self-Reflection

What thoughts spring to mind?

The Hardest Thing

It's easy to behave like someone else. It's harder to behave like the real you. The easy path goes around obstacles while the harder path goes through obstacles. You decide whether you will learn from adversity or learn little during your journey. Being you is easily the hardest thing you will ever do.

Self-Reflection

What thoughts spring to mind?

Logic Over Emotions

You can edit your social media posts to obtain more colourful, crisper images and to add catchy sounds. You can't edit your life after taking actions that were solely based on emotions and were not well thought-out. Use logic over emotions to make decisions and avoid undesired consequences. Now that's worth posting!

Self-Reflection

What thoughts spring to mind?

Decide and Go

Now is the time. Logic is the way. Decide and go. If you are still sitting there thinking about it, read that again.

Self–Reflection

What thoughts spring to mind?

The Storm

Stop getting angry about temporary problems, and develop the skill to deal with the situation and eliminate the underlying fear. Start embracing peace amid the storm. This will place you on a path to happiness, but staying on the path takes repeated choices as you encounter new and old obstacles along your journey.

Self-Reflection

What thoughts spring to mind?

Applause and Accolades

Stop looking for applause and accolades. Focus on taking action and checking your progress. When you look for applause, you will also find constructive and non-constructive criticism. Incorporate the feedback you know is true for you and block out all the other voices. Start celebrating and appreciating yourself.

Self-Reflection

What thoughts spring to mind?

____

____

____

____

____

____

____

____

Who's Fooling Who?

Waiting for someone to come along and make you happy is like knowingly purchasing fool's gold. You know you are lying to yourself, and you know it has no value. Decide for yourself to be happy and share your fortune with the unfortunate souls who continue to trade in worthless commodities of happiness. Who's fooling who?

Self-Reflection

What thoughts spring to mind?

Your Counterfeit Self

Being fake will ultimately get you fake relationships, unsatisfying goals, and will waste irreplaceable time. Being real will ultimately get you the right relationships, the goals meant for you, and true satisfaction during your limited lifespan. Your counterfeit self is worthless and is of value to NOBODY!

Self-Reflection

What thoughts spring to mind?

Embrace the Storm

Stop focusing on figuring out how to stop the storms in your life. Instead, ask God for the wisdom and guidance required to navigate the treacherous waters. Start taking action on what you can do right now, embrace the storm, and use the energy to power your epic journey. Land ahoy!

Self-Reflection

What thoughts spring to mind?

How to Fly

No one remembers the birds that didn't figure out how to fly. Except the cats!

Self-Reflection

What thoughts spring to mind?

Procrastinators

Assemble the right team around you to climb those mountains. Decide which thoughts you will act on after reading this message. Victory evades procrastinators.

Self-Reflection

What thoughts spring to mind?

Chewing Gum

When you focus on extracting happiness from someone else, you have already lost. The temporary satisfaction is like chewing gum to obtain the juicy, fruity flavours. In the end, you will be left with a tasteless rubbery material. Make the choice to infuse yourself with natural long-lasting flavours by being true to your values. Chewing on that will win you a lifetime of happiness.

Self-Reflection

What thoughts spring to mind?

You Be You

When I do something that you don't like, that's me. When I do something that you do like, that's me. And when I do nothing, that's still me. You liking what I do or don't do has nothing to do with me. You be you and I'll continue to be me. Now that's something that I like!

Self-Reflection

What thoughts spring to mind?

Healthy Habit

Your mind, your soul, your body, and your spirit combine to make the real you. Treating yourself with continuous doses of your true self every day is an addictive, healthy habit. Staying true to your real self will help you make decisions that are both healing and motivating.

Self-Reflection

What thoughts spring to mind?

Starring Role

Turning down your light to avoid blinding someone else will leave you lost in the dark. You will continue to stumble about through life and accomplish little. Turn up your light to its full brightness and you will light the way for yourself and the world. It's your choice to play the understudy or the starring role before the curtain closes.

Self-Reflection

What thoughts spring to mind?

Actionable Steps

I will help you transform the vision in your mind into actionable steps. I will then hold you accountable to your own words even when it gets uncomfortable. This will allow you to achieve the progress you said you wanted.

Self-Reflection

What thoughts spring to mind?

Attitude Drives Change

Eight years ago, I got a call from a recruiter, offering a position at a new company. The job was appealing. It would pay well, allowing me to better provide for my family. But it would involve moving a few hours away. Which would mean uprooting not just my own life, but that of my wife and children. My son and daughter would need to switch schools, bid farewell to friends and build new connections. My wife would have to change jobs to accommodate my own shift. It would be asking a lot of my family.

We considered it. Discussed it. And ultimately decided to go through with it. It would be a lot of work, would likely involve some stress and tension, as big changes tend to do. But we'd move into a small town, taking us out of the bustling bigger town and nearby city life, which I'd never particularly had a taste for, in addition to gaining stronger financial stability.

Instead of allowing the fear of the unknown grasp our hearts, we treated the move as an adventure—to help our children find the positives in the changes coming their way, but also to keep our own perspectives clean of worry and doubt.

My grandmother helped with the decision as well. She approved of the company, liked some of their products. Her offered blessing eased my lingering concerns about moving away from my extended family. But the timing couldn't have been more tailored to our needs. My daughter was about to start grade nine, so the transition into high school would usher her into a new school district regardless. And soon enough, my children would be able to get their driver's licenses, which would allow for even more visits with friends and family.

It wasn't just a choice about whether to accept the job and move, but also to seek the silver lining, to find the good. We could've approached the move with grumbles and groans, with heads down and tempers bubbling. But what purpose would that have served? Other than to drag us all emotionally through the mud and cause us to butt heads. And we were already going to pay the price of being farther away from our loved ones, so keeping our own family unit strong was what mattered most.

Ultimately, we chose to move. We chose happiness. We chose to embrace the new journey with open minds and open arms. And that alone made the choice the best we could have made.

Rejuvenate Your Mind

The only activity that won't exhaust and deplete your physical resources is being still. Be still, then take the time to rejuvenate your mind and enrich your life. Now that's an activity worth running through your mind over and over again!

Self-Reflection

What thoughts spring to mind?

1% Chance

Having a vision for your life that you have a 99% chance of achieving will not feel very satisfying in the end. However, having a vision for your life with less than a 1% chance of achievement will feel unimaginably engaging. You decide whether your life will be a priceless experience or a non-event.

Self-Reflection

What thoughts spring to mind?

Mentally Bankrupt

When you think you know it all and that there is nothing of value to be learned from other people, this is proof that all the golden nuggets of knowledge you had previous stockpiled have turned into a tarnished, worthless pile of metal. You are not only sadly mistaken, but also mentally bankrupt and have diminished your value and currency in this world.

Self-Reflection

What thoughts spring to mind?

Complex Problems

The reality of life as an adult, which I imagined as a youth, was quite unimaginable. Real-life, challenging situations demand we use our imaginations to solve complex problems that have life-changing consequences. Now that's the real picture.

Self-Reflection

What thoughts spring to mind?

Eye to Eye

I trust you to be unworthy of trust on some occasions. However, I trust that something worthwhile will come from the occasions in which my trust in you was well placed. I trust we see eye to eye on this fact and expectation.

Self-Reflection

What thoughts spring to mind?

Artificial Sugary Thinking

Life is nothing like a box of chocolates. When eating a box of chocolates, we often pick again while looking for our favourites and skip over the flavours we don't like. In life, we often must digest all flavours, good and bad, whether we like them or not. Stop fooling yourself and lose the artificial, sugary thinking that is rotting your mind.

Self-Reflection

What thoughts spring to mind?

Easily Offended

When your feelings are easily hurt, think hard as why that happens. Hardly a day goes by without you being easily offended. It's hard to offend someone who can easily dismiss the opinions and words of other people. It's easy to see we are all selfish and hard to get along with at times.

Self-Reflection

What thoughts spring to mind?

True Happiness

Your happiness is not my responsibility. Your sadness is not my responsibility. Your emotions are not my responsibility. My responsibility is to allow you to be responsible for yourself and me to be responsible for myself. Now that will bring us both true happiness!

Self-Reflection

What thoughts spring to mind?

My Thoughts

Whether I agree with you or disagree with you, my thoughts are my own and your thoughts are your own. The fact that they are aligned or misaligned is completely irrelevant. Think about it and let me know when you agree with me.

Self-Reflection

What thoughts spring to mind?

Nothing of Value

If you think my services are too expensive and you feel that you are entitled to receive them for free, let's agree that you likely have nothing of value to offer that would warrant us having a relationship, whether professional or otherwise.

Self-Reflection

What thoughts spring to mind?

Self-Worth

When a relationship no longer serves you and only serves the other person, the choice to continue or move on awaits you. Allowing yourself to stay in a one-sided relationship or not reflects the value you have placed on your own self-worth.

Self-Reflection

What thoughts spring to mind?

Appear Saintly

Offering unsolicited advice to someone has nothing to do with them. It has everything to do with stroking your own ego and wanting to appear saintly. What other people say or do has nothing to do with you. Clean up your own mess first and allow others to clean up their own.

Self-Reflection

What thoughts spring to mind?

____

____

____

____

____

____

____

____

What's On You

If I sound angry to you, that's on you. If I sound happy to you, that's on you. If I sound sad to you, that's on you. If I sound indifferent to you, that's also on you. How you perceive me has absolutely nothing to do with me and everything to do with your distorted expectations of how I should act in the movie script of your life.

Self-Reflection

What thoughts spring to mind?

Let It All Go

Let go of the expectations you have of the people in your life. Let go of the expectation that other people need to make you happy. Let go of the expectation that you need attention from other people. Let it all go! Now you've got something precious that cannot be held or seen. Hold on to your peace and enjoy your newfound light.

Self-Reflection

What thoughts spring to mind?

True Wisdom

True wisdom is knowing when, where, and how to be blunt with people. I have always found that being blunt with people on a one-to-one basis is welcomed and more effective versus delivering a bludgeoning in public. Wise words are only wise at the right time, in the right place.

Self-Reflection

What thoughts spring to mind?

Examine Your Reaction

If you ask me to do you a favour and my answer is "No," and you proceed to get upset or angry, I have done you a favour by allowing you the opportunity to examine your reaction. No need to say thank you. However, let me say you are welcome.

Self-Reflection

What thoughts spring to mind?

Legacy

Whether you feel alone or feel like you belong, it's more beneficial to focus on making progress on your goals. Wasting time on fleeting concerns adds zero value to your impact and legacy in this world.

Self-Reflection

What thoughts spring to mind?

Wise or Unwise Choice

Joy, anger, sadness, or indifference, whatever emotions you experience and allow to run your life are solely your own wise or unwise choice.

Self-Reflection

What thoughts spring to mind?

Lucky

Bad luck, good luck, or no luck, you decide how your life turns out by your choices or lack of choices. You were already lucky to be born you.

Self-Reflection

What thoughts spring to mind?

Blaze Your Own Trail

The only good luck you should count on is not being struck by lightning. Blaze your own trail like a comet across the sky.

Self-Reflection

What thoughts spring to mind?

Path to Freedom

Friends, family members, or foes, everyone is focused on finding their own fortune. Forget about competing with anybody and figure out your own path to freedom. Fulfilling your fate takes focus.

Self-Reflection

What thoughts spring to mind?

Meal of Humiliation

When someone serves you a meal of humiliation, it's no different than when someone serves you a banquet of honour. Do what you do, regardless of whether or not anyone values your contributions.

Self-Reflection

What thoughts spring to mind?

Cut the Chain

Cut the chain of expectations and free yourself. Look after your own happiness and let other people look after their own. Now you have strengthened your weakest link.

Self-Reflection

What thoughts spring to mind?

Excuses

When you consistently offer excuses for your failed goals, you have succeeded in achieving the mindset of a person who will continue to fail. Although, I bet you will have an explanation that says otherwise.

Self-Reflection

What thoughts spring to mind?

Take a Breath

Pause and take a breath before you respond. Respond after you have had a chance to breathe and think. Your delayed reply will cause a chill to run down the other person's spine. Chill out, speak your truth, and be real from your head to your toes.

Self-Reflection

What thoughts spring to mind?

Fight against Life

When you fight against life, life will fight against you. When you let go of worries, worries will let go of you. Relax and don't worry about fighting the urge to express the real you.

Self-Reflection

What thoughts spring to mind?

Inoculate Yourself

Your heart rate, your blood pressure, and your temperature are all naturally programmed to have your body function perfectly as yourself. Your conditioned mind has been infected by a virus and causes an unnatural heartbeat, elevated blood pressure, and an increased temperature. Inoculate yourself and stop the spread.

Self-Reflection

What thoughts spring to mind?

Approve of Yourself

Confidence in yourself comes from being you, especially when you are tempted to change what you want to say or do to get the approval of others. Approve of yourself and let other people change what they say or do. Now that's something special.

Self-Reflection

What thoughts spring to mind?

Borrow Belief, Then Cultivate Your Own

After my first year of university, my educational life seemed to have gone well. My highest grades were in physics and chemistry, and that first year set the expectation that the path forward would be, if not entirely smooth, at least only a little gravely.

But in second year, everything changed.

Nothing seemed to be going the way I wanted. I grappled with my studies. It was a struggle to take in my lectures and digest the coursework. I didn't know how to push forward or how I'd make it through the second year, let alone the two that would follow. I was losing hope, I was losing confidence.

My future was rapidly slipping out of my grasp.

One lifeline was my fellow chemistry classmates. Especially one friend in particular.

Around the time the rest of our classmates were ordering their school jackets, the reality of my situation weighed heavily on me as though I had the world on my shoulders. The jackets were a symbol of pride and glimpse into the future. With the university name "McMaster" on the back, the university emblem on the front, the sleeves were reserved for the year we were to graduate and the name of our program. But while the others in my program were excitedly ordering their jackets with 'HONS CHEM" on the left arm, and the planned graduating year "93" on the right arm, the idea made my stomach tighten.

I wasn't even sure I could pass my second year. How could I bring myself to anticipate graduation at all, honours or not?

That's when my friend stepped in.

She encouraged me to still buy my jacket, despite my reservations. "You've got this," she said. "Put 'HONS' on it anyway, and we'll make sure we get through this together."

We. Together.

She and I. But also the rest of our classmates. Because within our little group of chemists, no one was left behind. We were a team. When one of us struggled, the rest would be there to offer support. We studied together. Encouraged each other. Victories were shared wins and losses were never handled alone.

Which is exactly what I needed.

I needed confidence. Belief. But I had none left after the whiplash from my first to second year. So I leaned on my friend's belief in me. Borrowed it. As often as needed until I could slowly cultivate my own belief in myself naturally.

Because what were the alternatives?

I could give up entirely and drop out of school. Or, I could switch into the three year program instead, abandoning all hope of honours, and just do 'well enough' to pass. But either way, what would be the point of that? Then I'd never reach the goal I'd set out for myself early on. Because I'd no longer have the opportunity to prove my doubts wrong.

So I ordered my jacket. I put 'HONS' on it. And I continued to hold onto the support offered by my fellow chemists. The next three years were still stressful, challenging. Graduating didn't happen easily. But as promised, we stuck together and made it through our program.

Reflecting on it now, that was pivotal moment. Because any single change could have altered the entire course of my life. My career, the people I met, the relationships I formed. It all could have butterflied out in entirely different directions had I made any other decision. But with the help of my friend and classmates, I stuck with it. I accomplished my goal. And I'd never want to trade any of the hard work that went into getting to where I am today for any other version of myself or my life.

The Wrong Track

When you feel the consistent need to explain yourself to other people, you are on the wrong track. Take the time needed to study and understand yourself to get on the right track. All aboard!

Self-Reflection

What thoughts spring to mind?

Vegetables or Lollipops

Words provide the required nutrition for our lives. Most people prefer sugary words with artificial flavour and little or no value for personal growth. Words that are beneficial for growth are often hard to chew and hard to swallow, and they will leave a bad taste in your mouth. It's your choice to consume vegetables or lollipops, or perhaps both.

Self-Reflection

What thoughts spring to mind?

A Pretend Existence

The world we experience around us is well-scripted, photoshopped, and edited, and it is predominantly false. The true world is hidden in the background and is being experienced by only a few. Join it whenever you are sick and tired of a pretend existence.

Self-Reflection

What thoughts spring to mind?

____

____

____

____

____

____

____

____

I See You

I see you, I hear you, and I know you are there. You see me, you hear me, and you know I'm there. Our level of interaction depends on the potential value and benefits we both think exist between us.

Self-Reflection

What thoughts spring to mind?

Two Valid Expectations

Your reasonable or unreasonable expectations of me are only about you, and they have nothing to do with me. I decide what I do or don't do. You decide what you do or don't do. Those are the only two valid expectations between human beings.

Self-Reflection
What thoughts spring to mind?

Regrets

A life of no regrets, a life of fewer regrets, or a life overflowing with regrets. Only you can choose which will be your reality. Be real and let the world experience the real you. Stop reacting and start living.

Self-Reflection

What thoughts spring to mind?

Be Genuine

Lie to yourself, lie about yourself, or lie for yourself, regardless the truth will be buried inside you waiting to come out. Be genuine for the sake of your real self.

Self-Reflection

What thoughts spring to mind?

____

____

____

____

____

____

____

A Treasure Chest

Every day you spend pretending to be authentic is a day you have spent living a perfect lie. Living your imperfect truth pays dividends which results in a treasure chest that you won't be able to spend in a lifetime.

Self-Reflection

What thoughts spring to mind?

The Real You

Being the real you will get you the goals you want. Being the inauthentic you will get you the goals someone else wants. So when you decide to be the real you, that's a real achievement.

Self-Reflection

What thoughts spring to mind?

Own Your Vision

You know you better than anyone else knows you. However, you are looking to other people to tell you what's right for you. Those people can't see the vision you have for your life. Most of those people can't see the visions for their own lives. Own your vision and start walking into your future.

Self-Reflection

What thoughts spring to mind?

On Second Thought

People going for their dreams and taking risks are often worried about being embarrassed and looking bad to other people. Meanwhile those "other people" are not taking risks and are not taking action on their own dreams. Those worries sound ridiculous on second thought.

Self-Reflection

What thoughts spring to mind?

Keep Listening

Listen and then make your own decisions. Look and then make your own decisions. Decide and then go for it. Keep listening and looking along the way.

Self-Reflection

What thoughts spring to mind?

Make a Difference

Start making a difference, and make a difference by starting. Stop waiting to start and do it!

Self-Reflection

What thoughts spring to mind?

____

____

____

____

____

____

____

____

Sound Logic

Thank yourself for thinking clearly about your problems. The problem becomes clear when, thankfully, sound logic is applied instead of emotions. Clear out the emotion.

Self-Reflection

What thoughts spring to mind?

Offended

You are offended, you were offended, or you will be offended. Whether it happened today, happened yesterday, or will happen tomorrow, it will still be only your problem and none of my business.

Self-Reflection

What thoughts spring to mind?

Forget about Reacting

Forget about insults, forget about criticisms, forget about disappointments, and most importantly, remember to forget about reacting to other people's broken promises, empty words, or selfish actions. We are all self-serving.

Self-Reflection

What thoughts spring to mind?

Needlessly Stressful

Stressing out about the stress in your life is needlessly stressful. Approach the stress in your life in a logical way and you will find a logical solution to resolve those stressful situations.

Self-Reflection

What thoughts spring to mind?

Stop Overthinking

When your incessant, out-of-control habit of overthinking leads to confusion and worry, you need to rethink your approach. Stop overthinking and start living in peace. You are not as smart as you think you are. You heard me right.

Self-Reflection

What thoughts spring to mind?

Start Being Reasonable

Your reason for thinking you can figure out everything is the reason you have figured out nothing. Start being reasonable.

Self-Reflection

What thoughts spring to mind?

A Puppet

Compliments make you feel good, insults make you feel bad, sunshine makes you feel good, and stormy weather makes you feel bad. You need to decide how you want to feel, instead of reacting like a puppet to everything in your environment.

Self-Reflection

What thoughts spring to mind?

People Liking You

People liking you, people respecting you, people appreciating you, and people admiring you are all great. However, those people are focusing solely on themselves and how you make them feel. It has zero to do with you.

Self-Reflection

What thoughts spring to mind?

Criticism Will Burn

Criticism will burn you if you are insecure, criticism will hurt you if you lack self-confidence, and criticism will sting you if you feel unworthy. However, criticism will be rendered useless if you know the value of being your unique and one-of-a-kind self.

Self-Reflection

What thoughts spring to mind?

My Attitude

If your attitude depends on my attitude, then I recommend you get an attitude adjustment. My attitude will remain as I choose, regardless of your choices.

Self-Reflection

What thoughts spring to mind?

Being Unkind

Being kind and being authentic are not mutually exclusive. Don't use being real as an excuse to be unkind. Being inauthentic is ultimately being unkind to yourself.

Self-Reflection

What thoughts spring to mind?

Pause and Think

Your immediate replies will be your downfall. Pause and think about your real response, and then reply at your own pace. Slow down and rise up.

Self-Reflection

What thoughts spring to mind?

The Truth

Knowing the truth means also knowing the lie. Take your time while deciding which is beneficial for the real you to speak out loud.

Self-Reflection

What thoughts spring to mind?

A Question

Ask someone a question if you are interested in what they are saying. Make a statement if you are interested in what you are saying. Listen for what is not being said and not being heard.

Self-Reflection

What thoughts spring to mind?

Let Yourself Down

When someone lets you down, you have two choices: one, make it an issue, or two, make it a non-issue. Either way it doesn't matter, because you were the one who let yourself down in the first place. Think about it.

Self-Reflection

What thoughts spring to mind?

The Road to Destruction is Paved in Lies

The phone rang. When I answered it, the man on the other end introduced himself as an officer of the RCMP (Royal Canadian Mounted Police) and asked if I wouldn't mind meeting with him to answer some questions that may be able to assist in an open investigation.

As the manager of quality assurance for a pharmaceutical company, I agreed to meet with the officer a few days later.

While some might have been nervous about the meeting, I was the opposite. There was no reason to be nervous. I had nothing on my conscience. No guilt, no shame. I kept my nose clean professionally. So when I got the call, I knew the officer genuinely just wanted to get my perspective on the situation, whatever it might be about.

The benefit of always working with integrity in one's career.

A few days later, I drove about an hour out of town and met with the RCMP. The room I was guided to was nothing short of scene from a movie. The classic cold, hard, barren walls, a table in the middle of the room—I thought I noticed a tape recorder in the center, though I can't be entirely sure. What I was sure of was the stack of papers on the table, in front of where the officer sat.

I took the seat across from him.

A laboratory my company had contracted was under investigation for allegedly falsifying data. And said laboratory was familiar; my team too had picked up on some questionable actions on the lab's part a year or so prior and I'd even spoken with their president about my concerns. As it turned out, following the much more minor investigation my own company conducted, the RCMP had somehow caught word and taken over, beginning an even more thorough deep dive into the actions of that laboratory.

I answered their questions without hesitation. I explained the instance with my own company, where the lab was supposed to have run some tests for us but the analyst responsible never actually did. That my company had to check the product ourselves as a result, to ensure where was no sketchy or misleading information.

Perhaps some would argue whether that was the right thing to do, being so transparent with the officer. But what would the alternative have been? There are often two choices: to act with integrity or to not.

As long as one always moves forward with honesty and a clear conscience, there's nothing to fear. No roads paved in worry and lies. Behaving in illegitimate ways might seem like a smooth ride initially, but eventually, the pavement will crack, the rubble will rock and shake your trek. No good deed goes unrewarded, and no bad deed goes unpunished.

Karma will always come around to gnaw on you later, especially when you least expect it.

The laboratory in question was eventually found guilty and shut down, charges and arrests abound. Which just affirmed my decision to conduct myself and my business practices with integrity. One person really can make or break a system. Even in the largest of companies, all it takes is a single person on-high deciding to pave the wrong road. But, on the other hand, it goes both ways; all it takes is a single person along the chain of command deciding against following that path to shatter it into rocky rubble.

There is no 'have to'. Even the choices we make under pressure are still our choices. And every action has consequences. The question we must ask ourselves is whether we're willing to accept those consequences.

Short-Sighted

Take note of how someone conducts themselves while attempting to sell you a costly product or a service. Telling them that you are not interested in their services will bring out their real self. It's a costly and short-sighted financial mistake made by most inauthentic salespeople.

Self-Reflection

What thoughts spring to mind?

Taking Offence

Taking offence, being offended, feeling offended, and staying offended are all choices we are free to make. Likewise, not taking the offence, not feeling offended and not staying offended are also choices we are free to make. Go ahead and make your choice without offending yourself.

Self-Reflection

What thoughts spring to mind?

Relationships

Every relationship has a pre-determined expiry period, whether it's known or unknown to the people involved. The value of the mutual benefits being exchanged influences the length of the expiry period. Think about your relationships from the other person's point of view and act accordingly.

Self-Reflection

What thoughts spring to mind?

Your Voice

Capture your thoughts and add your voice in perpetuity to the tapestry of the world's consciousness, now and forever.

Self-Reflection

What thoughts spring to mind?

Be Yourself

The advice offered most frequently from one person to another is "Be yourself." However, this advice presumes to sum up this most complex human challenge using only two words. Being yourself is often the furthest thing from reality, even for the person offering the advice, and it often takes an ongoing commitment to oneself with frequent reminders from oneself.

Self-Reflection

What thoughts spring to mind?

Seek Wise Counselling

We spend a significant portion of our lives studying subjects such as history, geography, science, and mathematics. However, most people have never been taught how to be themselves. That's a lifelong course in which most people will unfortunately, receive an incomplete, unless they seek wise counselling.

Self-Reflection

What thoughts spring to mind?

Embrace the Freedom

Only once you are tired of failing, tired of faking, and tired of feeling like a fraud will you be provoked enough to be yourself. After that, you will embrace the freedom you had the whole time.

Self-Reflection

What thoughts spring to mind?

Applause and Accolades

Your real self is who you are when you remove the makeup, remove the costume, get off the stage, stop using rehearsed lines, and stop looking for applause and accolades from an audience.

Self-Reflection

What thoughts spring to mind?

Keep Getting Euchred

You were created by God to be you. You deciding that you prefer to be someone else other than who you were created to be doesn't trump God. Be you and play to win, or keep getting euchred.

Self-Reflection

What thoughts spring to mind?

Curtain of Fear

Once you push through the curtain of fear, you find your dreams on the other side.

Self-Reflection

What thoughts spring to mind?

Overthinking

The time you spend overthinking is time you have spent underachieving. Think, decide, and take action to increase the value of your time.

Self-Reflection

What thoughts spring to mind?

Denying Your Faults

Admitting your faults and doing something about them shows your humanity. Denying your faults and doing nothing about them shows your unchecked human nature.

Self-Reflection

What thoughts spring to mind?

Beware

People like to paint their intentions and actions as being saintly in nature. Beware, always pretending and acting like a saint reveals your true intentions.

Self-Reflection

What thoughts spring to mind?

Mistakes

Mistakes are mistakenly believed to be unwanted events, however the real mistake is overlooking the value of mistakes and taking them for granted.

Self-Reflection

What thoughts spring to mind?

Mediocrity

Give up, give in, or give it your all. Pick one and commit to it with full intensity. It's better than just sitting there in mediocrity.

Self-Reflection

What thoughts spring to mind?

Your Gift

Your gift or your passion, your gift and your passion, your gift is your passion. Whichever way makes sense for you, start taking consistent action and focus on being you as you take steps forward every day.

Self-Reflection

What thoughts spring to mind?

Words

The power of words grows exponentially when aligned with actions that are consistent with the initial thought or idea.

Self-Reflection

What thoughts spring to mind?

Choose Your Fate

Act in life; don't re-act to people. Choose your fate.

Self-Reflection

What thoughts spring to mind?

Behaviours

Extremely violent or extremely peaceful behaviours exist as potential actions in human beings. The range of actual exhibited behaviours depends on the morals, values, and what's deemed acceptable by the individual's conscience and by society.

Self-Reflection

What thoughts spring to mind?

Fear Exists

The best thing about fear is that it exists. Without it, we humans would likely sit around talking about everything we were going to do but not actually doing any of those things. But wait, most people are not taking any action now, even though they know that fear exists. Interesting.

Self-Reflection

What thoughts spring to mind?

Lack of Action

Whether you are drifting aimlessly through life, or you have taken precise aim at your destinations in life, when and where you arrive are solely dependent on your own thoughts and actions. Saying it another way: it's more likely a lack of thought or lack of action for some people.

Self-Reflection

What thoughts spring to mind?

Saw Dust

Counting on some people is like counting on saw dust to turn back into solid wood. I suppose anything is possible, so keep relying on those unreliable people to assist with your goals, because you know deep down that you are lying to yourself about achieving them.

Self-Reflection

What thoughts spring to mind?

____

____

____

____

____

____

____

____

Blazing Inferno

Whether the cup is half empty or half full, it doesn't really matter. All that matters is whether your desire to take action and fill the cup is a blazing inferno or if your pilot light has long been extinguished. Light your own fire!

Self-Reflection

What thoughts spring to mind?

Valuable and Untarnished

Whether you fail to succeed or succeed in failing, as long as you were focused on your primary job, which is being you, then you have truly got something valuable and untarnished.

Self-Reflection

What thoughts spring to mind?

Unsightly Stretchmarks

You were born into this world to grow and become comfortable in your own skin. However, some people seem to prefer growing into someone else's skin by copying them in every way. Ultimately, this will leave unsightly stretchmarks and will become uncomfortable.

Self-Reflection

What thoughts spring to mind?

I Prefer Freedom

Keep your platinum, gold, and diamonds, I prefer freedom, peace, and yes, money. Let's keep it real, at the end of the day money alone may not buy happiness, but it serves as the much-needed down payment.

Self-Reflection

What thoughts spring to mind?

The Magic

Assembling the right team around you will allow you to focus on the things directly related to your purpose. The magic happens when each member of your team is also focused on their purpose, which dovetails perfectly with yours.

Self-Reflection

What thoughts spring to mind?

Unlived Moments

You are living this exact moment only once. Each minute you spend dwelling on the past or being anxious about the future was a lost opportunity to live. Those unlived moments add up and are costly during a limited lifespan.

Self-Reflection

What thoughts spring to mind?

The Missing Piece

There I was, riding the airport escalator, at twenty-seven years old, looking at my father for the very first time.

Ever since childhood, I'd wanted to meet my father. Raised by my grandmother essentially since birth, I couldn't shake the unsettling feeling that something was missing from my life. My mother tried her best, but she was young; only in her early twenties when I was born. So she placed me in the capable hands of my grandparents, who took good care of and loved me. My grandmother became my rock through my early years, but that alone wasn't enough to stave off the insecurity that had been seeded in me as I grew older.

With my mother in Canada and no knowledge of my father, finding value in myself was a challenge on the best of days. It was easy to become complacent and feel left behind, wondering if I had place in the world at all and, if so, what that could possibly be. Frustration and rage were the emotions I felt in place of the affection I craved.

My lacking self-esteem and tendency toward feeling frustrated took more hits around the age of nine or ten when my grandmother too immigrated to Canada. For one year, I stayed with the minister of our local church while she settled. And when I was finally able to follow suit and move to Canada the following year, there were conversations as to where I should live. Or rather, with whom.

During her time in Canada, my mother had built a life for herself. Understandably. Ten years is a long time. She had a husband and additional children. Two sons and a daughter. My half-siblings. Which, objectively, is lovely and wonderful. On some level, I was happy for her. Or perhaps I can say that now, but to my younger self, it was kindle added to the flames of my frustration and discomfort.

Regardless, I stayed with my mother for a little while. A few years. But I never fit in, it never felt right for me to infiltrate the household she'd built while I'd been in Jamaica. They had a rhythm I struggled to integrate into. It was akin to living with strangers, despite the shared blood—or at least partially—that ran through our veins.

So, eventually, I returned to my saving grace: my grandmother.

Through all that time, I spent my youth wondering about my father as well. Not quite fantasizing, but with no concept of who my biological father was, my brain occasionally took liberties while trying to paint a picture of him.

I didn't know his name, where he lived, how he met my mother, nothing. She never spoke about him, and she and I didn't spend a lot of time together as it was, with us living such separate lives. Yet, despite having nowhere to begin, the fire in my heart to at some point, one day, meet my father wouldn't die out.

At twenty-three, just after finishing university, I decided it was time to put my desire into action. But I needed something to start me off. So, I asked my mother—for at least a name.

Armed with what little information she could provide, I turned to 1-800-US-SEARCH and received about a hundred or so names. A blessing and a curse. Having a list helped, but it was a lot of people to sort through, one at a time.

Still, I went forward.

I picked out the men sharing my father's name that lived in New York State and developed a plan to go there myself and visit each of those men to, theoretically, locate my father. I drove from Southern Ontario across the border and began my search. But in the end, I never made it to my destination to begin my hunt properly. I reached a police station and asked if they might be able to assist me, but with such a large task, despite narrowing down my list, it would be exhausting and time consuming—not to mention financially straining—to seek out each person.

Disappointed, I returned home.

Four years later, I received a call from a relative on Mother's Day. Somehow, they'd learned where my father was. Both where in the United States he lived and that he was visiting Jamaica as we spoke, to attend the funeral of his own father; my grandfather. I was even provided his phone number.

The timing might not have been the best, but I dialed the number.

And my father answered.

Perhaps there could have been a more tactful manner of introduction, but I didn't sugarcoat my reason for contacting him. How could I? I was hearing my sire's voice for the first time in my twenty-seven years of life. The truth just burst out.

"My name is Garnet Thompson, and I'm your son."

He was surprised. And not entirely convinced. Of course he wouldn't be. I can't imagine being in his shoes, receiving an anonymous phone call from an unknown number while attending a funeral, informing him of the existence of a child he never knew existed. He asked about me and my age, about how I was sure he was my father, and my mother's name. It wasn't a long conversation considering the loss of his own father, but we agreed to speak again once he returned to the United States in a few weeks.

As promised, three or four weeks later, he called me back.

During our second call, I assured him I didn't want anything from him: no money, I didn't want to interject myself into his life or disrupt his own possibly family. All I wanted was to meet him, even if only once. Something he was surprisingly open to after our conversations.

We arranged an in-person meeting, which happened to be on Father's Day weekend, at a resort in the Poconos in Pennsylvania.

Which is how I ended up riding the airport escalator, at twenty-seven years old, looking at my father for the very first time.

Dressed sharply, with pressed slacks and a clean, tucked in shirt, the man who greeted me was the picture-perfect image of successful. Our face-to-face introduction was a quiet affair. Soft voices, loose hugs. Accompanying me was my now-wife and with my father was his own wife. It was a little surreal, and yet, it was one of the most grounding experiences of my life.

We stayed at a resort and spent time getting to know one another. The more we talked, the clearer it became that the details did, indeed, line up. That there was no doubt I was his son.

At one point, by a beautiful lake, I admitted our meeting would have been very different had it happened only a few years prior. At the time, when I initially tried to search for him at twenty-three, I was still consumed with frustration and anger that accompanied me through most of my life. Perhaps I would've tried to fight him; I can't be sure. But I'm glad the universe, that God, ultimately delayed our meeting until I was ready to greet my father with a much more level head and open mind.

By the end of our first visit, my father offered me one of his rings. The first ring he'd ever purchased for himself after immigrating to the United States and beginning his career. It had been a reward for his efforts, for the time and energy and care he put into building a somewhat stable life for himself in those early years.

I still have that ring today.

Since that fateful meeting between myself and my father, we've seen each other several more times. The following year, my wife and I got married, and I invited my father and his own wife to the cruise ship where we were wed. My grandmother and a few other maternal and paternal family members were there as well, which was an interesting experience to navigate, but ultimately, my heart was flooded with gratitude at having them in attendance.

It wasn't all that long after our first meeting, when my father's mother passed away as well. I flew to Jamaica to attend the funeral for the grandmother I never met, to support my father and to meet some of my paternal family. It was there I met up with my other half-siblings. Two brothers and one sister. The time we spent together should possibly have been awkward. Maybe uncomfortable. After all, they were no more or less strangers to me than my maternal siblings when we first met. But instead, the opportunity to connect with a side of my family I'd always dreamt of was pleasant and calm.

Reflecting on it now, after finally meeting my father, the trajectory of my life changed. The goal I'd chased all my life was finally complete, and I could then focus on additional experiences I wanted in life. A successful career, a family of my own. I'm not sure where I would be today had I never sought my father out.

Leave an Impression

When you make a conscious effort to impress other people, the time you spent was lost doing something completely unimpressive. Just keep living and being you to leave an impression.

Self-Reflection

What thoughts spring to mind?

Life without Regrets

Choose to live your life while you can do so. The day will come when you will want to live your life, but the choice will no longer be yours to make. Live your life without regrets starting right now.

Self-Reflection

What thoughts spring to mind?

One Hundred Percent

People make impulsive decisions that they guess only impact their own lives, oblivious to the truth that they are correct. It's one hundred percent your decision if you allow someone else's decision to impact how you choose to live your life.

Self-Reflection

What thoughts spring to mind?

Brilliant Thoughts

During those moments when your mind feels like an incubator of thoughts being superheated by the universal energy of life, get out of your own way and capture the brilliant thoughts being channeled through your mind.

Self-Reflection

What thoughts spring to mind?

Intricate Puzzle

The problem is we view problems as problems, instead of as intricate puzzle pieces that need to be placed into the right position, with the right thought, at the right time, by the right person, with the right team.

Self-Reflection

What thoughts spring to mind?

Your Emotions

Once you have mastered your emotions and mastered being logical during every interaction with every person who crosses your path during your lifetime, you can then comeback and spend the rest of eternity criticizing other people.

Self-Reflection

What thoughts spring to mind?

Endless Overtime

We each have only two jobs in life: one is to be ourselves and the other is to let everyone else be themselves. Some people will be working endless overtime on both jobs and may never finish the work.

Self-Reflection

What thoughts spring to mind?

Fake News

The past, the present, and the future are all fake news as long as you continue to act like everyone else and refuse to just be yourself. Read the obituaries or the comics, either way it's a tragic and short-lived diversion.

Self-Reflection

What thoughts spring to mind?

Ask Permission

The best relationships are the ones in which individuals don't need permission to simply be themselves. The worst relationships are the ones in which individuals must ask permission to simply be themselves.

Self-Reflection

What thoughts spring to mind?

Ignore Them

When someone repeatedly tells you that you are so selfish, what they are really saying is that they haven't figured out how to control you and they are about to give up trying. Ignore them and let them keep wasting their own time.

Self-Reflection

What thoughts spring to mind?

An Imaginary World

Imagine if everyone in the world decided to be real, to stop acting, and to just be themselves. No, really, close your eyes and take a few minutes to imagine it. That will definitely remain an imaginary world.

Self-Reflection

What thoughts spring to mind?

Best Gifts

The most enjoyable experiences people have are often related to them fulfilling their purposes. Having fun doing what you like to do and enjoying time in your own company are often the best gifts to give yourself.

Self-Reflection

What thoughts spring to mind?

Courage to Act

Have the courage to act. Once you have woken up to life, there is no way to go back to sleep. So, figure it out, decide what's right for you, and have the courage to act.

Self-Reflection

What thoughts spring to mind?

Treat Yourself

Put the pieces together and treat yourself to your truth. Forget about being a poor copy of someone else.

Self-Reflection

What thoughts spring to mind?

____

____

____

____

____

____

____

Mindless Cyborg

Our capacity to think for ourselves is the most valuable asset every human being has, but not everyone knows they have the right to use it and not everyone chooses to use it. Think for yourself and don't be a mindless cyborg.

Self-Reflection

What thoughts spring to mind?

Self-Serving Creatures

Most people in your life are looking out for their own self-interests. Instead of counting on them and being disappointed, understand and accept that most humans are self-serving creatures. Learn to count on yourself and on your own God-given talents and skills.

Self-Reflection

What thoughts spring to mind?

Win the War

Your conditioned reaction to reacting will make you the guaranteed loser in every interaction. Start acting on what's right for you in every instance. Win the war and stop losing minor skirmishes and battles.

Self-Reflection

What thoughts spring to mind?

Depleting Resources

People waste precious words and time every day in living lies. Time spent and words spoken are gone forever. It's tragic that people use words and time as if they are unlimited resources of no value. Don't allow yourself to rob yourself of these depleting resources.

Self-Reflection

What thoughts spring to mind?

One Idea

Think about that one idea you have and know it's right for you, but you have been delaying taking action on it. Tell it to someone else and give them a chance to take action on it, since you are wasting the thought.

Self-Reflection

What thoughts spring to mind?

Save Your Breath

People speak with other people every day, yet they rarely tell them what they truly want to say. People listen to other people every day, yet they rarely hear what the other person is truly saying. Say what you truly mean, otherwise save your breath and everyone's time.

Self-Reflection

What thoughts spring to mind?

Invest in Your Own Voice

The value you bring to the table depends on the value you place on your own thoughts. Invest in your own voice and raise the stakes in the game of life. The surest path to winning the jackpot is to go all in and bet on yourself.

Self-Reflection

What thoughts spring to mind?

Rise Like a Phoenix

During those sudden moments when you are amid an inferno of problems, you have a choice to either peer through the blinding smoke and rise like a phoenix out of the flames, or resign yourself to rest defeated among the pile of ashes. Either way, the decision is solely yours to make.

Self-Reflection

What thoughts spring to mind?

Leave the Doubters

Recognizing the potential in yourself keeps you on the road for greater satisfaction and success. Stay focused and on course to catch up with even greater experiences ahead. Leave the doubters at the side of the road.

Self-Reflection

What thoughts spring to mind?

____

____

____

____

____

____

____

Learner for Life

Learning to learn is a learned skill. Once you have learned that and become a learner for life, then you truly have something. The lessons never stop until you do.

Self-Reflection

What thoughts spring to mind?

Second Impressions

After second impressions, the new shiny object honeymoon might be over. This is when you decide if that new person will go back to being a stranger, remain an acquaintance, become a friend, or become something more. First impressions aren't everything.

Self-Reflection

What thoughts spring to mind?

Mirror Mirror

Despite the fact that you look at yourself in a mirror hundreds or thousands of times during your life, you most likely have never seen your true self. However, there will come a day when you won't recognize the person looking back at you. Say hello to your real self when that happens. Let's hope you like the person you find staring back at you.

Self-Reflection

What thoughts spring to mind?

____

____

____

____

____

____

____

Investing In Umbrellas

It feels so refreshing to be myself and let the hurricane of chips rain down and fall wherever they land. I'll deal with getting wet in a logical way. Thinking about investing in umbrellas.

Self-Reflection

What thoughts spring to mind?

____

____

____

____

____

____

____

____

Reel It In

Brilliant ideas are like a gigantic fish on the line. If you take too long to reel it in or write it down, it will likely slip away and be gone forever.

Self-Reflection

What thoughts spring to mind?

One Step At A Time

Setting goals and then achieving them can be challenging, even for adults. Which is why I offered a specific approach to help my children learn how to work through their goals, one step at a time.

A pair of black hardbound notebooks and a pen were all that were needed.

They could write whatever goals they wanted, whatever came to mind or spoke to their hearts. Although, at the time, they were still young, so their goals were age appropriate, but the point wasn't to gatekeep what they wished to achieve or experience. The point was to allow them to put their thoughts on paper, to give them an outlet to collect and organize their goals, regardless of how lofty or modest they would be. And to help them put words to the things their hearts desired.

They scribbled in their notebooks, and with about twenty or so goals each, the next task was to categorize their lists into what could be realistically achievable within a week. Or rather, specifically, within the following week.

Some goals were easily sorted out due to the length of time they'd take to accomplish, while others were trickier. But that's when the next condition came in handy: asking themselves what they already had access to, on hand or in the house perhaps, that could help them reach some of their goals. What tools or assistance could they rely on? Whose expertise or guidance could they lean on? Myself, my wife, someone else (perhaps family or friends)? And how realistic would asking for that help within the one-week time frame be?

With those guidelines, they were able to narrow their lists down to a select few goals. And in the process, they learned to prioritize and practiced time management and decision-making skills. But that system also taught them goals don't have to be far off, unreachable dreams. That while some goals will take much longer and involve much more intensive effort to achieve, a simpler goal can be just as desirable and valuable as one that can't be as quickly reached.

As adults, we can ask ourselves the same questions when evaluating which of our goals to seek out in the here and now, but we can also add why we want a specific goal and thoughts on how we want to accomplish it. Armed with both sets of insights, we can more easily determine which concepts on our own lists are accomplishable through a metaphorical 100-meter sprint instead of a 42k marathon.

My children were also encouraged to add goals to their list as they achieve them, even if they never wrote those tasks down initially. Celebrating the little wins along the way is a fantastic motivator to keep reaching for and crossing out successes. It teaches our brain to see value in even the so-called 'smallest' of accomplishments, which in turn, makes the loftier goals more realistic to eventually complete as well. You can look back at all you've already achieved to boost your confidence as you climb another step closer to something larger.

And, often times, the smaller goals are necessary to build the staircase to the grander items on our lists.

The stories scattered throughout each held messages from my authentic self to your own. Take a moment to reflect on them and see if you can identify the themes in each.

Relationships. Goals. Choices. Actions. Freedom.

One Step At A Time:

____

____

The Missing Piece:

____

____

Embrace the World and
It Will Embrace You:

____

____

The Road to Destruction
is Paved in Lies:

____

____

Attitude Drives Change:

____

____

You're Never Alone:

____

____

Borrow Belief, Then
Cultivate Your Own:

____

____

About the Author

Garnet Thompson, a corporate executive, is the author of *20/20 Vision Dreams* for individuals young in age (or at heart), a children's book titled *Why the Bricklayer Smiles,* and this new, internationally-available book, *Looking into the Mirror: Messages from the Authentic Self to the Inauthentic Self.*

Canadian author Garnet Thompson emigrated from Jamaica when he was ten years old and met his father for the first time at the age of twenty-seven. His inspirations for writing are his children, Jasmine and Anthony.

Inspired by his children to pass on lessons learned while growing up, Thompson desires to equip the present and future generations of young adults with the mindset necessary to achieve their dreams. Growing up with his maternal grandparents in a non-traditional family setting provided a unique opportunity to learn vital life lessons.

Many young people in the world are without parental figures to provide the necessary coaching required to develop and maintain the right mindset and perspective. Thompson's books help equip the next generation with the tools and the mindset necessary to achieve their goals.

These books provide guided pages for readers to have an interactive experience resulting in a personalized record rich with cherished memories to keep for many years.

"Confidence in yourself comes from being you!" says Thompson.